AF372924

Clifford D. Simak

Unknown Guests

e-artnow 2020

Clifford D. Simak

Unknown Guests

Three Alien Contact Stories: Empire, The World That Couldn't Be, Hellhounds of the Cosmos

Illustrator: Gaughan

e-artnow, 2020
Contact: info@e-artnow.org

ISBN 978-80-273-0896-5

Contents

Empire

CHAPTER I

Spencer Chambers frowned at the spacegram on the desk before him. John Moore Mallory. That was the man who had caused so much trouble in the Jovian elections. The troublemaker who had shouted for an investigation of Interplanetary Power. The man who had said that Spencer Chambers and Interplanetary Power were waging economic war against the people of the Solar System.

Chambers smiled. With long, well-kept fingers, he rubbed his iron-gray mustache.

John Moore Mallory was right; for that reason, he was a dangerous man. Prison was the place for him, but probably a prison outside the Jovian confederacy. Perhaps one of the prison ships that plied to the edge of the System, clear to the orbit of Pluto. Or would the prison on Mercury be better?

Spencer Chambers leaned back in his chair and matched his fingertips, staring at them, frowning again.

Mercury was a hard place. A man's life wasn't worth much there. Working in the power plants, where the Sun poured out its flaming blast of heat, and radiations sucked the energy from one's body, in six months, a year at most, any man was finished.

Chambers shook his head. Not Mercury. He had nothing against Mallory. He had never met the man but he rather liked him. Mallory was just a man fighting for a principle, the same as Chambers was doing.

He was sorry that it had been necessary to put Mallory in prison. If the man only had listened to reason, had accepted the proposals that had been made, or just had dropped out of sight until the Jovian elections were over ... or at least had moderated his charges. But when he had attempted to reveal the offers, which he termed bribery, something had to be done.

Ludwig Stutsman had handled that part of it. Brilliant fellow, this Stutsman, but as mean a human as ever walked on two legs. A man utterly without mercy, entirely without principle. A man who would stoop to any depth. But a useful man, a good one to have around to do the dirty work. And dirty work sometimes was necessary.

Chambers picked up the spacegram again and studied it. Stutsman, out on Callisto now, had sent it. He was doing a good job out there. The Jovian confederacy, less than one Earth year under Interplanetary domination, was still half rebellious, still angry at being forced to turn over its government to the hand-picked officials of Chambers' company. An iron heel was needed and Stutsman was that iron heel.

So the people on the Jovian satellites wanted the release of John Moore Mallory. "They're getting ugly," the spacegram said. It had been a mistake to confine Mallory to Callisto. Stutsman should have thought of that.

Chambers would instruct Stutsman to remove Mallory from the Callisto prison, place him on one of the prison ships. Give instructions to the captain to make things comfortable for him. When this furor had blown over, after things had quieted down in the Jovian confederacy, it might be possible to release Mallory. After all, the man wasn't really guilty of any crime. It was a shame that he should be imprisoned when racketeering rats like Scorio went scot-free right here in New York.

A buzzer purred softly and Chambers reached out to press a stud.

"Dr. Craven to see you," his secretary said. "You asked to see him, Mr. Chambers."

"All right," said Chambers. "Send him right in."

He clicked the stud again, picked up his pen, wrote out a spacegram to Stutsman, and signed it.

Dr. Herbert Craven stood just inside the door, his black suit wrinkled and untidy, his sparse sandy hair standing on end.

"You sent for me," he said sourly.

"Sit down, Doctor," invited Chambers.

Craven sat down. He peered at Chambers through thick-lensed glasses.

"I haven't much time," he declared acidly.

"Cigar?" Chambers offered.

"Never smoke."

"A drink, then?"

"You know I don't drink," snapped Craven.

"Doctor," said Chambers, "you're the least sociable man I've ever known. What do you do to enjoy yourself?"

"I work," said Craven. "I find it interesting."

"You must. You even begrudge the time it takes to talk with me."

"I won't deny it. What do you want this time?"

Chambers swung about to face him squarely across the desk. There was a cold look in the financier's gray eyes and his lips were grim.

"Craven," he said, "I don't trust you. I've never trusted you. Probably that's no news to you."

"You don't trust anyone," countered Craven. "You're watching everybody all the time."

"You sold me a gadget I didn't need five years ago," said Chambers. "You outfoxed me and I don't hold it against you. In fact, it almost made me admire you. Because of that I put you under a contract, one that you and all the lawyers in hell can't break, because someday you'll find something valuable, and when you do, I want it. A million a year is a high price to pay to protect myself against you, but I think it's worth it. If I didn't think so, I'd have turned you over to Stutsman long ago. Stutsman knows how to handle men like you."

"You mean," said Craven, "that you've found I'm working on something I haven't reported to you."

"That's exactly it."

"You'll get a report when I have something to report. Not before."

"That's all right," said Chambers. "I just wanted you to know."

Craven got to his feet slowly. "These talks with you are so refreshing," he remarked.

"We'll have to have them oftener," said Chambers.

Craven banged the door as he went out.

Chambers stared after him. A queer man, the most astute scientific mind anywhere, but not a man to be trusted.

The president of Interplanetary Power rose from his chair and walked to the window. Below spread the roaring inferno of New York, greatest city in the Solar System, a strange place of queer beauty and weighty materialism, dreamlike in its super-skyscraper construction, but utilitarian in its purpose, for it was a port of many planets.

The afternoon sunlight slanted through the window, softening the iron-gray hair of the man who stood there. His shoulders almost blocked the window, for he had the body of a fighting man, one, moreover, in good condition. His short-clipped mustache rode with an air of dignity above his thin, rugged mouth.

His eyes looked out on the city, but did not see it. Through his brain went the vision of a dream that was coming true. His dream spun its fragile net about the planets of the Solar System, about their moons, about every single foot of planetary ground where men had gone to build and create a second homeland-the mines of Mercury and the farms of Venus, the pleasure-lands of Mars and the mighty domed cities on the moons of Jupiter, the moons of Saturn and the great, cold laboratories of Pluto.

Power was the key, supplied by the accumulators owned and rented by Interplanetary Power. A monopoly of power. Power that Venus and Mercury had too much of, must sell on the market, and that the other planets and satellites needed. Power to drive huge spaceships across the void, to turn the wheels of industry, to heat the domes on colder worlds. Power to make possible the life and functioning of mankind on hostile worlds.

In the great power plants of Mercury and Venus, the accumulators were charged and then shipped out to those other worlds where power was needed. Accumulators were rented, never sold. Because they belonged at all times to Interplanetary Power, they literally held the fate of all the planets in their cells.

A few accumulators were manufactured and sold by other smaller companies, but they were few and the price was high. Interplanetary saw to that. When the cry of monopoly was raised, Interplanetary could point to these other manufacturers as proof that there was no restraint of trade. Under the statute no monopoly could be charged, but the cost of manufacturing accumulators alone was protection against serious competition from anyone.

Upon a satisfactory, efficient power-storage device rested the success or failure of space travel itself. That device and the power it stored were for sale by Interplanetary ... and, to all practical purposes, by Interplanetary only.

Accordingly, year after year, Interplanetary had tightened its grip upon the Solar System. Mercury was virtually owned by the company. Mars and Venus were little more than puppet states. And now the government of the Jovian confederacy was in the hands of men who acknowledged Spencer Chambers as their master. On Earth the agents and the lobbyists representing Interplanetary swarmed in every capital, even in the capital of the Central European Federation, whose people were dominated by an absolute dictatorship. For even Central Europe needed accumulators.

"Economic dictatorship," said Spencer Chambers to himself. "That's what John Moore Mallory called it." Well, why not? Such a dictatorship would insure the best business brains at the heads of the governments, would give the Solar System a business administration, would guard against the mistakes of popular government.

Democracies were based on a false presumption-the theory that all people were fit to rule. It granted intelligence where there was no intelligence. It presumed ability where there was not the slightest trace of any. It gave the idiot the same political standing as the wise man, the crackpot the same political opportunity as the man of well-grounded common sense, the weakling the same voice as the strong man. It was government by emotion rather than by judgment.

Spencer Chambers' face took on stern lines. There was no softness left now. The late afternoon sunlight painted angles and threw shadows and created highlights that made him look almost like a granite mask on a solid granite body.

There was no room for Mallory's nonsense in a dynamic, expanding civilization. No reason to kill him-even he might have value under certain circumstances, and no really efficient executive destroys value-but he had to be out of the way where his mob-rousing tongue could do no damage. The damned fool! What good would his idiotic idealism do him on a prison spaceship?

CHAPTER II

Russell Page squinted thoughtful eyes at the thing he had created —a transparent cloud, a visible, sharply outlined cloud of *something*. It was visible as a piece of glass is visible, as a globe of water is visible. There it lay, within his apparatus, a thing that shouldn't be.

"I believe we have something there, Harry," he said slowly.

Harry Wilson sucked at the cigarette that drooped from the corner of his mouth, blew twin streams of smoke from his nostrils. His eyes twitched nervously.

"Yeah," he said. "Anti-entropy."

"All of that," said Russell Page. "Perhaps a whole lot more."

"It stops all energy change," said Wilson, "as if time stood still and things remained exactly as they were when time had stopped."

"It's more than that," Page declared. "It conserves not only energy *in toto*, not only the energy of the whole, but the energy of the part. It is perfectly transparent, yet it has refractive qualities. It won't absorb light because to do so would change its energy content. In that field, whatever is hot stays hot, whatever is cold can't gain heat."

He scraped his hand over a week's growth of beard, considering. From his pocket he took a pipe and a leather pouch. Thoughtfully he filled the pipe and lit it.

It had started with his experiments in Force Field 348, an experiment to observe the effects of heating a conductor in that field. It had been impossible to heat the conductor electrically, for that would have upset the field, changed it, twisted it into something else. So he had used a Bunsen burner.

Through half-closed eyes, he still could see that slender strand of imperm wire, how its silvery length had turned to red under the blue flame. Deep red at first and then brighter until it flamed in almost white-hot incandescence. And all the while the humming of the transformer as the force field built up. The humming of the transformer and the muted roaring of the burner and the glowing heat in the length of wire.

Something had happened then ... an awesome something. A weird wrench as if some greater power, some greater law had taken hold. A glove of force, invisible, but somehow sensed, had closed about the wire and flame. Instantly the roaring of the burner changed in tone; an odor of gas spewed out of the vents at its base. Something had cut off the flow of flame in the brass tube. Some force, *something* ...

The flame was a transparent cloud. The blue and red of flame and hot wire had changed, in the whiplash of a second, to a refractive but transparent cloud that hung there within the apparatus.

The red color had vanished from the wire as the blue had vanished from the flame. The wire was shining. It wasn't silvery; it wasn't white. There was no hint of color, just a refractive blur that told him the wire was there. Colorless reflection. *And that meant perfect reflection!* The most perfect reflectors reflect little more than 98 per cent of the light incident and the absorption of the two per cent colors those reflectors as copper or gold or chromium. But the imperm wire within that force field that had been flame a moment before, was reflecting *all* light.

He had cut the wire with a pair of shears and it had still hung, unsupported, in the air, unchanging within the shimmer that constituted something no man had ever seen before.

"You can't put energy in," said Page, talking to himself, chewing the bit of his pipe. "You can't take energy out. It's still as hot as it was at the moment the change came. But it can't radiate any of that heat. It can't radiate any kind of energy."

Why, even the wire was reflective, so that it couldn't absorb energy and thus disturb the balance that existed within that bit of space. Not only energy itself was preserved, but the very form of energy.

But why? That was the question that hammered at him. Why? Before he could go ahead, he had to know why.

Perhaps the verging of the field toward Field 349? Somewhere in between those two fields of force, somewhere within that almost non-existent borderline which separated them, he might find the secret.

Rising to his feet, he knocked out his pipe.

"Harry," he announced, "we have work to do."

Smoke drooled from Wilson's nostrils.

"Yeah," he said.

Page had a sudden urge to lash out and hit the man. That eternal drooling of smoke out of his nostrils, that everlasting cigarette dangling limply from one corner of his mouth, the shifty eyes, the dirty fingernails, got on his nerves.

But Wilson was a mechanical genius. His hands were clever despite the dirty nails. They could fashion pinhead cameras and three-gram electroscopes or balances capable of measuring the pressure of electronic impacts. As a laboratory assistant he was unbeatable. If only he wouldn't answer every statement or question with that nerve-racking 'yeah'!

Page stopped in front of a smaller room, enclosed by heavy quartz. Inside that room was the great bank of mercury-vapor rectifiers. From them lashed a blue-green glare that splashed against his face and shoulders, painting him in angry, garish color. The glass guarded him from the terrific blast of ultra-violet light that flared from the pool of shimmering molten metal, a terrible emanation that would have flayed a man's skin from his body within the space of seconds.

The scientist squinted his eyes against the glare. There was something in it that caught him with a deadly fascination. The personification of power-the incredibly intense spot of incandescent vapor, the tiny sphere of blue-green fire, the spinning surge of that shining pool, the intense glare of ionization.

Power ... the breath of modern mankind, the pulse of progress.

In an adjacent room were the accumulators. Not Interplanetary accumulators, which he would have had to rent, but ones he had bought from a small manufacturer who turned out only ten or fifteen thousand a year ... not enough to bother Interplanetary.

Gregory Manning had made it possible for him to buy those accumulators. Manning had made many things possible in this little laboratory hidden deep within the heart of the Sierras, many miles from any other habitation.

Manning's grandfather, Jackson Manning, had first generated the curvature field and overcome gravity, had left his grandson a fortune that approached the five-billion mark. But that had not been all. From his famous ancestor, Manning had inherited a keen, sharp, scientific mind. From his mother's father, Anthony Barret, he had gained an astute business sense. But unlike his maternal grandfather, he had not turned his attention entirely to business. Old Man Barret had virtually ruled Wall Street for almost a generation, had become a financial myth linked with keen business sense, with an uncanny ability to handle men and money. But his grandson, Gregory Manning, had become known to the world in a different way. For while he had inherited scientific ability from one side of the family, financial sense from the other, he likewise had inherited from some other ancestor-perhaps remote and unknown —a wanderlust that had taken him to the farthest outposts of the Solar System.

It was Gregory Manning who had financed and headed the rescue expedition which took the first Pluto flight off that dark icebox of a world when the exploration ship had crashed. It was he who had piloted home the winning ship in the Jupiter derby, sending his bulleting craft screaming around the mighty planet in a time which set a Solar record. It was Gregory Manning who had entered the Venusian swamps and brought back, alive, the mystery lizard that had been reported there. And he was the one who had flown the serum to Mercury when the lives of ten thousand men depended upon the thrumming engines that drove the shining ship inward toward the Sun.

Russell Page had known him since college days. They had worked out their experiments together in the school laboratories, had spent long hours arguing and wondering ...debating scientific theories. Both had loved the same girl, both had lost her, and together they had been bitter over it ...drowning their bitterness in a three-day drunk that made campus history.

After graduation Gregory Manning had gone on to world fame, had roamed over the face of every planet except Jupiter and Saturn, had visited every inhabited moon, had climbed Lunar mountains, penetrated Venusian swamps, crossed Martian deserts, driven by a need to see and experience that would not let him rest. Russell Page had sunk into obscurity, had buried himself in scientific research, coming more and more to aim his effort at the discovery of a new source of power ...power that would be cheap, that would destroy the threat of Interplanetary dictatorship.

Page turned away from the rectifier room.

"Maybe I'll have something to show Greg soon," he told himself. "Maybe, after all these years...."

Forty minutes after Page put through the call to Chicago, Gregory Manning arrived. The scientist, watching for him from the tiny lawn that surrounded the combined home and laboratory, saw his plane bullet into sight, scream down toward the little field and make a perfect landing.

Hurrying toward the plane as Gregory stepped out of it, Russell noted that his friend looked the same as ever, though it had been a year or more since he had seen him. The thing that was discomfiting about Greg was his apparently enduring youthfulness.

He was clad in jodhpurs and boots and an old tweed coat, with a brilliant blue stock at his throat. He waved a hand in greeting and hurried forward. Russ heard the grating of his boots across the gravel of the walk.

Greg's face was bleak; it always was. A clean, smooth face, hard, with something stern about the eyes.

His grip almost crushed Russ's hand, but his tone was crisp. "You sounded excited, Russ."

"I have a right to be," said the scientist. "I think I have found something at last."

"Atomic power?" asked Manning. There was no flutter of excitement in his voice, just a little hardening of the lines about his eyes, a little tensing of the muscles in his cheeks.

Russ shook his head. "Not atomic energy. If it's anything, it's material energy, the secret of the energy of matter."

They halted before two lawn chairs.

"Let's sit down here," invited Russ. "I can tell it to you out here, show it to you afterward. It isn't often I can be outdoors."

"It is a fine place," said Greg. "I can smell the pines."

The laboratory perched on a ledge of rugged rock, nearly 7,000 feet above sea level. Before them the land swept down in jagged ruggedness to a valley far below, where a stream flashed in the noonday sun. Beyond climbed pine-clad slopes and far in the distance gleamed shimmering spires of snow-capped peaks.

From his leather jacket Russ hauled forth his pipe and tobacco, lighted up.

"It was this way," he said. Leaning back comfortably he outlined the first experiment. Manning listened intently.

"Now comes the funny part," Russ added. "I had hopes before, but I believe this is what put me on the right track. I took a metal rod, a welding rod, you know. I pushed it into that solidified force field, if that is what you'd call it ...although that doesn't describe it. The rod went in. Took a lot of pushing, but it went in. And though the field seemed entirely transparent, you couldn't see the rod, even after I had pushed enough of it in so it should have come out the other side. It was as if it hadn't entered the sphere of force at all. As if I were just telescoping the rod and its density were increasing as I pushed, like pushing it back into itself, but that, of course, wouldn't have been possible."

He paused and puffed at his pipe, his eyes fixed on the snowy peaks far in the purple distance. Manning waited.

"Finally the rod came out," Russ went on. "Mind you, it came out, even after I would have sworn, if I had relied alone upon my eyes, that it hadn't entered the sphere at all. *But it came out ninety degrees removed from its point of entry!*"

"Wait a second," said Manning. "This doesn't check. Did you do it more than once?"

"I did it a dozen times and the results were the same each time. But you haven't heard the half of it. When I pulled that rod out-yes, I could pull it out-it was a good two inches shorter than when I had pushed it in. I couldn't believe that part of it. It was even harder to believe than that the rod should come out ninety degrees from its point of entry. I measured the rods after that and made sure. Kept an accurate record. Every single one of them lost approximately two inches by being shoved into the sphere. Every single one of them repeated the phenomenon of curving within the sphere to come out somewhere else than where I had inserted them."

"Any explanation of it?" asked Manning, and now there was a cold chill of excitement in his voice.

"Theories, no real explanations. Remember that you can't see the rod after you push it into the sphere. It's just as if it isn't there. Well, maybe it isn't. You can't disturb anything within that sphere or you'd change the sum of potential-kinetic-pressure energies within it. The sphere seems dedicated to that one thing … it cannot change. If the rod struck the imperm wire within the field, it would press the wire down, would use up energy, decrease the potential energy. So the rod simply had to miss it somehow. I believe it *moved into some higher plane of existence and went around.* And in doing that it had to turn so many corners, so many fourth-dimensional corners, that the length was used up. Or maybe it was increased in density. I'm not sure. Perhaps no one will ever know."

"Why didn't you tell me about this sooner?" demanded Manning. "I should have been out here helping you. Maybe I wouldn't be much good, but I might have helped."

"You'll have your chance," Russ told him. "We're just starting. I wanted to be sure I had something before I troubled you. I tried other things with that first sphere. I found that metal pushed through the sphere will conduct an electrical current, which is pretty definite proof that the metal isn't within the sphere at all. Glass can be forced through it without breaking. Not flexible glass, but rods of plain old brittle glass. It turns without breaking, and it also loses some of its length. Water can be forced through a tube inserted in the sphere, but only when terrific pressure is applied. What that proves I can't even begin to guess."

"You said you experimented on the first sphere," said Manning. "Have you made others?"
Russ rose from his chair.

"Come on in, Greg," he said, and there was a grin on his face. "I have something you'll have to see to appreciate."

The apparatus was heavier and larger than the first in which Russ had created the sphere of energy. Fed by a powerful accumulator battery, five power leads were aimed at it, centered in the space between four great copper blocks.

Russ's hand went out to the switch that controlled the power. Suddenly the power beams flamed, changed from a dull glow into an intense, almost intolerable brilliance. A dull grumble of power climbed up to a steady wail.

The beams had changed color, were bluish now, the typical color of ionized air. They were just power beams, meeting at a common center, but somehow they were queer, too, for though they were capable of slashing far out into space, they were stopped dead. Their might was pouring into a common center and going no farther. A splash of intensely glowing light rested over them, then began to rotate slowly as a motor somewhere hummed softly, cutting through the mad roar and rumble of power that surged through the laboratory.

The glowing light was spinning more swiftly now. A rotating field was being established. The power beams began to wink, falling and rising in intensity. The sphere seemed to grow, almost filling the space between the copper blocks. It touched one and rebounded slightly toward another. It extended, increased slightly. A terrible screaming ripped through the room, drowning out the titanic din as the spinning sphere came in contact with the copper blocks, as force and metal resulted in weird friction.

With a shocking wrench the beams went dead, the scream cut off, the roar was gone. A terrifying silence fell upon the room as soon as the suddenly thunking relays opened automatically.

The sphere was gone! In its place was a tenuous refraction that told where it had been. That and a thin layer of perfectly reflective copper ... colorless now, but Manning knew it was copper, for it represented the continuation of the great copper blocks.

His mind felt as if it were racing in neutral, getting nowhere. Within that sphere was the total energy that had been poured out by five gigantic beams, turned on full, for almost a minute's time. Compressed energy! Energy enough to blast these mountains down to the primal rock were it released instantly. Energy trapped and held by virtue of some peculiarity of that little borderline between Force Fields 348 and 349.

Russ walked across the room to a small electric truck with rubber caterpillar treads, driven by a bank of portable accumulators. Skillfully the scientist maneuvered it over to the other side of the room, picked up a steel bar four inches in diameter and five feet long. Holding it by the handler's magnetic crane, he fixed it firmly in the armlike jaws on the front of the machine, then moved the machine into a position straddling the sphere of force.

With smashing momentum the iron jaws thrust downward, driving the steel bar into the sphere. There was a groaning crash as the handler came to a halt, shuddering, with only eight inches of the bar buried in the sphere. The stench of hot insulation filled the room while the electric motor throbbed, the rubber treads creaked, the machine groaned and strained, but the bar would go no farther.

Russ shut off the machine and stood back.

"That gives you an idea," he said grimly.

"The trick now," Greg said, "is to break down the field."

Without a word, Russ reached for the power controls. A sudden roar of thunderous fury and the beams leaped at the sphere ... but this time the sphere did not materialize again. Again the wrench shuddered through the laboratory, a wrench that seemed to distort space and time.

Then, as abruptly as it had come, it was gone. But when it ended, something gigantic and incomprehensibly powerful seemed to rush soundlessly by ... something that was felt and sensed. It was like a great noiseless, breathless wind in the dead of night that rushed by them and through them, all about them in space and died slowly away.

But the vanished steel did not reappear with the disappearance of the sphere and the draining away of power. Almost grotesquely now, the handler stood poised above the place where the sphere had been and in its jaws it held the bar. But the end of the bar, the eight inches that had been within the sphere, was gone. It had been sliced off so sharply that it left a highly reflective concave mirror on the severed surface.

"Where is it?" demanded Manning. "In that higher dimension?"

Russ shook his head. "You noticed that rushing sensation? That may have been the energy of matter rushing into some other space. It may be the key to the energy of matter!"

Gregory Manning stared at the bar. "I'm staying with you, Russ. I'm seeing this thing through."

"I knew you would," said Russ.

Triumph flamed briefly in Manning's eyes. "And when we finish, we'll have something that will break Interplanetary. We'll smash their stranglehold on the Solar System." He stopped and looked at Page. "Lord, Russ," he whispered, "do you realize what we'll have?"

"I think I do, Greg," the scientist answered soberly. "Material energy engines. Power so cheap that you won't be able to give it away. More power than anybody could ever need."

CHAPTER III

Russ hunched over the keyboard set in the control room of the *Comet* and stared down at the keys. The equation was set and ready. All he had to do was tap that key and they would know, beyond all argument, whether or not they had dipped into the awful heart of material energy; whether, finally, they held in their grasp the key to the release of energy that would give the System power to spare.

His glance lifted from the keyboard, looked out the observation port. Through the inkiness of space ran a faint blue thread, a tiny line that stretched from the ship and away until it was lost in the darkness of the void.

One hundred thousand miles away, that thread touched the surface of a steel ball bearing ... a speck in the immensity of space.

He thought about that little beam of blue. It took power to do that, power to hold a beam tight and strong and steady through the stress of one hundred thousand miles. But it had to be that far away ... and they had that power. From the bowels of the ship came the deep purr of it, the angry, silky song of mighty engines throttled down.

He heard Harry Wilson shuffling impatiently behind him, smelled the acrid smoke that floated from the tip of Wilson's cigarette.

"Might as well punch that key, Russ," said Manning's cool voice. "We have to find out sooner or later."

Russ's finger hovered over the key, steadied and held. When he punched that key, if everything worked right, the energy in the tiny ball bearing would be released instantaneously. The energy of a piece of steel, weighing less than an ounce. Over that tight beam of blue would flash the impulse of destruction....

His fingers plunged down.

Space flamed in front of them. For just an instant the void seemed filled with an angry, bursting fire that lapped with hungry tongues of cold, blue light toward the distant planets. A flare so intense that it was visible on the Jovian worlds, three hundred million miles away. It lighted the night-side of Earth, blotting out the stars and Moon, sending astronomers scurrying for their telescopes, rating foot-high streamers in the night editions.

Slowly Russ turned around and faced his friend.

"We have it, Greg," he said. "We really have it. We've tested the control formulas all along the line. We know what we can do."

"We don't know it all yet," declared Greg. "We know we can make it work, but I have a feeling we haven't more than skimmed the surface possibilities."

Russ sank into a chair and stared about the room. They knew they could generate alternating current of any frequency they chose by use of a special collector apparatus. They could release radiant energy in almost any quantity they desired, in any wave-length, from the longest radio to the incredibly hard cosmics. The electrical power they could measure accurately and easily by simple voltmeters and ammeters. But radiant energy was another thing. When it passed all hitherto known bonds, it would simply fuse any instrument they might use to measure it.

But they knew the power they generated. In one split second they had burst the energy bonds of a tiny bit of steel and that energy had glared briefly more hotly than the Sun.

"Greg," he said, "it isn't often you can say that any event was the beginning of a new era. You can with this-the era of unlimited power. It kind of scares me."

Up until a hundred years ago coal and oil and oxygen had been the main power sources, but with the dwindling of the supply of coal and oil, man had sought another way. He had turned back to the old dream of snatching power direct from the Sun. In the year 2048 Patterson had perfected the photo-cell. Then the Alexanderson accumulators made it possible to pump the life-blood of power to the far reaches of the System, and on Mercury and Venus, and to a lesser extent on Earth, great accumulator power plants had sprung up, with Interplanetary, under the driving genius of Spencer Chambers, gaining control of the market.

The photo-cell and the accumulator had spurred interplanetary trade and settlement. Until it had been possible to store Sun-power for the driving of spaceships and for shipment to the outer planets, ships had been driven by rocket fuel, and the struggling colonies on the outer worlds had fought a bitter battle without the aid of ready power.

Coal and oil there were in plenty on the outer worlds, but one other essential was lacking ... oxygen. Coal on Mars, for instance, had to burned under synthetic air pressures, like the old carburetor. The result was inefficiency. A lot of coal burned, not enough power delivered.

Even the photo-cells were inefficient when attempts were made to operate them beyond the Earth; that was the maximum distance for maximum Solar efficiency.

Russ dug into the pocket of his faded, scuffed leather jacket and hauled forth pipe and pouch. Thoughtfully he tamped the tobacco into the bowl.

"Three months," he said. "Three months of damn hard work."

"Yeah," agreed Wilson, "we sure have worked."

Wilson's face was haggard, his eyes red. He blew smoke through his nostrils.

"When we get back, how about us taking a little vacation?" he asked.

Russ laughed. "You can if you want to. Greg and I are keeping on."

"We can't waste time," Manning said. "Spencer Chambers may get wind of this. He'd move all hell to stop us."

Wilson spat out his cigarette. "Why don't you patent what you have? That would protect you."

Russ grinned, but it was a sour one.

"No use," said Greg. "Chambers would tie us up in a mile of legal red tape. It would be just like walking up and handing it to him."

"You guys go ahead and work," Wilson stated. "I'm taking a vacation. Three months is too damn long to stay out in a spaceship."

"It doesn't seem long to me," said Greg, his tone cold and sharp.

No, thought Russ, it hadn't seemed long. Perhaps the hours had been rough, the work hard, but he hadn't noticed. Sleep and food had come in snatches. For three months they had worked in space, not daring to carry out their experiments on Earth ... frankly afraid of the thing they had.

He glanced at Manning.

The three months had left no mark upon him, no hint of fatigue or strain. Russ understood now how Manning had done the things he did. The man was all steel and flame. Nothing could touch him.

"We still have a lot to do," said Manning.

Russ leaned back and puffed at his pipe.

Yes, there was a lot to do. Transmission problems, for instance. To conduct away such terrific power as they knew they were capable of developing would require copper or silver bars as thick as a man's thigh, and even so at voltages capable of jumping a two-foot spark gap.

Obviously, a small machine such as they now had would be impractical. No matter how perfectly it might be insulated, the atmosphere itself would not be an insulator, with power such as this. And if one tried to deliver the energy as a mechanical rotation of a shaft, what shaft could transmit it safely and under control?

"Oh, hell," Russ burst out, "let's get back to Earth."

Harry Wilson watched the couple alight from the aero-taxi, walk up the broad steps and pass through the magic portals of the Martian Club. He could imagine what the club was like, the deference of the management, the exotic atmosphere of the dining room, the excellence of the long, cold drinks served at the bar. Mysterious drinks concocted of ingredients harvested in the jungles of Venus, spiced with produce from the irrigated gardens of Mars.

He puffed on the dangling cigarette and shuffled on along the airy highwalk. Below and above him, all around him flowed the beauty and the glamor, the bravery and the splendor of New York. The city's song was in his ears, the surging noises that were its voice.

Two thousand feet above his head reared giant pinnacles of shining metal, glinting in the noonday sun, architecture that bore the alien stamp of other worlds.

Wilson turned around, stared at the Martian Club. A man needed money to pass through those doors, to taste the drinks that slid across its bar, to sit and watch its floor shows, to hear the music of its orchestras.

For a moment he stood, hesitating, as if he were trying to make up his mind. He flipped away the cigarette, turned on his heel, walked briskly to the automatic elevator which would take him to the lower levels.

There, on the third level, he entered a Mecho restaurant, sat down at a table and ordered from the robot waiter, pushing ivory-tipped buttons on the menu before him.

He ate leisurely, smoked ferociously, thinking. Looking at his watch, he saw that it was nearly two o'clock. He walked to the cashier machine, inserted the metallic check with the correct change and received from the clicking, chuckling register the disk that would let him out the door.

"Thank you, come again," the cashier-robot fluted.

"Don't mention it," growled Wilson.

Outside the restaurant he walked briskly. Ten blocks away he came to a building roofing four square blocks. Over the massive doorway, set into the beryllium steel, was a map of the Solar System, a map that served as a cosmic clock, tracing the movement of the planets as they swung in their long arcs around the Sun. The Solar System was straddled by glowing, golden letters. They read: Interplanetary Building.

It was from here that Spencer Chambers ruled his empire built on power.

Wilson went inside.

CHAPTER IV

The new apparatus was set up, a machine that almost filled the laboratory ... a giant, compact mass of heavy, solidly built metal work, tied together by beams of girderlike construction. It was meant to stand up under the hammering of unimaginable power, the stress of unknown spatial factors.

Slowly, carefully, Russell Page tapped keys on the control board, setting up an equation. Sucking thoughtfully at his pipe, he checked and rechecked them.

Harry Wilson regarded him through squinted eyes.

"What the hell is going to happen now?" he asked.

"We'll have to wait and see," Russ answered. "We know what we want to happen, what we hope will happen, but we never can be sure. We are working with conditions that are entirely new."

Sitting beside a table littered with papers, staring at the gigantic machine before him, Gregory Manning said slowly: "That thing simply has to adapt itself to spaceship drive. There's everything there that's needed for space propulsion. Unlimited power from a minimum of fuel. Split-second efficiency. Entire independence of any set condition, because the stuff creates its own conditions."

He slowly wagged his head.

"The secret is some place along the line," he declared. "I feel that we must be getting close to it."

Russ walked from the control board to the table, picked up a sheaf of papers and leafed through them. He selected a handful and shook them in his fist.

"I thought I had it here," he said. "My math must have been wrong, some factor that I didn't include in the equation."

"You'll keep finding factors for some time yet," Greg prophesied.

"Repulsion would have been the answer," said Russ bitterly. "And the Lord knows we have it. Plenty of it."

"Too much," observed Wilson, smoke drooling from his nostrils.

"Not too much," corrected Greg. "Inefficient control. You jump at conclusions, Wilson."

"The math didn't show that progressive action," said Russ. "It showed repulsion, negative gravity that could be built up until it would shoot the ship outside the Solar System within an hour's time. Faster than light. We don't know how many times faster."

"Forget it," advised Greg. "The way it stands, it's useless. You get repulsion by progressive steps. A series of squares with one constant factor. It wouldn't be any good for space travel. Imagine trying to use it on a spaceship. You'd start with a terrific jolt. The acceleration would fade and just when you were recovering from the first jolt, you'd get a second one and that second one would iron you out. A spaceship couldn't take it, let alone a human body."

"Maybe this will do it," said Wilson hopefully.

"Maybe," agreed Russ. "Anyhow we'll try it. Equation 578."

"It might do the trick," said Greg. "It's a new approach to the gravity angle. The equation explains the shifting of gravitational lines, the changing and contortion of their direction. Twist gravity and you have a perfect space drive. As good as negative gravity. Better, perhaps, more easily controlled. Would make for more delicate, precise handling."

Russ laid down the sheaf of papers, lit his pipe and walked to the apparatus.

"Here goes," he said.

His hand went out to the power lever, eased it in. With a roar the material energy engine built within the apparatus surged into action, sending a flow of power through the massive leads. The thunder mounted in the room. The laboratory seemed to shudder with the impact.

Wilson, watching intently, cried out, a brief, choked-off cry. A wave of dizziness engulfed him. The walls seemed to be falling in. The room and the machine were blurring. Russ, at the controls, seemed horribly disjointed. Manning was a caricature of a man, a weird, strange figure that moved and gestured in the mad room.

Wilson fought against the dizziness. He tried to take a step and the floor seemed to leap up and meet his outstretched foot, throwing him off balance. His cigarette fell out of his mouth, rolled along the floor.

Russ was shouting something, but the words were distorted, loud one instant, rising over the din of the apparatus, a mere whisper the next. They made no sense.

There was a peculiar whistling in the air, a sound such as he had never heard before. It seemed to come from far away, a high, thin shriek that was torture in one's ears.

Giddy, seized with deathly nausea, Wilson clawed his way across the floor, swung open the laboratory door and stumbled outdoors. He weaved across the lawn and clung to a sun dial, panting.

He looked back at the laboratory and gasped in disbelief. All the trees were bent toward the building, as if held by some mighty wind. Their branches straining, every single leaf standing at rigid attention, the trees were bending in toward the structure. *But there was no wind.*

And then he noticed something else. No matter where the trees stood, no matter in what direction from the laboratory, they all bent inward toward the building ... and the whining, thundering, shrieking machine.

Inside the laboratory an empty bottle crashed off a table and smashed into a thousand fragments. The tinkling of the broken glass was a silvery, momentary sound that protested against the blasting thrum of power that shook the walls.

Manning fought along the floor to Russ's side. Russ roared in his ear: "Gravitational control! Concentration of gravitational lines!"

The papers on the desk started to slide, slithering onto the floor, danced a crazy dervish across the room. Liquids in the laboratory bottles were climbing the sides of glass, instead of lying at rest parallel with the floor. A chair skated, bucking and tipping crazily, toward the door.

Russ jerked the power lever back to zero. The power hum died. The liquids slid back to their natural level, the chair tipped over and lay still, papers fluttered gently downward.

The two men looked at one another across the few feet of floor space between them. Russ wiped beads of perspiration from his forehead with his shirt sleeve. He sucked on his pipe, but it was dead.

"Greg," Russ said jubilantly, "we have something better than anti-gravity! We have something you might call *positive* gravity ... gravity that we can control. Your grandfather nullified gravity. We've gone him one better."

Greg gestured toward the machine. "You created an attraction center. What else?"

"But the center itself is not actually an attracting force. The fourth dimension is mixed up in this. We have a sort of fourth-dimensional lens that concentrates the lines of any gravitational force. Concentration in the fourth dimension turns the force loose in three dimensions, but we can take care of that by using mirrors of our anti-entropy. We can arrange it so that it turns the force loose in only one dimension."

Greg was thoughtful for a moment. "We can guide a ship by a series of lenses," he declared at last. "But here's the really important thing. That field concentrates the forces of gravity already present. Those forces exist throughout all of space. There are gravitational lines everywhere. We can concentrate them in any direction we want to. In reality, we fall toward the body which originally caused the force of gravitation, not to the concentration."

Russ nodded. "That means we can create a field immediately ahead of the ship. The ship would fall into it constantly, with the concentration moving on ahead. The field would tend to break down in proportion to the strain imposed and a big ship, especially when you are building up speed, would tend to enlarge it, open it up. But the field could be kept tight by supplying energy and we have plenty of that ... far more than we'd ever need. We supply the energy, but that's only a small part of it. The body emitting the gravitational force supplies the fulcrum that moves us along."

"It would operate beyond the planets," said Greg. "It would operate equally well anywhere in space, for all of space is filled with gravitational stress. We could use gravitational bodies many light years away as the driver of our ships."

A half-wild light glowed momentarily in his eyes.

"Russ," he said, "we're going to put space fields to work at last."

He walked to the chair, picked it up and sat down in it.

"We'll start building a ship," he stated, "just as soon as we know the mechanics of this gravity concentration and control. Russ, we'll build the greatest ship, the fastest ship, the most powerful ship the Solar System has ever known!"

"Damn," said Russ, "that thing's slipped again."

He glared at the offending nut. "I'll put a lock washer on it this time."

Wilson stepped toward the control board. From his perch on the apparatus, Russ motioned him away.

"Never mind discharging the field," he said. "I can get around it somehow."

Wilson squinted at him. "This tooth is near killing me."

"Still got a toothache?" asked Russ.

"Never got a wink of sleep last night."

"You better run down to Frisco and have it yanked out," suggested the scientist. "Can't have you laid up."

"Yeah, that's right," agreed Wilson. "Maybe I will. We got a lot to do."

Russ reached out and clamped his wrench on the nut, quickly backed it off and slipped on the washer. Viciously he tightened it home. The wrench stuck.

Gritting his teeth on the bit of his pipe, Russ cursed soundlessly. He yanked savagely at the wrench. It slipped from his hand, hung for a minute on the nut and then plunged downward, falling straight into the heart of the new force field they had developed.

Russ froze and watched, his heart in his throat, mad thoughts in his brain. In a flash, as the wrench fell, he remembered that they knew nothing about this field. All they knew was that any matter introduced in it suddenly acquired an acceleration in the dimension known as time, with its normal constant of duration reduced to zero.

When that wrench struck the field, it would cease to exist! But something else might happen, too, something entirely unguessable.

The wrench fell only a few feet, but it seemed to take long seconds as Russ watched, frozen in fascination.

He saw it strike the hazy glow that defined the limits of the field, saw it floating down, as if its speed had been slowed by some dense medium.

In the instant that hazy glow intensified a thousand times-became a blinding sun-burst! Russ ducked his head, shielded his eyes from the terrible blast of light. A rending, shuddering thud seemed to echo …in space rather than in air …and both field and wrench were gone!

A moment passed, then another, and there was the heavy, solid clanging thud of something striking metal. This time the thud was not in space, but a commonplace noise, as if someone had dropped a tool on the floor above.

Russ turned around and stared at Wilson. Wilson stared back, his mouth hanging open, the smoldering, cigarette dangling from his mouth.

"Greg!" Russ shouted, his cry shattering the silence in the laboratory.

A door burst open and Manning stepped into the main laboratory room, a calculation pad in one hand, a pencil in the other.

"What's the matter?" he demanded.

"We have to find my wrench!"

"Your wrench?" Greg was puzzled. "Can't you get another?"

"I dropped it into the field. Its time-dimension was reduced to zero. It became an 'instantaneous wrench'."

"Nothing new in that," said Greg, unruffled.

"But there is," persisted Russ. "The field collapsed, you see. Maybe the wrench was too big for it to handle. And when the field collapsed the wrench gained a new time-dimension. I heard it. We have to find it."

The three of them pounded up the stairs to the room where Russ had heard the thump. There was nothing on the floor. They searched the room from end to end, then the other rooms. There was no wrench.

At the end of an hour Greg went back to the main laboratory, brought back a portable fluoroscope.

"Maybe this will do the trick," he announced bleakly.

It did. They found the wrench *inside the space between the walls*!

Russ stared at the shadow in the fluoroscope plate. Undeniably it was the shadow of the wrench.

"Fourth dimension," he said. "Transported in time."

The muscles in Greg's cheeks were tensed, that old flame of excitement burning in his eyes, but otherwise his face was the mask of old, the calm, almost terrible mask that had faced a thousand dangers.

"Power and time," he corrected.

"If we can control it," said Russ.

"Don't worry. We can control it. And when we can, it's the biggest thing we've got."

Wilson licked his lips, dredged a cigarette out of a pocket.

"If you don't mind," he said, "I'll hit for Frisco tonight. This tooth of mine is getting worse."

"Sure, can't keep an aching tooth," agreed Russ, thinking of the wrench while talking.

"Can I take your ship?" asked Wilson.

"Sure," said Russ.

Back in the laboratory they rebuilt the field, dropped little ball bearings in it. The ball bearings disappeared. They found them everywhere-in the walls, in tables, in the floor. Some, still existing in their new time-dimension, hung in mid-air, invisible, intangible, but there.

Hours followed hours, with the sheet of data growing. Math machines whirred and chuckled and clicked. Wilson departed for San Francisco with his aching tooth. The other two worked on. By dawn they knew what they were doing. Out of the chaos of happenstance they were finding rules of order, certain formulas of behavior, equations of force.

The next day they tried heavier, more complicated things and learned still more.

A radiogram, phoned from the nearest spaceport, forty miles distant, informed them that Wilson would not be back for a few days. His tooth was worse than he had thought, required an operation and treatment of the jaw.

"Hell," said Russ, "just when he could be so much help."

With Wilson gone the two of them tackled the controlling device, labored and swore over it. But finally it was completed.

Slumped in chairs, utterly exhausted, they looked proudly at it.

"With that," said Russ, "we can take an object and transport it any place we want. Not only that, we can pick up any object from an indefinite distance and bring it to us."

"What a thing for a lazy burglar," Greg observed sourly.

Worn out, they gulped sandwiches and scalding coffee, tumbled into bed.

The outdoor camp meeting was in full swing. The evangelist was in his top form. The sinners' bench was crowded. Then suddenly, as the evangelist paused for a moment's silence before he drove home an important point, the music came. Music from the air. Music from somewhere in the sky. The soft, heavenly music of a hymn. As if an angels' chorus were singing in the blue.

The evangelist froze, one arm pointing upward, with index finger ready to sweep down and emphasize his point. The sinners kneeling at the bench were petrified. The congregation was astounded.

The hymn rolled on, punctuated, backgrounded by deep celestial organ notes. The clear voice of the choir swept high to a bell-like note.

"Behold!" shrieked the evangelist. "Behold, a miracle! Angels singing for us! Kneel! Kneel and pray!"

Nobody stood.

Andy McIntyre was drunk again. In the piteous glare of mid-morning, he staggered homeward from the poker party in the back of Steve Abram's harness shop. The light revealed him to the scorn of the entire village.

At the corner of Elm and Third he ran into a maple tree. Uncertainly he backed away, intent on making another try. Suddenly the tree spoke to him:

"Alcohol is the scourge of mankind. It turns men into beasts. It robs them of their brains, it shortens their lives..."

Andy stared, unable to believe what he heard. The tree, he had no doubt, was talking to him personally.

The voice of the tree went on: "...takes the bread out of the mouths of women and children. Fosters crime. Weakens the moral fiber of the nation."

"Stop!" screamed Andy. "Stop, I tell you!"

The tree stopped talking. All he could hear was the whisper of wind among its autumn-tinted leaves.

Suddenly running, Andy darted around the corner, headed home.

"Begad," he told himself, "when trees start talkin' to you it's time to lay off the bottle!"

In another town fifty miles distant from the one in which the tree had talked to Andy McIntyre, another miracle happened that same Sunday morning.

Dozens of people heard the bronze statue of the soldier in the courtyard speak. The statue did not come to life. It stood as ever, a solid piece of golden bronze, in spots turned black and green by weather. But from its lips came words ...words that burned themselves into the souls of those who heard. Words that exhorted them to defend the principles for which many men had died, to grasp and hold high the torch of democracy and liberty.

In somber bitterness, the statue called Spencer Chambers the greatest threat to that liberty and freedom. For, the statue said, Spencer Chambers and Interplanetary Power were waging an economic war, a bloodless one, but just as truly war as if there were cannons firing and bombs exploding.

For a full five minutes the statue spoke and the crowd, growing by the minute, stood dumbfounded.

Then silence fell over the courtyard. The statue stood as before, unmoving, its timeless eyes staring out from under the ugly helmet, its hands gripping the bayoneted rifle. A blue and white pigeon fluttered softly down, alighted on the bayonet, looked the crowd over and then flew to the courthouse tower.

Back in the laboratory, Russ looked at Greg.

"That radio trick gives me an idea," he said. "If we can put a radio in statues and trees without interfering with its operation, why can't we do the same thing with a television set?"

Greg started. "Think of the possibilities of that!" he burst out.

Within an hour a complete television sending apparatus was placed within the field and a receptor screen set up in the laboratory.

The two moved chairs in front of the screen and sat down. Russ reached out and pulled the switch of the field control. The screen came to life, but it was only a gray blur.

"It's traveling too fast," said Greg. "Slow it down."

Russ retarded the lever. "When that thing's on full, it's almost instantaneous. It travels in a time dimension and any speed slower than instantaneity is a modification of that force field."

On the screen swam a panorama of the mountains, mile after mile of snow-capped peaks and valleys ablaze with the flames of autumn foliage. The mountains faded away. There was desert now and then a city. Russ dropped the televisor set lower, down into a street. For half an hour they sat comfortably in their chairs and watched men and women walking, witnessed one dog fight, cruised slowly up and down, looking into windows of homes, window-shopping in the business section.

"There's just one thing wrong," said Greg. "We can see everything, but we can't hear a sound."

"We can fix that," Russ told him.

He lifted the televisor set from the streets, brought it back across the desert and mountains into the laboratory.

"We have two practical applications now," said Greg. "Space drive and television spying. I don't know which is the best. Do you realize that with this television trick there isn't a thing that can be hidden from us?"

"I believe we can go to Mars or Mercury or anywhere we want to with this thing. It doesn't seem to have any particular limits. It handles perfectly. You can move it a fraction of an inch as easily as a hundred miles. And it's fast. Almost instantaneous. Not quite, for even with our acceleration within time, there is a slight lag."

By evening they had an audio apparatus incorporated in the set, had wired the screen for sound.

"Let's put this to practical use," suggested Greg. "There's a show at the New Mercury Theater in New York I've been wanting to see. Let's knock off work and take in that show."

"Now," said Russ, "you really have an idea. The ticket scalpers are charging a fortune, and it won't cost us a cent to get in!"

Pine roots burned brightly in the fireplace, snapping and sizzling as the blaze caught and flamed on the resin. Deep in an easy chair, Greg Manning stretched his long legs out toward the fire and lifted his glass, squinting at the flames through the amber drink.

"There's something that's been worrying me a little," he said. "I hadn't told you about it because I figured it wasn't as serious as it looked. Maybe it isn't, but it looks funny."

"What's that?" asked Russ.

"The stock market," replied Greg. "There's something devilish funny going on there. I've lost about a billion dollars in the last two weeks."

"A *billion* dollars?" gasped Russ.

Greg swirled the whiskey in his glass. "Don't sound so horrified. The loss is all on paper. My stocks have gone down. Most of them cut in half. Some even less than that. Martian Irrigation is down to 75. I paid 185 for it. It's worth 200."

"You mean something has happened to the market?"

"Not to the market. If that was it, I wouldn't worry. I've seen the market go up and down. That's nothing to worry about. But the market, except for a slight depression, has behaved normally in these past two weeks. It almost looks as if somebody was out to get me."

"Who'd want to and why?"

Greg sighed. "I wish I knew. I haven't really lost a cent, of course. My shares can't stay down for very long. The thing is that right now I can't sell them even for what I paid for them. If I sold now I'd lose that billion. But as long as I don't have to sell, the loss is merely on paper."

He sipped at the drink and stared into the fire.

"If you don't have to, what are you worrying about?" asked Russ.

"Couple of things. I put that stock up as collateral to get the cash to build the spaceship. At present prices, it will take more securities than I thought. If the prices continue to go down, I'll have the bulk of my holdings tied up in the spaceship. I might even be forced to liquidate some of it and that would mean an actual loss."

He hunched forward in the chair, stared at Russ.

"Another thing," he said grimly, "is that I hate the idea of somebody singling me out as a target. As if they were going to make a financial example of me."

"And it sounds as if someone has," agreed Russ.

Greg leaned back again, drained his glass and set it down.

"It certainly does," he said.

Outside, seen through the window beside the fireplace, the harvest moon was a shield of silver hung in the velvet of the sky. A lonesome wind moaned in the pines and under the eaves.

"I got a report from Belgium the other day," said Greg. "The spaceship is coming along. It'll be the biggest thing afloat in space."

"The biggest and the toughest," said Russ, and Greg nodded silent agreement.

The ship itself was being manufactured at the great Space Works in Belgium, but other parts of it, apparatus, engines, gadgets of every description, were being manufactured at other widely scattered points. Anyone wondering what kind of ship the finished product would be would have a hard time gathering the correct information, which, of course, was the idea. The "anyone" they were guarding against was Spencer Chambers.

"We need a better television set," said Russ. "This one we have is all right, but we need the best there is. I wonder if Wilson could get us one in Frisco and bring it back."

"I don't see why not," said Greg. "Send him a radio."

Russ stepped to the phone, called the spaceport and filed the message.

"He always stays at the Greater Martian," he told Greg. "We'll probably catch him there."

Two hours later the phone rang. It was the spaceport.

"That message you sent to Wilson," said the voice of the operator, "can't be delivered. Wilson isn't at the Greater Martian. The clerk said he checked out for New York last night."

"Didn't he leave a forwarding address?" asked Russ.

"Apparently not."

Russ hung up the receiver, frowning. "Wilson is in New York."

Greg looked up from a sheet of calculations.

"New York, eh?" he said and then went back to work, but a moment later he straightened from his work. "What would Wilson be doing in New York?"

"I wonder ..." Russ stopped and shook his head.

"Exactly," said Greg. He glanced out of the window, considering, the muscles in his cheeks knotting. "Russ, we both are thinking the same thing."

"I hate to think it," said Russ evenly. "I hate to think such a thing about a man."

"One way to find out," declared Greg. He rose from the chair and walked to the television control board, snapped the switch. Russ took a chair beside him. On the screen the mountains danced weirdly as the set rocketed swiftly away and then came the glint of red and yellow desert. Blackness blanked out the screen as the set plunged into the ground, passing through the curvature of the Earth's surface. The blackness passed and fields and farms were beneath them on the screen, a green and brown checkerboard with tiny white lines that were roads.

New York was in the screen now. Greg's hand moved the control and the city rushed up at them, the spires speeding toward them like plunging spears. Down into the canyons plunged the set, down into the financial district with its beetling buildings that hemmed in the roaring traffic.

Grimly, surely, Greg drove his strange machine through New York. Through buildings, through shimmering planes, through men. Like an arrow the television set sped to its mark and then Greg's hand snapped back the lever and in the screen was a building that covered four whole blocks. Above the entrance was the famous Solar System map and straddling the map were the gleaming golden letters: Interplanetary Building.

"Now we'll see," said Greg.

He heard the whistle of the breath in Russ's nostrils as the television set began to move, saw the tight grip Russ had upon the chair arms.

The interior of the building showed on the screen as he drove the set through steel and stone, offices and corridors and brief glimpses of steel partitions, until it came to a door marked: Spencer Chambers, President.

Greg's hand twisted the control slightly and the set went through the door, into the office of Spencer Chambers.

Four men were in the room-Chambers himself; Craven, the scientist; Arnold Grant, head of Interplanetary's publicity department, *and Harry Wilson*!

Wilson's voice came out of the screen, a frantic, almost terrified voice.

"I've told you all I know. I'm not a scientist. I'm a mechanic. I've told you what they're doing. I can't tell you how they do it."

Arnold Grant leaned forward in his chair. His face was twisted in fury.

"There were plans, weren't there?" he demanded. "There were equations and formulas. Why didn't you bring us some of them?"

Spencer Chambers raised a hand from the desk, waved it toward Grant. "The man has told us all he knows. Obviously, he can't be any more help to us."

"You told him to go back and see if he couldn't find something else, didn't you?" asked Grant.

"Yes, I did," Chambers told him. "But apparently he couldn't find it."

"I tried," pleaded Wilson. Perspiration stood out on his forehead. The cigarette in his mouth was limp and dead. "One of them was always there. I never could get hold of any papers. I asked questions, but they were too busy to answer. And I couldn't ask too much, because then they would have suspected me."

"No, you couldn't do that," commented Craven with an open sneer.

In the laboratory Russ pounded the arm of his chair with a clenched fist. "The rat sold us out!"

Greg said nothing, but his face was stony and his eyes were crystal-hard.

On the screen Chambers was speaking to Wilson. "Do you think you could find something out if you went back again?"

Wilson squirmed in his chair.

"I'd rather not." His voice sounded like a whimper. "I'm afraid they suspect me now. I'm afraid of what they'd do if they found out."

"That's his conscience," breathed Russ in the laboratory. "I never suspected him."

"He's right about one thing, though," Greg said. "He'd better not come back."

Chambers was talking again: "You realize, of course, that you haven't been much help to us. You have only warned us that another kind of power generation is being developed. You've set us on our guard, but other than that we're no better off than we were before."

Wilson bristled, like a cowardly animal backed into a corner. "I told you what was going on. You can be ready for it now. I can't help it if I couldn't find out how all them things worked."

"Look here," said Chambers. "I made a bargain with you and I keep my bargains. I told you I would pay you twenty thousand dollars for the information you gave me when you first came to see me. I told you I'd pay you for any further additional information you might give. Also I promised you a job with the company."

Watching the financier, Wilson licked his lips. "That's right," he said.

Chambers reached out and pulled a checkbook toward him, lifted a pen from its holder. "I'm paying you the twenty thousand for the warning. I'm not paying you a dime more, because you gave me no other information."

Wilson leaped to his feet, started to protest.

"Sit down," said Chambers coldly.

"But the job! You said you'd give me a job!"

Chambers shook his head. "I wouldn't have a man like you in my organization. If you were a traitor to one man, you would be to another."

"But ... but ..." Wilson started to object and then sat down, his face twisted in something that came very close to fear.

Chambers ripped the check out of the book, waved it slowly in the air to dry it. Then he arose and held it out to Wilson, who reached out a trembling hand and took it.

"And now," said Chambers, "good day, Mr. Wilson."

For a moment Wilson stood uncertain, as if he intended to speak, but finally he turned, without a word, and walked through the door.

In the laboratory Russ and Greg looked at one another.

"Twenty thousand," said Greg. "Why, that was worth millions."

"It was worth everything Chambers had," said Russ, "because it's the thing that's going to wreck him."

Their attention snapped back to the screen.

Chambers was hunched over his desk, addressing the other two.

"Now, gentlemen," he asked, "what are we to do?"

Craven shrugged his shoulders. There was a puzzled frown in the eyes back of the thick-lensed glasses. "We haven't much to go on. Wilson doesn't know a thing about it. He hasn't the brain to grasp even the most fundamental ideas back of the whole thing."

Chambers nodded. "The man knew the mechanical setup perfectly, but that was all."

"I've constructed the apparatus," said Craven. "It's astoundingly simple. Almost too simple to do the things Wilson said it would do. He drew plans for it, so clear that it was easy to duplicate the apparatus. He himself checked the machine and says it is the same as Page and Manning have. But there are thousands of possible combinations for hookups and control board settings. Too many to try to go through and hit upon the right answer. Because, you see, one slight adjustment in any one of a hundred adjustments might do the trick ... but which of those adjustments do you have to make? We have to have the formulas, the equations, before we can even move."

"He seemed to remember a few things," said Grant hopefully. "Certain rules and formulas."

Craven flipped both his hands angrily. "Worse than nothing," he exploded. "What Page and Manning have done is so far in advance of anything that anyone else has even thought about that we are completely at sea. They're working with space fields, apparently, and we haven't even scratched the surface in that branch of investigation. We simply haven't got a thing to go on."

"No chance at all?" asked Chambers.

Craven shook his head slowly.

"At least you could try," snapped Grant.

"Now, wait," Chambers snapped back. "You seem to forget Dr. Craven is one of the best scientists in the world today. I'm relying on him."

Craven smiled. "I can't do anything with what Page and Manning have, but I might try something of my own."

"By all means do so," urged Chambers. He turned to Grant. "I observed you have carried out the plans we laid. Martian Irrigation hit a new low today."

Grant grinned. "It was easy. Just a hint here and there to the right people."

Chambers looked down at his hands, slowly closing into fists. "We have to stop them some way, any way at all. Keep up the rumors. We'll make it impossible for Greg Manning to finance this new invention. We'll take away every last dollar he has."

He glared at the publicity man. "You understand?"

"Yes, sir," said Grant, "I understand perfectly."

"All right," said Chambers. "And your job, Craven, is to either develop what Page has found or find something we can use in competition."

Craven growled angrily. "What happens if your damn rumors can't ruin Manning? What if I can't find anything?"

"In that case," said Chambers, "there are other ways."

"Other ways?"

Chambers suddenly smiled at them. "I have a notion to call Stutsman back to Earth."

Craven drummed his fingers idly on the arm of his chair. "Yes, I guess you do have other ways," he said.

Greg's hand snapped the switch and the screen suddenly was blank as the televisor set returned instantly to the laboratory.

"That explains a lot of things," he said. "Among them what has happened to my stocks."

Russ sat in his chair, numbed. "That little weak-kneed, ratting traitor, Wilson. He'd sell his mother for a new ten-dollar bill."

"We know," said Greg, "and Chambers doesn't know we know. We'll follow every move he makes. We'll know every one of his plans."

Pacing up and down the room, he was already planning their campaign.

"There are still a few things to do," he added. "A few possibilities we may have overlooked."

"But will we have time?" asked Russ.

"I think so. Chambers is going to go slow. The gamble is too big to risk any slip. He doesn't want to get in bad with the law. There won't be any strong-arm stuff ... not until he recalls Stutsman from Callisto."

He paused in mid-stride, stood planted solidly on the floor.

"When Stutsman gets into the game," he said, "all hell will break loose."

He took a deep breath.

"But we'll be ready for it then!"

CHAPTER VI

"If we can get television reception with this apparatus of ours," asked Greg, "what is to prevent us from televising? Why can't we send as well as receive?"

Russ drew doodles on a calculation sheet. "We could. Just something else to work out. You must remember we're working in a four-dimensional medium. That would complicate matters a little. Not like working in three dimensions alone. It would..."

He stopped. The pencil fell from his finger and he swung around slowly to face Manning.

"What's the matter now?" asked Greg.

"Look," said Russ excitedly. "We're working in four dimensions. And if we televised through four dimensions, what would we get?"

Greg wrinkled his brow. Suddenly his face relaxed. "You don't mean we can televise in *three* dimensions, do you?"

"That's what it should work out to," declared Russ. He swung back to the table again, picked up his pencil and jotted down equations. He looked up from the sheet. "Three-dimensional television!" he almost whispered.

"Something new again," commented Greg.

"I'll say it's new!"

Russ reached out and jerked a calculator toward him. Rapidly he set up the equations, pressed the tabulator lever. The machine gurgled and chuckled, clicked out the result. Bending over to read it, Russ sucked in his breath.

"It's working out right," he said.

"That'll mean new equipment, lots of it," Greg pointed out. "Wilson's gone, damn him. Who's going to help us?"

"We'll do it ourselves," said Russ. "When we're the only ones here, we can be sure there won't be any leak."

It took hours of work on the math machines, but at the end of that time Russ was certain of his ground.

"Now we go to work," he said, gleefully.

In a week's time they had built a triple televisor, but simplifications of the standard commercial set gave them a mechanism that weighed little more and was far more efficient and accurate.

During the time the work went on they maintained a watch over both the office of Spencer Chambers and the laboratory in which Dr. Herbert Craven worked 16 hours a day. Unseen, unsuspected, they were silent companions of the two men during many hours. They read what the men wrote, read what was written to them, heard what they said, saw how they acted. Doing so, the pair in the high mountain laboratory gained a deep insight into the characters of unsuspecting quarries.

"Both utterly ruthless," declared Greg. "But apparently men who are sincere in thinking that the spoils belong to the strong. Strange, almost outdated men. You can't help but like Chambers. He's good enough at heart. He has his pet charities. He really, I believe, wants to help the people. And I think he actually believes the best way to do it is to gain a dictatorship over the Solar System. That ambition rules everything in his life. It has hardened him and strengthened him. He will crush ruthlessly, without a single qualm, anything that stands in his path. That's why we'll have a fight on our hands."

Craven seemed to be making little progress. They could only guess at what he was trying to develop.

"I think," said Russ, "he's working on a collector field to suck in radiant energy. If he really gets that, it will be something worth having."

For hours Craven sat, an intent, untidy, unkempt man, sunk deep in the cushions of an easy chair. His face was calm, with relaxed jaw and eyes that seemed vacant. But each time he would rouse himself from the chair to pencil new notations on the pads of paper that littered his desk. New ideas, new approaches.

The triple televisor was completed except for one thing.

"Sound isn't so easy," said Russ. "If we could only find a way to transmit it as well as light."

"Listen," said Greg, "why don't you try a condenser speaker."

"A condenser speaker?"

"Sure, the gadget developed way back in the 1920s. It hasn't been used for years to my knowledge, but it might do the trick."

Russ grinned broadly. "Hell, why didn't I think of that? Here I've been racking my brain for a new approach, a new wrinkle … and exactly what I wanted was at hand."

"Should work," declared Greg. "Just the opposite of a condenser microphone. Instead of radiating sound waves mechanically, it radiates a changing electric field and this field becomes audible directly within the ear. Even yet no one seems to understand just how it works, but it does … and that's good enough."

"I know," said Russ. "It really makes no sound. In other words it creates an electric field that doubles for sound. It ought to be just the thing because nothing can stop it. Metal shielding can, I guess, if it's thick enough, but it's got to be pretty damn thick."

It took time to set the mechanism up. Ready, the massive apparatus, within which glowed a larger and more powerful force field, was operated by two monstrous material energy engines. The controls were equipped with clockwork drives, designed so that the motion of the Earth could be nullified completely and automatically for work upon outlying planets.

Russ stood back and looked at it. "Stand in front of that screen, Greg," he said, "and we'll try it on you."

Greg stepped in front of the screen. The purr of power came on. Suddenly, materializing out of the air, came Greg's projection. Hazy and undefined at first, it rapidly assumed apparent solidity. Greg waved his arm; the image moved its arm.

Russ left the controls and walked across the laboratory to inspect the image. Examined from all sides, it looked solid. Russ walked through it and felt nothing. There was nothing there. It was just a three-dimensional image. But even from two feet away, it was as if the man himself stood there in all the actuality of flesh and blood.

"Hello, Russ," the image whispered. It held out a hand. "Glad to see you again."

Laughing, Russ thrust out his hand. It closed on nothing in mid-air, but the two men appeared to shake hands.

They tested the machine that afternoon. Their images strode above the trees, apparently walking on thin air. Gigantic replicas of Greg stood on a faraway mountain top and shouted with a thunderous voice. Smaller images, no more than two inches high, shinnied up a table leg.

Satisfied, they shut off the machine.

"That's one of the possibilities you mentioned," suggested Russ.

Greg nodded grimly.

An autumn gale pelted the windows with driving rain, and a wild, wet wind howled through the pines outside. The fire was leaping and flaring in the fireplace.

Deep in his chair, Russ stared into the flame and puffed at his pipe.

"The factory wants more money on the spaceship," said Greg from the other chair. "I had to put up some more shares as collateral on a new loan."

"Market still going down?" asked Russ.

"Not the market," replied Greg. "My stocks. All of them hit new lows today."

Russ dragged at the pipe thoughtfully. "I've been thinking about that stock business, Greg."

"So have I, but it doesn't seem to do much good."

"Look," said Russ slowly, "what planets have exchanges?"

"All of them except Mercury. The Jovian exchange is at Ranthoor. There's even one out at Pluto. Just mining and chemical shares listed, though."

Russ did not reply. Smoke curled up from his pipe. He was staring into the fire.

"Why do you ask?" Greg wanted to know.

"Just something stirring around in my mind. I was wondering where Chambers does most of his trading."

"Ranthoor now," said Greg. "Used to do it on Venus. The listing is larger there. But since he took over the Jovian confederacy, he switched his business to it. The transaction tax is lower. He saw to that."

"And the same shares are listed on the Callisto market as on the New York boards?"

"Naturally," said Greg, "only not as many."

Russ watched the smoke from his pipe. "How long does it take light to travel from Callisto to Earth?"

"Why, about 45 minutes, I guess. Somewhere around there." Greg sat upright. "Say, what's light got to do with this?"

"A lot," said Russ. "All commerce is based on the assumption that light is instantaneous, but it isn't. All business, anywhere throughout the Solar System, is based on Greenwich time. When a noon signal sent out from Earth reaches Mars, it's noon there, but as a matter of fact, it is actually 15 minutes or so past noon. When the same signal reaches Callisto, the correct time for the chronometer used in commerce would be noon when it is really a quarter to one. That system simplifies things. Does away with varying times. And it has worked all right so far because there has been, up to now, nothing that could go faster than light. No news can travel through space, no message, no signal can be sent at any speed greater than that. So everything has been fine."

Greg had come out of the chair, was standing on his feet, the glow of the blaze throwing his athletic figure into bold relief. That calm exterior had been stripped from him now. He was excited.

"I see what you are getting at! We have something that is almost instantaneous!"

"Almost," said Russ. "Not quite. There's a time lag somewhere. But it isn't noticeable except over vast distances."

"But it would beat ordinary light signals to Callisto. It would beat them there by almost 45 minutes."

"Almost," Russ agreed. "Maybe a split second less."

Greg strode up and down in front of the fireplace like a caged lion. "By heaven," he said, "we've got Chambers where we want him. We can beat the stock quotations to Callisto. With that advance knowledge of what the board is doing in New York, we can make back every dime I've lost. We can take Mr. Chambers to the cleaners!"

Russ grinned. "Exactly," he said. "We'll know 45 minutes in advance of the other traders what the market will be. Let's see Chambers beat that."

CHAPTER VII

Ben Wrail was taking things easy. Stretched out in his chair, with his cigar lit and burning satisfactorily, he listened to a radio program broadcast from Earth.

Through the window beside him, he could look out of his skyscraper apartment over the domed city of Ranthoor. Looming in the sky, slightly distorted by the heavy quartz of the distant dome, was massive Jupiter, a scarlet ball tinged with orange and yellow. Overwhelmingly luminous, monstrously large, it filled a large portion of the visible sky, a sight that brought millions of tourists to the Jovian moons each year, a sight that even the old-timers still must stare at, drawn by some unfathomable fascination.

Ben Wrail stared at it now, puffing at his cigar, listening to the radio. An awe-inspiring thing, a looming planet that seemed almost ready to topple and crash upon this airless, frigid world.

Wrail was an old-timer. For thirty years-Earth years-he had made his home in Ranthoor. He had seen the city grow from a dinky little mining camp enclosed by a small dome to one that boasted half a million population. The dome that now covered the city was the fourth one. Four times, like the nautilus, the city had outgrown its shell, until today it was the greatest domed city in the Solar System. Where life had once been cheap and where the scum of the system had held rendezvous, he had seen Ranthoor grow into a city of dignity, capital of the Jovian confederacy.

He had helped build that confederacy, had been elected a member of the constitution commission, had helped create the government and for over a decade had helped to make its laws.

But now ...Ben Wrail spat angrily and stuffed the cigar back in his mouth again, taking a fresh and fearsome grip. Now everything had changed. The Jovian worlds today were held in bond by Spencer Chambers. The government was in the hands of his henchmen. Duly elected, of course, but in an election held under the unspoken threat that Interplanetary Power would withdraw, leaving the moons circling the great planet without heat, air, energy. For the worlds of the Jovian confederacy, every single one of them, depended for their life upon the accumulators freighted outward from the Sun.

Talk of revolt was in the air, but, lacking a leader, it would get nowhere. John Moore Mallory was imprisoned on one of the prison spaceships that plied through the Solar System. Mallory, months ago, had been secretly transferred from the Callisto prison to the spaceship, but in a week's time the secret had been spread in angry whispers. If there had been riots and bloodshed, they would have been to no purpose. For revolution, even if successful, would gain nothing. It would merely goad Interplanetary Power into withdrawing, refusing to service the domed cities on the moons.

Ben Wrail stirred restlessly in his chair. The cigar had gone out. The radio program blared unheard. His eyes still looked out the window without seeing Jupiter.

"Damn," said Ben Wrail. Why did he have to go and spoil an evening thinking about this damned political situation? Despite his part in the building of the confederacy, he was a businessman, not a politician. Still, it hurt to see something torn down that he had helped to build, though he knew that every pioneering strike in history had been taken over by shrewd, ruthless, powerful operators. Knowing that should have helped, but it didn't. He and the other Jovian pioneers had hoped it wouldn't happen and, of course, it had.

"Ben Wrail," said a voice in the room.

Wrail swung around, away from the window.

"Manning!" he yelled, and the man in the center of the room grinned bleakly at him. "How did you come in without me hearing you? When did you get here?"

"I'm not here," said Greg. "I'm back on Earth."

"You're what?" asked Wrail blankly. "That's a pretty silly statement, isn't it, Manning? Or did you decide to loosen up and pull a gag now and then?"

"I mean it," said Manning. "This is just an image of me. My body is back on Earth."

"You mean you're dead? You're a ghost?"

The grin widened, but the face was bleak as ever.

"No, Ben, I'm just alive as you are. Let me explain. This is a television image of me. Three-dimensional television. I can travel anywhere like this."

Wrail sat down in the chair again. "I don't suppose there'd be any use trying to shake hands with you."

"No use," agreed Manning's image. "There isn't any hand."

"Nor asking you to have a chair?"

Manning shook his head.

"Anyhow," said Wrail, "I'm damn glad to see you-or think I see you. I don't know which. Figure you can stay and talk with me a while?"

"Certainly," said Manning. "That is what I came for. I want to ask your help."

"Listen," declared Wrail, "you can't be on Earth, Manning. I say something to you and you answer right back. That isn't possible. You can't hear anything I say until 45 minutes after I say it, and then I'd have to wait another 45 minutes to hear your answer."

"That's right," agreed the image, "if you insist upon talking about the velocity of light. We have something better than that."

"We?"

"Russell Page and myself. We have a two-way television apparatus that works almost instantaneously. To all purposes, so far as the distance between Earth and Callisto is concerned, it is instantaneous."

Wrail's jaw fell. "Well, I be damned. What have you two fellows been up to now?"

"A lot," said Manning laconically. "For one thing we are out to bust Interplanetary Power. Bust them wide open. Hear that, Wrail?"

Wrail stared in stupefaction. "Sure, I hear. But I can't believe it."

"All right then," said Manning grimly, "we'll give you proof. What could you do, Ben, if we told you what was happening on the stock market in New York ... *without you having to wait the 45 minutes it takes the quotations to get here?*"

Wrail sprang to his feet. "What could I do? Why, I could run the pants off every trader in the exchange! I could make a billion a minute!" He stopped and looked at the image. "But this isn't like you. This isn't the way you'd do things."

"I don't want you to hurt anyone but Chambers," said Manning. "If somebody else gets in the way, of course they have to take the rap along with him. But I do want to give Chambers a licking. That's what I came here to see you about."

"By Heaven, Greg, I'll do it," said Wrail. He stepped quickly forward, held out his hand to close the deal, and encountered only air.

Manning's image threw back its head and laughed.

"That's your proof, Ben. Good enough?"

"I'll say it is," said Wrail shakily, looking down at the solid-seeming hand that his own had gone right through.

November 6, 2153, was a day long remembered in financial circles throughout the Solar System. The Ranthoor market opened easy with little activity. Then a few stocks made fractional gains. Mining dropped fractionally. Martian Irrigation still was unexplainably low, as was Pluto Chemical and Asteroid Mining.

Trading through two brokers, Ben Wrail bought 10,000 shares of Venus Farms, Inc. when the market opened at 83½. A few minutes later they bought 10,000 shares of Spacesuits Ltd. at 106¼. The farm stocks dropped off a point. Spacesuits gained a point. Then suddenly both rose. In the second hour of trading the Venus stocks had boomed a full five points and Wrail sold. Ten minutes later they sagged. At the end of the day they were off two points from the opening. In late afternoon Wrail threw his 10,000 shares of Spacesuits on the market, sold them at an even 110. Before the close they had dropped back with a gain of only half a point over the opening.

Those were only two transactions. There were others. Spaceship Fabrication climbed three points before it fell and Wrail cashed in on that. Mercury Metals rose two points and crashed back to close with a full point loss. Wrail sold just before the break. He had realized a cool half million in the day's trade.

The next day it was a million and then the man who had always been a safe trader, who had always played the conservative side of the market, apparently sure of his ground now, plunged deeper and deeper. It was uncanny. Wrail knew when to buy and when to sell. Other traders watched closely, followed his lead. He threw them off by using different brokers to disguise his transactions.

Hectic day followed hectic day. Ben Wrail did not appear on the floor. Calls to his office netted exactly nothing. Mr. Wrail was not in. So sorry.

His brokers, well paid, were close-mouthed. They bought and sold. That was all.

Seated in his office, Ben Wrail was busy watching two television screens before him. One showed the board in the New York exchange. In the other was the image of Gregory Manning, hunched in a chair in Page's mountain laboratory back on Earth. And before Greg likewise were two screens, one showing the New York exchange board, the other trained on Ben Wrail's office.

"That Tourist stuff looks good," said Greg. "Why not buy a block of it? I happen to know that Chambers owns a few shares. He'll be dabbling in it."

Ben Wrail grinned. "It's made a couple of points, hasn't it? It's selling here for 60 right now. In 45 minutes it'll be quoted at 62."

He picked up a telephone. "Buy all you can of Tourist," he said. "Right away. I'll tell you when to sell. Get rid of whatever you have in Titan Copper at 10:30."

"Better let go of your holdings of Ranthoor Dome," suggested Greg. "It's beginning to slip."

"I'll watch it," promised Ben. "It may revive."

They lapsed into silence, watching the board in New York.

"You know, Greg," said Ben finally, "I really didn't believe all this was true until I saw those credit certificates materialize on my desk."

"Simple," grunted Greg. "This thing we've got can take anything any place. I could reach out there, grab you up and have you down here in a split second."

Ben sucked his breath in between his teeth. "I'm not doubting anything any more. You sent me half a billion two days ago. It's more than doubled now."

He picked up the phone again and spoke to his broker on the other end.

"Unload Ranthoor Dome when she reaches 79."

The real furor came on the Ranthoor floor when Wrail cornered Titan Copper. Striking swiftly, he purchased the stock in huge blocks. The shares rocketed as the exchanges throughout the System were thrown into an uproar. Under the cover of the excitement he proceeded to corner Spacesuits Ltd. Spacesuits zoomed.

For two days the main exchanges on four worlds were in a frenzy as traders watched the shares climb swiftly. Operators representing Interplanetary Power made offerings. No takers were reported. The shares climbed.

Within one hour, however, the entire Wrail holdings in both stocks were dumped on the market. The Interplanetary Power traders, frantic over the prospect of losing control of the two important issues, bought heavily. The price plummeted.

Spencer Chambers lost three billion or more on the deal. Overnight Ben Wrail had become a billionaire many times over. Greg Manning added to his own fortune.

"We have enough," said Greg. "We've given Chambers what he had coming to him. Let's call it off."

"Glad to," agreed Ben. "It was just too damned easy."

"Be seeing you, Ben."

"I'll get down to Earth some day. Come see me when you have a minute. Drop in for an evening."

"That's an invitation," said Greg. "It's easy with this three-dimension stuff."

He reached out a hand, snapped a control. The screens in Wrail's office went dead.
Wrail reached for a cigar, lit it carefully. He leaned back in his chair, put his feet on the desk.
"By Heaven," he said satisfiedly, "I've never enjoyed anything so much in all my life."

CHAPTER VIII

A giant cylindrical hull of finest beryl steel, the ship loomed in the screen. A mighty ship, braced into absolute rigidity by monster cross beams of shining steel. Glowing under the blazing lamps that lighted the scene, it towered into the shadows of the factory, dwarfing the scurrying workmen who swarmed over it.

"She's a beauty," said Russ, puffing at his pipe.

Greg nodded agreement. "They're working on her day and night to get her finished. We may need it some day and need it in a hurry. If Chambers really gets that machine of his to rolling, space will be the only place big enough to hide in."

He chuckled, a grim chuckle, deep in his throat.

"But we won't have to hide long. Just until we get organized and then will come the time when we'll call for the showdown. Chambers will have to spread his cards."

Russ snapped the television switch and the screen went blank. The laboratory suddenly was a place of queer lights and shadows, bulging with grotesque machines, with sprawling apparatus, a place that hinted darkly of vast power and mighty forces.

The scientist sat up in his chair. "We've come a long way, Greg. A long, long way. We have the greatest power man has ever known; we have an almost incomprehensible space drive; we have three-dimensional television."

"And," said Greg dryly, "we took Chambers to the cleaners on the market."

They sat in silence. Greg smelled the smoke from Russ's pipe, mixed with the taint of lubricant and the faint lingering scent of ionized air.

"We mustn't underrate Chambers, however," he declared. "The man made one mistake. He underrated us. We can't repeat his mistake. He is dangerous all the time. He will stop at nothing. Not even murder."

"He's going easy now," said Russ. "He's hoping Craven can find something that will either equal our stuff or beat it. But Craven isn't having any luck. He's still driving himself on the radiation theory, but he doesn't seem to make much headway."

"If he got it, just what would it mean?"

"Plenty. With that he could turn all radiations in space to work. The cosmics, heat, light, everything. Space is full of radiation."

"If it hadn't been for Wilson," Greg said, his voice a snarl, "we wouldn't have to be worrying about Chambers. Chambers wouldn't know until we were ready to let him know."

"Wilson!" ejaculated Russ, suddenly leaning forward. "I had forgotten about Wilson. What do you say we try to find him?"

Harry Wilson sat at his table in the Martian Club and watched the exotic Martian dance, performed by near-nude girls. Smoke trailed up lazily from his drooping cigarette as he watched through squinted eyes. There was something about the dance that got under Wilson's skin.

The music rose, then fell to whispering undertones and suddenly, unexpectedly, crashed and stopped. The girls were running from the floor. A wave of smooth, polite applause rippled around the tables.

Wilson sighed and reached for his wine glass. He crushed the cigarette into a tray and sipped his wine. He glanced around the room, scanning the bobbing, painted faces of the night-the great, the near-great, the near-enough-to-touch-the-great. Brokers and businessmen, artists and writers and actors. There were others, too, queer night-life shadows that no one knew much about, or that one heard too much about ... the playboys and the ladies of family and fortune, correctly attired men, gorgeously, sleekly attired women.

And-Harry Wilson. The waiters called him Mr. Wilson. He heard people whispering about him asking who he was. His soul soaked it in and cried for more. Good food, good drinks, the pastels of the walls, the soft lights and weird, exotic music. The cold but colorful correctness of it all.

Just two months ago he had stood outside the club, a stranger in the city, a mechanic from a little out-of-the-way laboratory, a man who was paid a pittance for his skill. He had stood outside and watched his employers walk up the steps and through the magic doors. He had watched in bitterness....

But now!

The orchestra was striking up a tune. A blonde nodded at him from a near-by table. Solemnly, with the buzz of wine in his brain and its hotness in his blood, he returned the nod.

Someone was speaking to him, calling him by name. He looked around, but there was no one looking at him now. And once again, through that flow of music, through the hum of conversation, through the buzzing of his own brain, came the voice, cold and sharp as steel:

"Harry Wilson!"

It sent a shudder through him. He reached for the wine glass again, but his hand stopped half-way to the stem, paused and trembled at what he saw.

For there was a gray vagueness in front of him, a sort of shimmer of nothingness, and out of that shimmer materialized a pencil.

As he watched, in stricken terror, the point of the pencil dropped to the tablecloth and slowly, precisely, it started to move. He stared, hypnotized, unbelieving, with the fingers of madness probing at his brain. The pencil wrote:

> Wilson, you sold me out.

The man at the table tried to speak, tried to shriek, but his tongue and throat were dry and only harsh breath rattled in his mouth.

The pencil moved on mercilessly:

> But you will pay. No matter where you go, I will find you. You cannot hide from me.

The pencil slowly lifted its point from the table and suddenly was gone, as if it had never been. Wilson, eyes wide and filled with terrible fear, stared at the black words on the cloth.

> Wilson, you sold me out. But you will pay. No matter where you go, I will find you. You cannot hide from me.

The music pulsated in the room, the hum of conversation ran like an undertone, but Wilson did not hear. His entire consciousness was centered on the writing, the letters and the words that filled his soul with dread.

Something seemed to snap within him. The cold wind of terror reached out and struck at him. He staggered from the chair. His hand swept the wine glass from the table and it shattered into chiming shards.

"They can't do this to me!" he shrieked.

There was a silence in the room a silence of terrible accusation. Everyone was staring at him. Eyebrows raised.

A waiter was at his elbow. "Do you feel ill, sir?"

And then, on unsteady feet, he was being led away. Behind him he heard the music once again, heard the rising hum of voices.

Someone set his hat on his head, was holding his coat. The cold air of the night struck his face and the doors sighed closed behind him.

"I'd take it easy going down the step, sir," counseled the doorman.

An aero-taxi driver held open the door of the cab and saluted.

"Where to, sir?"

Wilson stumbled in and stammered out his address. The taxi droned into the traffic lane.

Hands twitching, Wilson fumbled with the key, took minutes to open the door into his apartment. Finally the lock clicked and he pushed open the door. His questing finger found the wall switch. Light flooded the room.

Wilson heaved a sigh of relief. He felt safe here. This place belonged to him. It was his home, his retreat....

A low laugh, hardly more than a chuckle, sounded behind him. He whirled and for a moment, blinking in the light, he saw nothing. Then something stirred by one of the windows, gray and vague, like a sheet of moving fog.

As he watched, shrinking back against the wall, the grayness deepened, took the form of a man. And out of that mistiness a face was etched, a face that had no single line of humor in it, a bleak face with the fire of anger in the eyes.

"Manning!" shrieked Wilson. "Manning!" He wheeled and sprinted for the door, but the gray figure moved, too ...incredibly fast, as if it were wind-blown vapor, and barred his path to the door.

"Why are you running away?" Manning's voice mocked. "Certainly you aren't afraid of me."

"Look," Wilson whimpered, "I didn't think of what it meant. I just was tired of working the way Page made me work. Tired of the little salary I got. I wanted money. I was hungry for money."

"So you sold us out," said Manning.

"No," cried Wilson, "I didn't think of it that way. I didn't stop to think."

"Think now, then," said Manning gravely. "Think of this. No matter where you are, no matter where you go, no matter what you do, I'll always be watching you, I'll never let you rest. I'll never give you a minute's peace."

"Please," pleaded Wilson. "Please, go away and leave me. I'll give you back the money ... there's some of it left."

"You sold out for twenty thousand," said Manning. "You could have gotten twenty million. Chambers would have paid that much to know what you could tell him, because it was worth twenty billion."

Wilson's breath was coming in panting gasps. He dropped his coat and backed away. The back of his knees collided with a chair and he folded up, sat down heavily, still staring at the gray mistiness that was a man.

"Think of that, Wilson," Manning went on sneeringly. "You could have been a millionaire. Maybe even a billionaire. You could have had all the fine things these other people have. But you only got twenty thousand."

"What can I do?" begged Wilson.

The misty face split in a sardonic grin.

"I don't believe there's anything left for you to do."

Before Wilson's eyes the face dissolved, lost its lines, seemed to melt away. Only streaming, swirling mist, then a slight refraction in the air and then nothing.

Slowly Wilson rose to his feet, reached for the bottle of whiskey on the table. His hand shook so that the liquor splashed. When he raised the glass to his mouth, his still-shaking hand poured half the drink over his white shirt front.

CHAPTER IX

Ludwig Stutsman pressed his thin, straight lips together. "So that's the setup," he said.

Across the desk Spencer Chambers studied the man. Stutsman was like a wolf, lean and cruel and vicious. He even looked like a wolf, with his long, thin face, his small, beady eyes, the thin, bloodless lips. But he was the kind of man who didn't always wait for instructions, but went ahead and used his own judgment. And in a ruthless sort of way, his judgment was always right.

"Only as a last resort," cautioned Chambers, "do I want you to use the extreme measures you are so fond of using. If they should prove necessary, we can always use them. But not yet. I want to settle this thing in the quietest way possible. Page and Manning are two men who can't simply disappear. There'd be a hunt, an investigation, an ugly situation."

"I understand," agreed Stutsman. "If something should happen to their notes, if somebody could find them. Perhaps you. If you found them on your desk one morning."

The two men measured one another with their eyes, more like enemies than men working for the same ends.

"Not my desk," snapped Chambers, "Craven's. So that Craven could discover this new energy. Whatever Craven discovers belongs to Interplanetary."

Chambers rose from his chair and walked to the window, looked out. After a moment's time, he turned and walked back again, sat down in his chair. Leaning back, he matched his fingertips, his teeth flashing in a grin under his mustache.

"I don't know anything about what's going on," he said. "I don't even know someone has discovered material energy. That's up to Craven. He has to find it. Both you and Craven work alone. I know nothing about either of you."

Stutsman's jaw closed like a steel trap. "I've always worked alone."

"By the way," said Chambers, the edge suddenly off his voice, "how are things going in the Jovian confederacy? I trust you left everything in good shape."

"As good as could be expected," Stutsman replied. "The people are still uneasy, half angry. They still remember Mallory."

"But Mallory," objected Chambers, "is on a prison ship. In near Mercury now, I believe."

Stutsman shook his head. "They still remember him. We'll have trouble out there one of these days."

"I would hate to have that happen," remarked Chambers softly. "I would regret it very much. I sent you out there to see that nothing happened."

"The trouble out there won't be a flash to this thing you were telling me about," snapped Stutsman.

"I'm leaving that in your hands, too," Chambers told him. "I know you can take care of it."

Stutsman rose. "I can take care of it."

"I'm sure you can," Chambers said.

He remained standing after Stutsman left, looking at the door through which the man had gone. Maybe it had been a mistake to call Stutsman in from Callisto. Maybe it was a mistake to use Stutsman at all. He didn't like a lot of things the man did ... or the way he did them. Brutal things.

Slowly Chambers sat down again and his face grew hard.

He had built an empire of many worlds. That couldn't be done with gentle methods and no sure goal. Fighting every inch from planet to planet, he had used power to gain power. And now that empire was threatened by two men who had found a greater power. That threat had to be smashed! It would be smashed!

Chambers leaned forward and pressed a buzzer.

"Yes, Mr. Chambers?" said a voice in the communicator.

"Send Dr. Craven in," commanded Chambers.

Craven came in, slouchily, his hair standing on end, his eyes peering through the thick-lensed glasses.

"You sent for me," he growled, taking a chair.

"Yes, I did," said Chambers. "Have a drink?"

"No. And no smoke either."

Chambers took a long cigar from the box on his desk, clipped off the end and rolled it in his mouth.

"I'm a busy man," Craven reminded him.

Puckering lines of amusement wrinkled Chambers' eyes as he lit up, watching Craven.

"You do seem to be busy, Doctor," he said. "I only wish you had something concrete to report."

The scientist bristled. "I may have in a few days, if you leave me alone and let me work."

"I presume that you are still working on your radiation collector. Any progress?"

"Not too much. You can't expect a man to turn out discoveries to order. I'm working almost night and day now. If the thing can be solved, I'll solve it."

Chambers glowed. "Keep up the good work. But I wanted to talk to you about something else. You heard, I suppose, that I lost a barrel of money on the Ranthoor exchange."

Craven smiled, a sardonic twisting of his lips. "I heard something about it."

"I thought you had," said Chambers sourly. "If not, you would have been the only one who hadn't heard how Ben Wrail took Chambers for a ride."

"He really took you then," commented Craven. "I thought maybe it was just one of those stories."

"He took me, but that's not what's worrying me. I want to know how he did it. No man, not even the most astute student of the market, could have foretold the trend of the market the way he did. And Wrail isn't the most astute. It isn't natural when a man who has always played the safe side suddenly turns the market upside down. Even less natural when he never makes a mistake."

"Well," demanded Craven, "what do you want me to do about it? I'm a scientist. I've never owned a share of stock in my life."

"There's an angle to it that might interest you," said Chambers smoothly, leaning back, puffing at the cigar. "Wrail is a close friend of Manning. And Wrail himself didn't have the money it took to swing those deals. Somebody furnished that money."

"Manning?" asked Craven.

"What do you think?"

"If Manning's mixed up in it," said Craven acidly, "there isn't anything any of us can do about it. You're bucking money and genius together. This Manning is no slouch of a scientist himself and Page is better. They're a combination."

"You think they're good?" asked Chambers.

"Good? Didn't they discover material energy?" The scientist glowered at his employer. "That ought to be answer enough."

"Yes, I know," Chambers agreed irritably. "But can you tell me how they worked this market deal?"

Craven grimaced. "I can guess. Those boys didn't stop with just finding how to harness material energy. They probably have more things than you can even suspect. They were working with force fields, you remember, when they stumbled onto the energy. Force fields are something we don't know much about. A man monkeying around with them is apt to find almost anything."

"What are you getting at?"

"My guess would be that they have a new kind of television working in the fourth dimension, using time as a factor. It would penetrate anything. Nothing could stop it. It could go anywhere, at a speed many times the speed of light ...almost instantaneously."

Chambers sat upright in his chair. "Are you *sure* about this?"

Craven shook his head. "Just a guess. I tried to figure out what I would do if I were Page and Manning and had the things they had. That's all."

"And what would you do?"

Craven smiled dourly. "I'd be using that television right in this office," he said. "I'd keep you and me under observation all the time. If what I think is true, Manning is watching us now and has heard every word we said."

Chambers' face was a harsh mask of anger. "I don't believe it could be done!"

"Doctor Craven is right," said a quiet voice.

Chambers swung around in his chair and gasped. Greg Manning stood inside the room, just in front of the desk.

"I hope you don't mind," said Greg. "I've been wanting to have a talk with you."

Craven leaped to his feet, his eyes shining. "Three dimensions!" he whispered. "How did you do it?"

Greg chuckled. "I haven't patented the idea, Doctor. I'd rather not tell you just now."

"You will accept my congratulations, however?" asked Craven.

"That's generous of you. I really hadn't expected this much."

"I mean it," said Craven. "Damned if I don't." Chambers was on his feet, leaning across the desk, with his hand held out. Greg's right hand came out slowly.

"Sorry, I really can't shake hands," he said. "I'm not here, you know. Just my image."

Chambers' hand dropped to the desk. "Stupid of me not to realize that. You looked so natural." He sat back in his chair again, brushed his gray mustache. A smile twisted his lips. "So you've been watching me?"

"Off and on," Greg said.

"And what is the occasion of this visit?" asked Chambers. "You could have held a distinct advantage by remaining unseen. I didn't entirely believe what Craven told me, you know."

"That isn't the point at all," declared Greg. "Maybe we can get to understand one another."

"So you're ready to talk business."

"Not in the sense you mean," Greg said. "I'm not willing to make concessions, but there's no reason why we have to fight one another."

"Why, no," said Chambers, "there's no reason for that. I'll be willing to buy your discovery."

"I wouldn't sell it to you," Greg told him.

"You wouldn't? Why not? I'm prepared to pay for it."

"You'd pay the price, all right. Anything I asked … even if it bankrupted you. Then you'd mark it down to loss, and scrap material energy. And I'll tell you why."

A terrible silence hung in the room as the two men eyed one another across the table.

"You wouldn't use it," Greg went on, "because it would remove the stranglehold you have on the planets. It would make power too cheap. It would eliminate the necessity of your rented accumulators. The Jovian moons and Mars could stand on their feet without the power you ship to them. You could make billions in legitimate profits selling the apparatus to manufacture the energy … but you wouldn't want that. You want to be dictator of the Solar System. And that is what I intend to stop."

"Listen, Manning," said Chambers, "you're a reasonable man. Let's talk this thing over without anger. What do you plan to do?"

"I could put my material engines on the market," said Greg. "That would ruin you. You wouldn't move an accumulator after that. Your Interplanetary stock wouldn't be worth the paper it is written on. Material energy would wipe you out."

"You forget I have franchises on those planets," Chambers reminded him. "I'd fight you in the courts until hell froze over."

"I'd prove convenience, economy and necessity. Any court in any land, on any planet, would rule for me."

Chambers shook his head. "Not Martian or Jovian courts. I'd tell them to rule for me and the courts outside of Earth do what I tell them to."

Greg straightened and backed from the desk. "I hate to ruin a man. You've worked hard. You've built a great company. I would be willing, in return for a hands-off policy on your part, to hold up any announcement of my material energy until you had time to get out, to save what you could."

Hard fury masked Chambers' face. "You'll never build a material energy engine outside your laboratory. Don't worry about ruining me. I won't allow you to stand in my way. I hope you understand."

"I understand too well. But even if you are a dictator out on Mars and Venus, even if you do own Mercury and boss the Jovian confederacy, you're just a man to me. A man who stands for things that I don't like."

Greg stopped and his eyes were like ice crystals.

"You talked to Stutsman today," he said. "If I were you, I wouldn't let Stutsman do anything rash. Russ Page and I might have to fight back."

Mockery tinged Chambers' voice. "Am I to take this as a declaration of war, Mr. Manning?"

"Take it any way you like," Greg said. "I came here to give you a proposition, and you tell me you're going to smash me. All I have to say to you, Chambers, is this-when you get ready to smash me, you'd better have a deep, dark hole all picked out for yourself to hide in. Because I'll hand you back just double anything you hand out."

CHAPTER X

"One of us will have to watch all the time," Greg told Russ. "We can't take any chances. Stutsman will try to reach us sooner or later and we have to be ready for him."

He glanced at the new radar screen they had set up that morning beside the bank of other controls. Any ship coming within a hundred miles of the laboratory would be detected instantly and pinpointed.

The board flashed now. In the screen they saw a huge passenger ship spearing down toward the airport south of them.

"With the port that close," said Russ, "we'll get a lot of signals."

"I ordered the Belgium factory to rush work on the ship," said Greg. "But it will be a couple of weeks yet. We just have to sit tight and wait. As soon as we have the ship we'll start in on Chambers; but until we get the ship, we just have to dig in and stay on the defensive."

He studied the scene in the screen. The ship had leveled off, was banking in to the port. His eyes turned away, took in the laboratory with its crowding mass of machinery.

"We don't want to fool ourselves about Chambers," he said. "He may not have the power here on Earth that he does on the other planets, but he's got plenty. Feeling the way he does, he'll try to finish us off in a hurry now."

Russ reached out to the table that stood beside the bank of controls and picked up a small, complicated mechanism. Its face bore nine dials, with the needles on three of them apparently registering, the other six motionless.

"What is that?" asked Greg.

"A mechanical detective," said Russ. "A sort of mechanical shadow. While you were busy with the stock market stunt, I made several of them. One for Wilson and another for Chambers and still another for Craven." He hoisted and lowered the one in his hand. "This one is for Stutsman."

"A shadow?" asked Greg. "Do you mean that thing will trail Stutsman?"

"Not only trail him," said Russ. "It will find him, wherever he may be. Some object every person wears or carries is made of iron or some other magnetic metal. This 'shadow' contains a tiny bit of that ridiculous military decoration that Stutsman never allows far away from him. Find that decoration and you find Stutsman. In another one I have a chunk of Wilson's belt buckle, that college buckle, you know, that he's so proud of. Chambers has a ring made of a piece of meteoric iron and that's the bait for another machine. Have a tiny piece off Craven's spectacles in his machine. It was easy to get the stuff. The force field enables a man to reach out and take anything he wants to, from a massive machine to a microscopic bit of matter. It was a cinch to get the stuff I needed."

Russ chuckled and put the machine back on the table. He gestured toward it.

"It maintains a tiny field similar to our television field," he explained. "But it's modified along a special derivation with a magnetic result. It can follow and find the original mass of any metallic substance it may contain."

"Clever," commented Greg.

Russ lit his pipe, puffed comfortably. "We needed something like that."

The red light on the board snapped on and blinked. Russ reached out and slammed home the lever, twirled dials. It was only another passenger ship. They relaxed, but not too much.

"I wonder what he's up to," said Russ.

Stutsman's car had stopped in the dock section of New York. Crumbling, rotting piers and old tumbledown warehouses, deserted and unused since the last ship sailed the ocean before giving way to air commerce, loomed darkly, like grim ghosts, in the darkness.

Stutsman had gotten out of the car and said: "Wait here."

"Yes, sir," said the voice of the driver.

Stutsman strode away, down a dark street. The televisor kept pace with him and on the screen he could be seen as a darker shape moving among the shadows of that old, almost forgotten section of the Solar System's greatest city.

Another shadow detached itself from the darkness of the street, shuffled toward Stutsman.

"Sir," said a whining voice, "I haven't eaten..."

There was a swift movement as Stutsman's stick lashed out, a thud as it connected with the second shadow's head. The shadow crumpled on the pavement. Stutsman strode on.

Greg sucked in his breath. "He isn't very sociable tonight."

Stutsman ducked into an alley where even deeper darkness lay. Russ, with a delicate adjustment, slid the televisor along, closer to Stutsman, determined not to lose sight of him for an instant.

The man suddenly turned into a doorway so black that nothing could be seen. Sounds of sharp, impatient rappings came out of the screen as Stutsman struck the door with his stick.

Brilliant illumination sprang out over the doorway, but Stutsman seemed not to see it, went on knocking. The colors on the screen were peculiarly distorted.

"Ultra-violet," grunted Greg. "Whoever he's calling on wants to have a good look before letting anybody in."

The door creaked open and a shaft of normal light spewed out into the street, turning its murkiness to pallid yellow.

Stutsman stepped inside.

The man at the door jerked his head. "Back room," he said.

The televisor slid through the door into the lighted room behind Stutsman. Dust lay thick on the woodwork and floors. Patches of plaster had broken away. Furrows zigzagged across the floor, marking the path of heavy boxes or furniture which had been pushed along in utter disdain of the flooring. Cheap wall-paper hung in tatters from the walls, streaked with water from some broken pipe.

But the back room was a startling contrast to the first. Rich, comfortable furniture filled it. The floor was covered with a steel-cloth rug and steel-cloth hangings, colorfully painted, hid the walls.

A man sat under a lamp, reading a newspaper. He rose to his feet, like the sudden uncoiling of springs.

Russ gasped. That face was one of the best known faces in the entire Solar System. A ratlike face, with cruel cunning printed on it that had been on front pages and TV screens often, but never for pay.

"Scorio!" whispered Russ.

Greg nodded and his lips were drawn tight.

"Stutsman," said Scorio, surprised. "You're the last person in the world I was expecting. Come in. Have a chair. Make yourself comfortable."

Stutsman snorted. "This isn't a social call."

"I didn't figure it was," replied the gangster, "but sit down anyway."

Gingerly Stutsman sat down on the edge of a chair, hunched forward. Scorio resumed his seat and waited.

"I have a job for you," Stutsman announced bluntly.

"Fine. It isn't often you have one for me. Three-four years ago, wasn't it?"

"We may be watched," warned Stutsman.

The mobster started from his chair, his eyes darting about the room.

Stutsman grunted disgustedly. "If we're watched, there isn't anything we can do about it."

"We can't, huh?" snarled the gangster. "Why not?"

"Because the watcher is on the West Coast. We can't reach him. If he's watching, he can see every move we make, hear every word we say."

"Who is it?"

"Greg Manning or Russ Page," said Stutsman. "You've heard of them?"

"Sure. I heard of them."

"They have a new kind of television," said Stutsman. "They can see and hear everything that's happening on Earth, perhaps in all the Solar System. But I don't think they're watching us now. Craven has a machine that can detect their televisor. It registers certain field effects they use. They weren't watching when I left Craven's laboratory just a few minutes ago. They may have picked me up since, but I don't think so."

"So Craven has made a detector," said Greg calmly. "He can tell when we're watching now."

"He's a clever cuss," agreed Russ.

"Take a look at that machine now," urged Scorio. "See if they're watching. You shouldn't have come here. You should have let me know and I would have met you some place. I can't have people knowing where my hideout is."

"Quiet down," snapped Stutsman. "I haven't got the machine. It weighs half a ton."

Scorio sank deeper into his chair, worried. "Do you want to take a chance and talk business?"

"Certainly. That's why I'm here. This is the proposition. Manning and Page are working in a laboratory out on the West Coast, in the mountains. I'll give you the exact location later. They have some papers we want. We wouldn't mind if something happened to the laboratory. It might, for example blow up. But we want the papers first."

Scorio said nothing. His face was quiet and cunning.

"Give me the papers," said Stutsman, "and I'll see that you get to any planet you want to. And I'll give you two hundred thousand in Interplanetary Credit certificates. Give me proof that the laboratory blew up or melted down or something else happened to it and I'll boost the figure to five hundred thousand."

Scorio did not move a muscle as he asked: "Why don't you have some of your own mob do this job?"

"Because I can't be connected with it in any way," said Stutsman. "If you slip up and something happens, I won't be able to do a thing for you. That's why the price is high."

The gangster's eyes slitted. "If the papers are worth that much to you, why wouldn't they be worth as much to me?"

"They wouldn't be worth a dime to you."

"Why not?"

"Because you couldn't read them," said Stutsman.

"I can read," retorted the gangster.

"Not the kind of language on those papers. There aren't more than two dozen people in the Solar System who could read it, perhaps a dozen who could understand it, maybe half a dozen who could follow the directions in the papers." He leaned forward and jabbed a forefinger at the gangster. "And there are only two people in the System who could write it."

"What the hell kind of a language is it that only two dozen people could read?"

"It isn't a language, really. It's mathematics."

"Oh, arithmetic."

"No," Stutsman said. "Mathematics. You see? You don't even know the difference between the two, so what good would the papers do you?"

Scorio nodded. "Yeah, you're right."

CHAPTER XI

The Paris-Berlin express thundered through the night, a gigantic ship that rode high above the Earth. Far below one could see the dim lights of eastern Europe.

Harry Wilson pressed his face against the window, staring down. There was nothing to see but the tiny lights. They were alone, he and the other occupants of the ship ...alone in the dark world that surrounded them.

But Wilson sensed some other presence in the ship, someone besides the pilot and his mechanics up ahead, the hostess and the three stodgy traveling men who were his fellow passengers.

Wilson's hair ruffled at the base of his skull, tingling with an unknown fear that left him shaken.

A voice whispered in his ear: "Harry Wilson. So you are running away!"

Just a tiny voice that seemed hardly a voice at all, it seemed at once to come from far away and yet from very near. The voice, with an edge of coldness on it, was one he never would forget.

He cowered in his seat, whimpering.

The voice came again: "Didn't I tell you that you couldn't run away? That no matter where you went, I'd find you?"

"Go away," Wilson whispered huskily. "Leave me alone. Haven't you hounded me enough?"

"No," answered the voice, "not enough. Not yet. You sold us out. You warned Chambers about our energy and now Chambers is sending men to kill us. But they won't succeed, Wilson."

"You can't hurt me," said Wilson defiantly. "You can't do anything but talk to me. You're trying to drive me mad, but you can't. I won't let you. I'm not going to pay any more attention to you."

The whisper chuckled.

"You can't," argued Wilson wildly. "All you can do is talk to me. You've never done anything but that. You drove me out of New York and out of London and now you're driving me out of Paris. But Berlin is as far as I will go. I won't listen to you any more."

"Wilson," whispered the voice, "look inside your bag. The bag, Wilson, where you are carrying that money. That stack of credit certificates. Almost eleven thousand dollars, what is left of the twenty thousand Chambers paid you."

With a wild cry Wilson clawed at his bag, snapped it open, pawed through it.

The credit certificates were gone!

"You took my money," he shrieked. "You took everything I had. I haven't got a cent. Nothing except a few dollars in my pocket."

"You haven't got that either, Wilson," whispered the voice.

There was a sound of ripping cloth as something like a great, powerful hand flung aside Wilson's coat, tore away the inside pocket. There was a brief flash of a wallet and a bundle of papers, which vanished.

The hostess was hurrying toward him.

"Is there something wrong?"

"They took ..." Wilson began and stopped.

What could he tell her? Could he say that a man half way across the world had robbed him?

The three traveling men were looking at him.

"I'm sorry, miss," he stammered. "I really am. I fell asleep and dreamed."

He sat down again, shaken. Shivering, he huddled back into the corner of his seat. His hands explored the torn coat pocket. He was stranded, high in the air, somewhere between Paris and Berlin ...stranded without money, without a passport, with nothing but the clothes he wore and the few personal effects in his bag.

Fighting to calm himself, he tried to reason out his plight. The plane was entering the Central European Federation and that, definitely, was no place to be without a passport or without visible means of support. A thousand possibilities flashed through his mind. They might think he was a spy. He might be cited for illegal entry. He might be framed by secret police.

Terror perched on his shoulder and whispered to him. He shivered violently and drew farther back into the corner of the seat. He clasped his hands, beat them against his huddled knees.

He would cable friends back in America and have them identify him and vouch for his character. He would borrow some money from them, just enough to get back to America. But whom would he cable? And with aching bitterness in his breast, Harry Wilson came face to face with the horrible realization that nowhere in the world, nowhere in the Solar System, was there a single person who was his friend. There was no one to help him.

He bowed his head in his hands and sobbed, his shoulders jerking spasmodically, the sobs racking his body.

The traveling men stared at him unable to understand. The hostess looked briskly helpless. Wilson knew he looked like a scared fool and he didn't care.

He *was* scared.

Gregory Manning riffled the sheaf of credit certificates, the wallet, the passport and pile of other papers that lay upon the desk in front of him.

"That closes one little incident," he said grimly. "That takes care of our friend Wilson."

"Maybe you were a bit too harsh with him, Greg," suggested Russell Page.

Greg shook his head. "He was a traitor, the lowest thing alive. He sold the confidence we placed in him. He traded something that was not his to trade. He did it for money and now I've taken that money from him."

He shoved the pile of certificates to one side.

"Now I've got this stuff," he said, "I don't know what to do with it. We don't want to keep it."

"Why not send it to Chambers?" suggested Russ. "He will find the passport and the money on his desk in the morning. Give him something to think about tomorrow."

CHAPTER XII

Scorio snarled at the four men: "I want you to get the thing done right. I don't want bungling. Understand?"

The bulky, flat-faced man with the scar across his cheek shuffled uneasily. "We went over it a dozen times. We know just what to do."

He grinned at Scorio, but the grin was lopsided, more like a sneering grimace. At one time the man had failed to side-step a heat ray and it had left a neat red line drawn across the right cheek, nipped the end of the ear.

"All right, Pete," said Scorio, glaring at the man, "your job is the heavy work, so just keep your mind on it. You've got the two heaters and the kit."

Pete grinned lopsidedly again. "Yeah, my own kit. I can open anything hollow with this rig."

"You got a real job tonight," snarled Scorio. "Two doors and a safe. Sure you can do it?"

"Just leave it to me," Pete growled.

"Chizzy, you're to pilot," Scorio snapped. "Know the coordinates?"

"Sure," said Chizzy, "know them by heart. Do it with my eyes shut."

"Keep your eyes open. We can't have anything go wrong. This is too important. You swoop in at top speed and land on the roof. Stand by the controls and keep a hand on the big heater just in case of trouble. Pete, Max and Reg will go to the lockdoor. Reg will stay there with the buzzer and three drums of ammunition."

He whirled on Reg. "You got that ammunition?"

Reg nodded emphatically. "Four drums of it," he said. "One solid round in the gun. Another drum of solid and two explosive."

"There's a thousand rounds in each drum," snapped Scorio, "but they last only a minute, so do your firing in bursts."

"I ain't handled buzzers all these years without knowing something about them."

"There's only two men there," said Scorio, "and they'll probably be asleep. Come down with your motor dead. The lab roof is thick and the plane landing on those thick tires won't wake them. But be on your guard all the time. Pete and Max will go through the lockdoor into the laboratory and open the safe. Dump all the papers and money and whatever else you find into the bags and then get out fast. Hop into the plane and take off. When you're clear of the building, turn the heaters on it. I want it melted down and the men and stuff inside with it. Don't leave even a button unmelted. Get it?"

"Sure, chief," said Pete. He dusted his hands together.

"Now get going. Beat it."

The four men turned and filed out of the room, through the door leading to the tumbledown warehouse where was hidden the streamlined metal ship. Swiftly they entered it and the ship nosed gently upward, blasting out through a broken, frameless skylight, climbing up and up, over the gleaming spires of New York.

Back in the room hung with steel-cloth curtains, alone, Scorio lit a cigarette and chuckled. "They won't have a chance," he said.

"Who won't?" asked a tiny voice from almost in front of him.

"Why, Manning and Page ..." said Scorio, and then stopped. The fire of the match burned down and scorched his fingers. He dropped it. "Who asked that?" he roared.

"I did," said the piping voice.

Scorio looked down. A three-inch man sat on a matchbox on the desk!

"Who are you?" the gangster shouted.

"I'm Manning," said the little man. "The one you're going to kill. Don't you remember?"

"Damn you!" shrieked Scorio. His hand flipped open a drawer and pulled out a flame pistol. The muzzle of the pistol came up and blasted. Screwed down to its smallest diameter, the gun's aim was deadly. A straight lance of flame, no bigger than a pencil, streamed out, engulfed the little man, bored into the table top. The box of matches exploded with a gush of red that was a dull flash against the blue blaze of the gun.

But the figure of the man stood *within the flame*! Stood there and waved an arm at Scorio. The piping voice came out of the heart of the gun's breath.

"Maybe I'd better get a bit smaller. Make me harder to hit. More sport that way."

Scorio's finger lifted from the trigger. The flame snapped off. Laboriously climbing out of the still smoking furrow left in the oaken table top was Greg Manning, not more than an inch tall now.

The gangster laid the gun on the table, stepped closer, warily. With the palm of a mighty hand he swatted viciously at the little figure.

"I got you now!"

But the figure seemed to ooze upright between his fingers, calmly stepped off his hand onto the table. And now it began to grow. Watching it, Scorio saw it grow to six inches and there it stopped.

"What are you?" he breathed.

"I told you," said the little image. "I'm Gregory Manning. The man you set out to kill. I've watched every move you've made and known everything you planned."

"But that isn't possible," protested Scorio. "You're out on the West Coast. This is some trick. I'm just seeing things."

"You aren't seeing anything imaginary. I'm really here, in this room with you. I could lift my finger and kill you if I wished ...and maybe I should."

Scorio stepped back a pace.

"But I'm not going to," said Manning. "I have something better saved for you. Something more appropriate."

"You can't touch me!"

"Look," said Manning sternly. He pointed his finger at a chair. It suddenly grew cloudy, became a wisp of trailing smoke, was gone.

The gangster backed away, eyes glued to the spot where the chair had vanished.

"Look here," piped the little voice. Scorio jerked his head around and looked.

The chair was in Manning's hand. A tiny chair, but the very one that had disappeared from the room a moment before.

"Watch out!" warned Manning, and heaved the chair. The tiny chair seemed to float in the air. Then with a rush it gathered speed, grew larger. In a split second it was a full-sized chair and it was hurtling straight at the gangster's head.

With a strangled cry Scorio threw up his arms. The chair crashed into him, bowled him over.

"Now do you believe me?" demanded Manning.

Scrambling to his feet, Scorio gibbered madly, for the six-inch figure was growing. He became as large as the average man, and then much larger. His head cleared the high ceiling by scant inches. His mighty hands reached out for the gangster.

Scorio scuttled away on hands and knees, yelping with terror.

Powerful hands seemed to seize and lift him. The room was blotted out. The Earth was gone. He was in a place where there was nothing. No light, no heat, no gravitation. For one searing, blasting second he seemed to be floating in strangely suspended animation. Then with a jolt he became aware of new surroundings.

He blinked his eyes and looked around. He was in a great laboratory that hummed faintly with the suggestion of terrific power, that smelled of ozone and seemed filled with gigantic apparatus.

Two men stood in front of him.

He staggered back.

"Manning!" he gasped.

Manning grinned savagely at him. "Sit down, Scorio. You won't have long to wait. Your boys will be along any minute now."

Chizzy crouched over the controls, his eyes on the navigation chart. Only the thin screech of parted air disturbed the silence of the ship. The high scream and the slow, precise snack-snack of cards as Reg and Max played a game of double solitaire with a cold, emotionless precision.

The plane was near the stratosphere, well off the traveled air lanes. It was running without lights, but the cabin bulbs were on, carefully shielded.

Pete sat in the co-pilot's chair beside Chizzy. His blank, expressionless eyes stared straight ahead.

"I don't like this job," he complained.

"Why not?" asked Chizzy.

"Page and Manning aren't the kind of guys a fellow had ought to be fooling around with. They ain't just chumps. You fool with characters like them and you got trouble."

Chizzy growled at him disgustedly, bent to his controls.

Straight ahead was a thin sliver of a dying Moon that gave barely enough illumination to make out the great, rugged blocks of the mountains, like dark, shadowy brush-strokes on a newly started canvas.

Pete shuddered. There was something about the thin, watery moonlight, and those brush-stroke hills....

"It seems funny up here," he said.

"Hell," growled Chizzy, "you're going soft in your old age."

Silence fell between the two. The snack-snack of the cards continued.

"You ain't got nothing to be afraid of," Chizzy told Pete. "This tub is the safest place in the world. She's overpowered a dozen times. She can outfly anything in the air. She's rayproof and bulletproof and bombproof. Nothing can hurt us."

But Pete wasn't listening. "That moonlight makes a man see things. Funny things. Like pictures in the night."

"You're balmy," declared Chizzy.

Pete started out of his seat. His voice gurgled in his throat. He pointed with a shaking finger out into the night.

"Look!" he yelled "Look!"

Chizzy rose out of his seat ... and froze in sudden terror.

Straight ahead of the ship, etched in silvery moon-lines against the background of the star-sprinkled sky, was a grim and terrible face.

It was as big and hard as a mountain.

CHAPTER XIII

The ship was silent now. Even the whisper of the cards had stopped. Reg and Max were on their feet, startled by the cries of Pete and Chizzy.

"It's Manning!" shrieked Pete. "He's watching us!"

Chizzy's hand whipped out like a striking snake toward the controls and, as he grasped them, his face went deathly white. For the controls were locked! They resisted all the strength he threw against them and the ship still bore on toward that mocking face that hung above the Earth.

"Do something!" screamed Max. "You damn fool, do something!"

"I can't," moaned Chizzy. "The ship is out of control."

It seemed impossible. That ship was fast and tricky and it had reserve power far beyond any possible need. It handled like a dream ... it was tops in aircraft. But there was no doubt that some force more powerful than the engines and controls of the ship itself had taken over.

"Manning's got us!" squealed Pete. "We came out to get him and now he has us instead!"

The craft was gaining speed. The whining shriek of the air against its plates grew thinner and higher. Listening, one could almost feel and hear the sucking of the mighty power that pulled it at an ever greater pace through the tenuous atmosphere.

The face was gone from the sky now. Only the Moon remained, the Moon and the brushstroke mountains far below.

Then, suddenly, the speed was slowing and the ship glided downward, down into the sawteeth of the mountains.

"We're falling!" yelled Max, and Chizzy growled at him.

But they weren't falling. The ship leveled off and floated, suspended above a sprawling laboratory upon a mountain top.

"That's Manning's laboratory," whispered Pete in terror-stricken tones.

The levers yielded unexpectedly. Chizzy flung the power control over, drove the power of the accumulator bank, all the reserve, into the engines. The ship lurched, but did not move. The engines whined and screamed in torture. The cabin's interior was filled with a blast of heat, the choking odor of smoke and hot rubber. The heavy girders of the frame creaked under the mighty forward thrust of the engines ... but the ship stood still, frozen above that laboratory in the hills.

Chizzy, hauling back the lever, turned around, pale. His hand began clawing for his heat gun. Then he staggered back. For there were only two men in the cabin with him-Reg and Max. Pete had gone!

"He just disappeared," Max jabbered. "He was standing there in front of us. Then all at once he seemed to fade, as if he was turning into smoke. Then he was gone."

Something had descended about Pete. There was no sound, no light, no heat. He had no sense of weight. It was as if, suddenly, his mind had become disembodied.

Seeing and hearing and awareness came back to him as one might turn on a light. From the blackness and the eventless existence of a split second before, he was catapulted into a world of light and sound.

It was a world that hummed with power, that was ablaze with light, a laboratory that seemed crammed with mighty banks of massive machinery, lighted by great globes of creamy brightness, shedding an illumination white as sunlight, yet shadowless as the light of a cloudy day.

Two men stood in front of him, looking at him, one with a faint smile on his lips, the other with lines of fear etched across his face. The smiling one was Gregory Manning and the one who was afraid was Scorio!

With a start, Pete snatched his pistol from its holster. The sights came up and lined on Manning as he pressed the trigger. But the lancing heat that sprang from the muzzle of the gun never reached Manning. It seemed to strike an obstruction less than a foot away. It mushroomed with a flare of scorching radiance that drove needles of agony into the gangster's body.

His finger released its pressure and the gun dangled limply from his hand. He moaned with the pain of burns upon his unprotected face and hands. He beat feebly at tiny, licking blazes that ran along his clothing.

Manning was still smiling at him.

"You can't reach me, Pete," he said. "You can only hurt yourself. You're enclosed within a solid wall of force that matter cannot penetrate."

A voice came from one corner of the room: "I'll bring Chizzy down next."

Pete whirled around and saw Russell Page for the first time. The scientist sat in front of a great control board, his swift, skillful fingers playing over the banks of keys, his eyes watching the instrument and the screen that slanted upward from the control banks.

Pete felt dizzy as he stared at the screen. He could see the interior of the ship he had been yanked from a moment before. He could see his three companions, talking excitedly, frightened by his disappearance.

His eyes flicked away from the screen, looked up through the skylight above him. Outlined against the sky hung the ship. At the nose and stern, two hemispheres of blue-white radiance fitted over the metal framework, like the jaws of a powerful vise, holding the craft immovable.

His gaze went back to the screen again, just in time to see Chizzy disappear. It was as if the man had been a mere figure chalked upon a board ...and then someone had taken a sponge and wiped him out.

Russ's fingers were flying over the keys. His thumb reached out and tripped a lever. There was a slight hum of power.

And Chizzy stood beside him.

Chizzy did not pull his gun. He whimpered and cowered within the invisible cradle of force.

"You're yellow," Pete snarled at him, but Chizzy only covered his eyes with his arms.

"Look, boss," said Pete, addressing Scorio, "what are you doing here? We left you back in New York."

Scorio did not answer. He merely glared. Pete lapsed into silence, watching.

Manning stood poised before the captives, rocking back and forth on his heels.

"A nice bag for one evening," he told Russ.

Russ grinned and stoked up his pipe.

Manning turned to the gangster chief. "What do you think we ought to do with these fellows? We can't leave them in those force shells too long because they'll die for lack of air. And we can't let them loose because they might use their guns on us."

"Listen, Manning," Scorio rasped hoarsely, "just name your price to let us loose. We'll do anything you want."

Manning drew his mouth down. "I can't think of a thing. We just don't seem to have any use for you."

"Then what in hell," the gangster asked shakily, "are you going to do with us?"

"You know," said Manning, "I may be a bit old-fashioned along some lines. Maybe I am. I just don't like the idea of killing people for money. I don't like people stealing things other people have worked hard to get. I don't like thieves and murderers and thugs corrupting city governments, taking tribute on every man, woman and child in our big cities."

"But look here, Manning," pleaded Scorio, "we'd be good citizens if we just had a chance."

Manning's face hardened. "You sent these men here to kill us tonight, didn't you?"

"Well, not exactly. Stutsman kind of wanted you killed, but I told the boys just to get the stuff in the safe and never mind killing you. I said to them that you were pretty good eggs and I didn't like to bump you off, see?"

"I see," said Manning.

He turned his back on Scorio and started to walk away. The gangster chief came half-way out of his chair, and as he did so, Russ reached out a single finger and tapped a key. Scorio screamed and beat with his fists against the wall of force that had suddenly formed about him.

That single tap on the great keyboard had sprung a trap, had been the one factor necessary to bring into being a force shell already spun and waiting for him.

Manning did not even turn around at Scorio's scream. He slowly paced his way down the line of standing gangsters. He stopped in front of Pete and looked at him.

"Pete," he said, "you've sprung a good many prisons, haven't you?"

"There ain't a jug in the System that can hold me," Pete boasted, "and that's a fact."

"I believe there's one that could," Greg told him. "One that no man has ever escaped from, or ever will."

"What's that?" demanded Pete.

"The Vulcan Fleet," said Greg.

Pete looked into the eyes of the man before him and read the purpose in those eyes. "Don't send me there! Send me any place but there!"

Greg turned to Russ and nodded. Russ's fingers played their tune of doom upon the keyboard. His thumb depressed a lever. With a roar five gigantic material energy engines screamed with thrumming power.

Pete disappeared.

The engines roared with thunderous throats, a roar that seemed to drown the laboratory in solid waves of sound. A curious refractive effect developed about the straining hulks as space near them bent under their lashing power.

Months ago Russ and Greg had learned a better way of transmitting power than by metal bars or through conducting beams. Beams of such power as were developing now would have smashed atoms to protons and electrons. Through a window in the side of the near engine, Greg could see the iron ingot used as fuel dwindling under the sucking force.

The droning died and only a hum remained.

"He's in a prison now he'll never get out of," said Greg calmly. "I wonder what they'll think when they find him, dressed in civilian clothes and carrying a heat gun. They'll clap him into a photo-cell and keep him there until they investigate. When they find out who he is, he won't get out-he has enough unfinished prison sentences to last a century or two."

For Pete was on one of the Vulcan Fleet ships, the hell-ships of the prison fleet. There were confined only the most vicious and the most depraved of the Solar System's criminals. He would be forced to work under the flaming whip-lashes of a Sun that hurled such intense radiations that mere spacesuits were no protection at all. The workers on the Vulcan Fleet ships wore suits that were in reality photo-cells which converted the deadly radiations into electric power. For electric power can be disposed of where heat cannot.

Quailing inside his force shell, Scorio saw his men go, one by one. Saw them lifted and whisked away, out through the depths of space by the magic touch upon the keyboards. With terror-widened eyes he watched Russ set up the equations, saw him trip the activating lever, saw the men disappear, listened to the thunderous rumbling of the mighty engines.

Chizzy went to the Outpost, the harsh prison on Neptune's satellite. Reg went to Titan, clear across the Solar System, where men in the infamous penal colony labored in the frigid wastes of that moon of Saturn. Max went to Vesta, the asteroid prison, which long had been the target of reformers, who claimed that on it 50 per cent of the prisoners died of boredom and fear.

Max was gone and only Scorio remained.

"Stutsman's the one who got us into this," wailed the gangster. "He's the man you want to get. Not me. Not the boys. Stutsman."

"I promise you," said Greg, "that we'll take care of Stutsman."

"And Chambers, too," chattered Scorio. "But you can't touch Chambers. You wouldn't dare."

"We're not worrying about Chambers," Greg told him. "We're not worrying about anyone. You're the one who had better start doing some."

Scorio cringed.

"Let me tell you about a place on Venus," said Greg. "It's in the center of a big swamp that stretches for hundreds of miles in every direction. It's a sort of mountain rising out of the swamp. And the swamp is filled with beasts and reptiles of every kind. Ravenous things, lusting for blood. But they don't climb the mountain. A man, if he stayed on the mountain, would be safe. There's food there. Roots and berries and fruits and even small animals one could kill. A man might go hungry for a while, but soon he'd find the things to eat.

"But he'd be alone. No one ever goes near that mountain. I am the only man who ever set foot on it. Perhaps no one ever will again. At night you hear the screaming and the crying of the things down in swamp, but you mustn't pay any attention to them."

Scorio's eyes widened, staring. "You won't send me *there!*"

"You'll find my campfires," Greg told him, "if the rain hasn't washed them away. It rains a lot. So much and so drearily that you'll want to leave that mountain and walk down into the swamp, of your own free will, and let the monsters finish you."

Scorio sat dully. He did not move. Horror glazed his eyes.

Greg signed to Russ. Russ, pipe clenched between his teeth, reached out his fingers for the keys. The engines droned.

Manning walked slowly to a television control, sat down in the chair and flipped over a lever. A face stared out of the screen. It was strangely filled with anger and a sort of half-fear.

"You watched it, didn't you, Stutsman?" Greg asked.

Stutsman nodded. "I watched. You can't get away with it, Manning. You can't take the law into your own hands that way."

"You and Chambers have been taking the law into your hands for years," said Greg. "All I did tonight was clear the Earth of some vermin. Every one of those men was guilty of murder ... and worse."

"What did you gain by it?" asked Stutsman.

Greg gave a bitter laugh. "I convinced you, Stutsman," he said, "that it isn't so easy to kill me. I think it'll be some time before you try again. Better luck next time."

He flipped the switch and turned about in the chair.

Russ jerked his thumb at the skylight. "Might as well finish the ship now."

Greg nodded.

An instant later there was a fierce, intolerably blue-white light that lit the mountains for many miles. For just an instant it flared, exploding into millions of brilliant, harmless sparks that died into darkness before they touched the ground. The gangster ship was destroyed beyond all tracing, disintegrated. The metal and quartz of which it was made were simply gone.

Russ brought his glance back from the skylight, looked at his friend. "Stutsman will do everything he can to wipe us out. By tomorrow morning the Interplanetary machine will be rolling. With only one purpose-to crush us."

"That's right," Greg agreed, "but we're ready for them now. Our ship left the Belgium factories several hours ago. The *Comet* towed it out in space and it's waiting for us now. In a few hours the *Comet* will be here to pick us up."

"War in space," said Russ, musingly. "That's what it will be."

"Chambers and his gang won't fight according to any rules. There'll be no holds barred, no more feeble attempts like the one they tried tonight. From now on we need a base that simply can't be located."

"The ship," said Russ.

CHAPTER XIV

The *Invincible* hung in space, an empty, airless hull, the largest thing afloat.

Chartered freighters, leaving their ports from distant parts of the Earth, had converged upon her hours before, had unloaded crated apparatus, storing it in the yawning hull. Then they had departed.

Now the sturdy little space-yacht, *Comet*, was towing the great ship out into space, 500,000 miles beyond the orbit of the Moon. Slowly the hull was being taken farther and farther away from possible discovery.

Work on the installation of the apparatus had started almost as soon as the *Comet* had first tugged at the ponderous mass. Leaving only a skeleton crew in charge of the *Comet*, the rest of the selected crew had begun the assembly of the mighty machines which would transform the *Invincible* into a thing of unimaginable power and speed.

The doors were closed and sealed and the air, already stored in the ship's tanks, was released. The slight acceleration of the *Comet's* towing served to create artificial weight for easier work, but not enough to handicap the shifting of the heavier pieces of apparatus. An electric cable was run back from the little yacht and the *Invincible* took her first breath of life.

The work advanced rapidly, for every man was more than a mere engineer or spacebuster. They were a selected crew, the men who had helped to make the name of Gregory Manning famous throughout the Solar System.

First the engines were installed, then the two groups of five massive power plants and the single smaller engine as an auxiliary supply plant for the light, heat, air.

The accumulators of the *Comet* were drained in a single tremendous surge and the auxiliary generator started. It in turn awoke to life the other power plants, to leave them sleeping, idling, but ready for instant use to develop power such as man never before had dreamed of holding and molding to his will.

Then, with the gigantic tools these engines supplied ... tools of pure force and strange space fields ... the work was rapidly completed. The power boards were set in place, welded in position by a sudden furious blast of white hot metal and as equally sudden freezing, to be followed by careful heating and recooling till the beryl-steel reached its maximum strength. Over the hull swarmed spacesuited men, using that strange new power, heat-treating the stubborn metal in a manner never before possible.

The generators were charging the atoms of the ship's beryl-steel hide with the same hazy force that had trapped and held the gangster ship in a mighty vise. Thus charged, no material thing could penetrate them. The greatest meteor would be crushed to drifting dust without so much as scarring that wall of mighty force ... meteors traveling with a speed and penetrative power that no gun-hurled projectile could ever hope to attain.

Riding under her own power, driven by the concentration of gravitational lines, impregnable to all known forces, containing within her hull the secrets of many strange devices, the *Invincible* wheeled in space.

Russell Page lounged in a chair before the control manual of the tele-transport machine. He puffed placidly at his pipe and looked out through the great sweep of the vision panel. Out there was the black of space and the glint of stars, the soft glow of distant Jupiter.

Greg Manning was hunched over the navigation controls, sharp eyes watching the panorama of space.

Russ looked at him and grinned. On Greg's face there was a smile, but about his eyes were lines of alert watchfulness and thought. Greg Manning was in his proper role at the controls of a ship such as the *Invincible*, a man who never stepped backward from danger, whose spirit hungered for the vast stretches of void that lay between the worlds.

Russ leaned back, blowing smoke toward the high-arched control room ceiling.

They had burned their bridges behind them. The laboratory back in the mountains was destroyed. Locked against any possible attack by a sphere of force until the tele-transport had lifted from it certain items of equipment, it had been melted into a mass of molten metal that formed a pool upon the mountain top, that ran in gushing, fiery ribbons down the mountain side, flowing in gleaming curtains over precipices. It would have been easier to have merely disintegrated in one bursting flash of energy, but that would have torn apart the entire mountain range, overwhelmed and toppled cities hundreds of miles away, dealt Earth a staggering blow.

A skeleton crew had taken the *Comet* back to Earth and landed it on Greg's estate. Once again the tele-transport had reached out, wrapped its fingers around the men who stepped from the little ship. In less than the flash of a strobe light, they had been snatched back to the *Invincible*, through a million miles of space, through the very walls of the ship itself. One second they had been on Earth, the next second they were in the control room of the *Invincible*, grinning, saluting Greg Manning, trotting back to their quarters in the engine rooms.

Russ stared out at space, puffed at his pipe, considering.

A thousand years ago men had held what they called tournaments. Armored knights rode out into the jousting grounds and broke their lances to prove which was the better man. Today there was to be another tournament. This ship was to be their charger, and the gauntlet had been flung to Spencer Chambers and Interplanetary Power. And all of space was to be the jousting grounds.

This was war. War without trappings, without fanfare, but bitter war upon which depended the future of the Solar System. A war to break the grip of steel that Interplanetary accumulators had gained upon the planets, to shatter the grim dream of empire held by one man, a war for the right to give to the people of the worlds a source of power that would forever unshackle them.

Back in those days, a thousand years ago, men had built a system of government that historians called the feudal system. By this system certain men were called lords or barons and other titles. They held the power of life and death over the men "under" them.

This was what Spencer Chambers was trying to do with the Solar System … what he would do if someone did not stop him.

Russ bit viciously on his pipe-stem.

The Earth, the Solar System, never could revert to that ancient way of government. The proud people spawned on the Earth, swarming outward to the other planets, must never have to bow their heads as minions to an overlord.

The thrum of power was beating in his brain, the droning, humming power from the engine rooms that would blast, once and forever, the last threat of dictatorship upon any world. The power that would free a people, that would help them on and up and outward to the great destiny that was theirs.

And this had come because, wondering, groping, curiously, he had sought to heat a slender thread of imperm wire within Force Field 348, because another man had listened and had made available his fortune to continue the experiments. Blind luck and human curiosity … perhaps even the madness of a human dream … and from those things had come this great ship, this mighty power, these many bulking pieces of equipment that would perform wonders never guessed at less than a year ago.

Greg Manning swiveled his chair. "Well, Russ, we're ready to begin. Let's get Wrail first."

Russ nodded silently, his mind still half full of fleeting thought. Absent-mindedly he knocked out his pipe and pocketed it, swung around to the manual of the televisor. His fingers reached out and tapped a pattern.

Callisto appeared within the screen, leaped upward at them. Then the surface of the frozen little world seemed to rotate swiftly and a dome appeared.

The televisor dived through the dome, sped through the city, straight for a penthouse apartment.

Ben Wrail sat slumped in a chair. A newspaper was crumpled at his feet. In his lap lay a mangled dead cigar.

"Greg!" yelled Russ. "Greg, there's something wrong!"

Greg leaped forward, stared at the screen. Russ heard his smothered cry of rage.

In Wrail's forehead was a tiny, neatly drilled hole from which a single drop of blood oozed.

"Murdered!" exclaimed Russ.

"Yes, murdered," said Greg, and there was a sudden calmness in his voice.

Russ grasped the televisor control. Ranthoor's streets ran beneath them, curiously silent and deserted. Here and there lay bodies. A few shop windows were smashed. But the only living that stirred was a dog that slunk across the street and into the shadows of an alley.

Swiftly the televisor swung along the streets. Straight into the screen clanked a marching detail of government police, herding before them a half dozen prisoners. The men had their hands bound behind their backs, but they walked with heads held high.

"Revolution," gasped Russ.

"Not a revolution. A purge. Stutsman is clearing the city of all who might be dangerous to him. This will be happening on every other planet where Chambers holds control."

Perspiration ran down Russ's forehead and dripped into his eyes as he manipulated the controls.

"Stutsman is striking first," said Greg, calmly ... far too calmly. "He's consolidating his position, possibly on the pretense that plots have been discovered."

A few buildings were bombed. A line of bodies were crumpled at the foot of a steel wall, marking the spot where men had been lined up and mowed down with one sweeping blast from a heater.

Russ turned the television controls. "Let's see about Venus and Mars."

The scenes in Ranthoor were duplicated in Sandebar on Mars, in New Chicago, the capital of Venus. Everywhere Stutsman had struck ... everywhere the purge was wiping out in blood every person who might revolt against the Chambers-dictated governments. Throughout the Solar System violence was on the march, iron-shod boots trampling the rights of free men to tighten the grip of Interplanetary.

In the control room of the *Invincible* the two men stared at one another.

"There's one man we need," said Greg. "One man, if he's still alive, and I think he is."

"Who is that?" asked Russ.

"John Moore Mallory," said Greg.

"Where is he?"

"I don't know. He was imprisoned in Ranthoor, but Stutsman transferred him some place else. Possibly to one of the prison fleet."

"If we had the records of the Callisto prison," suggested Russ, "we could find out."

"If we had the records..."

"We'll get them!" Russ said.

He swung back to the keyboard again.

A moment later the administration offices of the prison were on the screen.

The two men searched the vision plate.

"The records are most likely in that vault," said Russ. "And the vault is locked."

"Don't worry about the lock," snapped Greg. "Just bring the whole damn thing here-vault and records and all."

Russ nodded grimly. His thumb tripped the tele-transport control and from the engine rooms came a drone of power. In Ranthoor Prison, great bands of force wrapped themselves around the vault, clutching it, enfolding it within a sphere of power. Back in the *Invincible* the engines screamed and the vault was ripped out of the solid steel wall as easily as a man might rip a button from his shirt.

CHAPTER XV

John Moore Mallory sat on the single metal chair within his cell and pressed his face against the tiny vision port. For hours he had sat there, staring out into the blackness of space.

There was bitterness in John Moore Mallory's soul, a terrible and futile bitterness. So long as he had remained within the Ranthoor prison, there had always been a chance of escape. But now, aboard the penal ship, there was no hope. Nothing but the taunting reaches of space, the mocking pinpoints of the stars, the hooting laughter of the engines.

Sometimes he had thought he would go mad. The everlasting routine, the meaningless march of hours. The work period, the sleep period ... the work period, the sleep period ... endless monotony, an existence without a purpose. Men buried alive in space.

"John Moore Mallory," said a voice.

Mallory heard, but he did not stir. An awful thought crossed his mind. Now he was hearing voices calling his name!

"John Mallory," said the voice again.

Mallory slowly turned about and as he turned he started from his chair.

A man stood in the cell! A man he had never seen before, who had come silently, for there had been no screech of opening door.

"You are John Moore Mallory, aren't you?" asked the man.

"Yes, I am Mallory. Who are you?"

"Gregory Manning."

"Gregory Manning," said Mallory wonderingly. "I've heard of you. You're the man who rescued the Pluto Expedition. But why are you here? How did you get in?"

"I came to take you away with me," said Greg. "Back to Callisto. Back to any place you want to go."

Mallory flattened himself against the partition, his face white with disbelief. "But I'm in a prison ship. I'm not free to go and come as I please."

Greg chuckled. "You are free to go and come as you please from now on," he said. "Even prison ships can't hold you."

"You're mad," whispered Mallory. "Either you're mad or I am. You're a dream. I'll wake up and find you gone."

Manning stood in silence, looking at the man. Mallory bore the marks of prison on him. His eyes were haunted and his rugged face was pinched and thin.

"Listen closely, Mallory," said Greg softly. "You aren't going mad and I'm not mad. You aren't seeing things. You aren't hearing things. You're actually talking to me."

There was no change in the other's face.

"Mallory," Greg went on, "I have what you've always needed-means of generating almost unlimited energy at almost no cost, the secret of the energy of matter. A secret that will smash Interplanetary, that will free the Solar System from Spencer Chambers. But I can't make that secret available to the people until Chambers is crushed, until I'm sure that he can't take it from me. And to do that I need your help."

Mallory's face lost its expression of bewilderment, suddenly lighted with realization. But his voice was harsh and bitter.

"You came too late. I can't help you. Remember, I'm in a prison ship from which no one can escape. You have to do what you can ...you must do what you can. But I can't be with you."

Manning strode forward. "You don't get the idea at all. I said I'd get you out of here and I'm going to. I could pick up this ship and put it wherever I wanted. But I don't want to. I just want you."

Mallory stared at him.

"Just don't be startled," said Greg. "Something will happen soon. Get ready for it."

Feet drummed on the metal corridor outside.

"Hey, you, pipe down!" yelled the voice of the guard. "You know there's no talking allowed now. Go to sleep."

"That's the guard," Mallory whispered fiercely. "They'll stop us."

Greg grinned viciously. "No, they won't."

The guard came into view through the grilled door.

"So it's you, Mallory ..." he began, stopping in amazement. "Hey, you!" he shouted at Greg. "Who are you? How did you get in that cell?"

Greg flipped a hand in greeting. "Pleasant evening, isn't it?"

The guard grabbed for the door, but he did not reach the bars. Some force stopped him six inches away. It could not be seen, could not be felt, but his straining against it accomplished nothing.

"Mallory and I are leaving," Greg told the guard. "We don't like it here. Too stuffy."

The guard lifted a whistle and blew a blast. Feet pounded outside. A prisoner yelled from one of the cells. Another catcalled. Instantly the ship was in an uproar. The convicts took up the yammering, shaking the bars on their doors.

"Let's get started," Greg said to Mallory. "Hold tight."

Blackness engulfed Mallory. He felt a peculiar twisting wrench. And then he was standing in the control room of a ship and Gregory Manning and another man were smiling at him. White light poured down from a cluster of globes. Somewhere in the ship engines purred with the hum of power. The air was fresh and pure, making him realize how foul and stale the air of the prison ship had been.

Greg held out his hand. "Welcome to our ship."

Mallory gripped his hand, blinking in the light. "Where am I?"

"You are on the *Invincible*, five million miles off Callisto."

"But were you here all the time?" asked Mallory. "Were you in my cell back there or weren't you?"

"I was really in your cell," Greg assured him. "I could have just thrown my image there, but I went there personally to get you. Russ Page, here, sent me out. When I gave him the signal, he brought both of us back."

"I'm glad you're with us," Russ said. "Perhaps you'd like a cup of coffee, something to eat."

Mallory stammered. "Why, I really would." He laughed. "Rations weren't too good in the prison ship."

They sat down while Russ rang the galley for coffee and sandwiches.

Crisply, Greg informed Mallory of the situation.

"We want to start manufacturing these engines as soon as possible," he explained, "but I haven't even dared to patent them. Chambers would simply buy out the officials if I tried it on Earth, delay the patent for a few days and then send through papers copied from ours. You know what he'd do with it if he got the patent rights. He'd scrap it and the old accumulator business would go on as always. If I tried it on any other world, with any other government, he'd see that laws were passed to block us. He'd probably instruct the courts to rule against the manufacture of the engines on the grounds that they were dangerous."

Mallory's face was grave. "There's only one answer," he said. "With the situation on the worlds, with this purge you told me about, there's only one thing to do. We have to act at once. Every minute we wait gives Stutsman just that much longer to tighten his hold."

"And that answer?" asked Russ.

"Revolution," said Mallory. "Simultaneous revolution in the Jovian confederacy, on Mars and Venus. Once free, the planets will stay free with your material energy engines. Spencer Chambers and his idea of Solar System domination will be too late."

Greg's forehead was wrinkled in thought, his facial muscles tensed.

"First thing to do," he said, "is to contact all the men we can find ... men we can rely on to help us carry out our plans. We'll need more televisor machines, more teleport machines, some for use on Mars and Venus, others for the Jovian moons. We will have to bring the men here to learn to operate them. It'll take a few days. We'll get some men to work on new machines right away."

He started to rise from his chair, but at that moment the coffee and sandwiches arrived.

Greg grinned. "We may as well eat first."

Mallory looked grateful and tried to keep from wolfing the food. The others pretended not to notice.

Grim hours followed, an unrelenting search over two planets and four moons for men whom Mallory considered loyal to his cause-men willing to risk their lives to throw off the yoke of Interplanetary.

They were hard to find. Many of them were dead, victims of the purge. The others were in hiding and word of them was difficult to get.

But slowly, one by one, they were ferreted out, the plan explained to them, and then, by means of the tele-transport, they were brought to the *Invincible*.

Hour after hour men worked, stripped to their waists, in the glaring inferno of terrible force fields, fashioning new television units. As fast as the sets were constructed, they were placed in operation.

The work went faster than could be expected, yet it was maddeningly slow.

For with the passing of each hour, Stutsman clamped tighter his iron grip on the planets. Concentration camps were filled to overflowing. Buildings were bombed and burned. Murders and executions were becoming too common to be news.

Then suddenly there was a new development.

"Greg, Craven has found something!" Russ cried. "I can't get him!"

Supervising the installation of a new televisor set, Greg spun around. "What's that?"

"Craven! I can't reach him. He's blocking me out!"

Greg helped, but the apparatus was unable to enter the Interplanetary building in New York. Certain other portions of the city adjacent to the building also were blanketed out. In all the Solar System, the Interplanetary building was the only place they could not enter, except the Sun itself.

Craven had developed a field from which their field shied off. The televisor seemed to roll off it like a drop of mercury. That definitely ended all spying on Craven and Chambers.

Russ mopped his brow, sucked at his dead pipe.

"Light penetrates it," he said. "Matter penetrates it, electricity, all ordinary forces. But this field won't. It's ...well, whatever Craven has is similarly dissimilar. The same thing of opposite nature. It repels our field, but doesn't affect anything else. That means he has analyzed our fields. We have Wilson to thank for this."

Greg nodded gravely. "There's just one thing to be thankful for," he declared. "He probably isn't any nearer our energy than he was before. But now we can't watch him. And that field of his shows that he has tremendous power of some sort."

"We can't watch him, but we can follow him," corrected Russ. "He can't shake us. None of them can. The mechanical shadow will take care of that. I have one for Craven with a bit of 'bait' off his spectacles and he'll keep those spectacles, never fear. He's blind as a bat without them. And we can track Chambers with his ring."

"That's right," agreed Greg, "but we've got to speed up. Craven is getting under way now. If he does this, he can do something else. Something that will really hurt us. The man's clever ...too damn clever."

CHAPTER XVI

A miracle came to pass in Ranthoor when a man for whom all hope had been abandoned suddenly appeared within the city's streets. But he appeared to be something not quite earthly, for he did not have the solidity of a man. He was pale, like a wraith from out of space, and one could see straight through him, yet he still had all the old mannerisms and tricks.

In frightened, awe-stricken whispers the word was spread ... the spirit of John Moore Mallory had come back to the city once again. He bulked four times the height of a normal man and there was that singular ghostliness about him. From where he had come, or how, or why, no one seemed to know.

But when he reached the steps of the federation's administration building and walked straight through a line of troopers that suddenly massed to bar his way, and when he turned on those steps and spoke to the people who had gathered, there was none to doubt that at last a sign had come. The sign that now, if ever, was the time to avenge the purge. Now the time to take vengeance for the blood that flowed in gutters, for the throaty chortling of the flame guns that had snuffed out lives against a broad steel wall.

Standing on the steps, shadowy but plainly visible, John Moore Mallory talked to the people in the square below, and his voice was the voice they remembered. They saw him toss his black mane of hair, they saw his clenched fist raised in terrible anger, they heard the boom of the words he spoke.

Like a shrilling alarm the words spread through the city, reverberating from the dome, seeking out those who were in hiding. From every corner of the city, from its deepest cellars and its darkest alleys, poured out a mass of humanity that surrounded the capitol and blackened the square and the converging streets with a mob that shrieked its hatred, bellowed its anger.

"Power!" thundered the mighty shadow on the steps. "Power to burn! Power to give away. Power to heat the dome, to work your mines, to drive your spaceships!"

"Power!" answered the voice of the crowd. "Power!" It sounded like a battle cry.

"No more accumulators," roared the towering image. "Never again need you rely on Spencer Chambers for your power. Callisto is yours. Ranthoor is yours."

The black crowd surged forward, reached the steps and started to climb, wild cheers in their throat, the madness of victory in their eyes. Up the steps came men with nothing but bare hands, screaming women, jeering children.

Officers snapped orders at the troops that lined the steps, but the troopers, staring into the awful, raging maw of that oncoming crowd, dropped their guns and fled, back into the capitol building, with the mob behind them, shrilling blood lust and long-awaited vengeance.

Out of the red and yellow wilderness of the deserts, a man came to Sandebar on Mars. He had long been thought dead. The minions of the government had announced that he was dead. But he had been in hiding for six years.

His beard was long and gray, his eyes were curtained by hardship, his white hair hung about his shoulders and he was clothed in the tattered leather trappings of the spaceways.

But men remembered him.

Tom Brown had lead the last revolt against the Martian government, an ill-starred revolt that ended almost before it started when the troopers turned loose the heavy heaters and swept the streets with washing waves of flame.

When he climbed to the base of a statue in Techor Park to address the crowd that gathered, the police shouted for him to come down and he disregarded them. They climbed the statue to reach him and their hands went through him.

Tom Brown stood before the people, in plain view, and spoke, but he wasn't there!

Other things happened in Sandebar that day. A voice spoke out of thin air, a voice that told the people the reign of Interplanetary was over. It told of a mighty new source of power. Power that would cost almost nothing. Power that would make the accumulators unnecessary ...

would make them out of date. A voice that said the people need no longer submit to the yoke of Spencer Chambers' government in order to obtain the power they needed.

There was no one there ... no one visible at all. And yet that voice went on and on. A great crowd gathered, listening, cheering. The police tried to break it up and failed. The troops were ordered out and the people fought them until the voice told them to disband peaceably and go to their homes.

Throughout Mars it was the same.

In a dozen places in Sandebar the voice spoke. It spoke in a dozen places, out of empty air, in Malacon and Alexon and Adebron.

Tom Brown, vanishing into the air after his speech was done, reappeared a few minutes later in Adebron and there the police, warned of what had happened in Sandebar, opened fire upon him when he stood on a park bench to address the people. But the flames passed through and did not touch him. Tom Brown, his long white beard covering his chest, his mad eyes flashing, stood in the fiery blast that bellowed from the muzzles of the flame rifles and calmly talked.

The chief of police at New Chicago, Venus, called the police commissioner. "There's a guy out here in the park, just across the street. He's preaching treason. He's telling the people to overthrow the government."

In the ground glass the police commissioner's face grew purple.

"Arrest him," he ordered the chief. "Clap him in the jug. Do you have to call me up every time one of those fiery-eyed boys climbs a soap box? Run him in."

"I can't," said the chief.

The police commissioner seemed ready to explode. "You can't? Why the hell not?"

"Well, you know that hill in the center of the park? Memorial Hill?"

"What has a hill got to do with it?" the commissioner roared.

"He's sitting on top of that hill. He's a thousand feet tall. His head is way up in the sky and his voice is like thunder. How can you arrest anybody like that?"

Everywhere in the System, revolt was flaming. New marching songs rolled out between the worlds, wild marching songs that had the note of anger in them. Weapons were brought out of hiding and polished. New standards were raised in an ever-rising tide against oppression.

Freedom was on the march again. The right of a man to rule himself the way he chose to rule. A new declaration of independence. A Solar Magna Carta.

There were new leaders, led by the old leaders. Led by spirits that marched across the sky. Led by voices that spoke out of the air. Led by signs and symbols and a new-born courage and a great and a deep conviction that right in the end would triumph.

Spencer Chambers glared at Ludwig Stutsman. "This is one time you went too far."

"If you'd given me a free hand before, this wouldn't have been necessary," Stutsman said. "But you were soft. You made me go easy when I should have ground them down. You left the way open for all sorts of plots and schemes and leaders to develop."

The two men faced one another, one the smooth, tawny lion, the other the snarling wolf.

"You've built up hatred, Stutsman," Chambers said. "You are the most hated man in the Solar System. And because of you, they hate me. That wasn't my idea. I needed you because I needed an iron fist, but I needed it to use judiciously. And you have been ruthless. You've used force when conciliation was necessary."

Stutsman sneered openly. "Still that old dream of a benevolent dictatorship. Still figuring yourself a little bronze god to be set up in every household. A dictatorship can't be run that way. You have to let them know you're boss."

Chambers was calm again. "Argument won't do us any good now. The damage is done. Revolt is flaming through all the worlds. We have to do something."

He looked at Craven, who was slouched in a chair beside the desk across which he and Stutsman faced each other.

"Can you help us, doctor?" he asked.

Craven shrugged. "Perhaps," he said acidly. "If I could only be left to my work undisturbed, instead of being dragged into these stupid conferences, I might be able to do something."

"You already have, haven't you?" asked Chambers.

"Very little. I've been able to blank out the televisor that Manning and Page are using, but that is all."

"Do you have any idea where Manning and Page are?"

"How could I know?" Craven asked. "Somewhere in space."

"They're at the bottom of this," snarled Stutsman. "Their damned tricks and propaganda."

"We know they're at the bottom of it," said Craven. "That's no news to us. If it weren't for them, we wouldn't have this trouble now, despite your bungling. But that doesn't help us any. With this new discovery of mine I have shielded this building from their observation. They can't spy on us any more. But that's as far as I've got."

"They televised the secret meeting of the emergency council when it met in Satellite City on Ganymede the other day," said Chambers. "The whole Jovian confederacy watched and listened to that meeting, heard our secret war plans, for fully ten minutes before the trick was discovered. Couldn't we use your shield to prevent such a situation again?"

"Better still," suggested Stutsman, "let's shield the whole satellite. Without Manning's ghostly leaders, this revolt would collapse of its own weight."

Craven shook his head. "It takes fifty tons of accumulators to build up that field, and a ton of fuel a day to maintain it. Just for this building alone. It would be impossible to shield a whole planet, an entire moon."

"Any progress on your collector field?" asked Chambers.

"Some," Craven admitted. "I'll know in a day or two."

"That would give us something with which to fight Manning and Page, wouldn't it?"

"Yes," agreed Craven. "It would be something to fight them with. If I can develop that collector field, we would be able to utilize every radiation in space, from the heat wave down through the cosmics. Within the Solar System, our power would be absolutely limitless. Your accumulators depend for their power storage upon just one radiation ... heat. But with this idea I have you'd use all types of radiations."

"You say you could even put the cosmics to work?" asked Chambers.

Craven nodded. "If I can do anything at all with the field, I can."

"How?" demanded Stutsman.

"By breaking them up, you fool. Smash the short, high-powered waves into a lot of longer, lower-powered waves." Craven swung back to face Chambers. "But don't count on it," he warned. "I haven't done it yet."

"You have to do it," Chambers insisted.

Craven rose from his chair, his blue eyes blazing angrily behind the heavy lenses. "How often must I tell you that you cannot hurry scientific investigation? You have to try and try ... follow one tiny clue to another tiny clue. You have to be patient. You have to hope. But you cannot force the work."

He strode from the room, slammed the door behind him.

Chambers turned slowly in his chair to face Stutsman. His gray eyes bored into the wolfish face.

"And now," he suggested, "suppose you tell me just why you did it."

Stutsman's lips curled. "I suppose you would rather I had allowed those troublemakers to go ahead, consolidate their plans. There was only one thing to do-root them out, liquidate them. I did it."

"You chose a poor time," said Chambers softly. "You would have to do something like this, just at the time when Manning is lurking around the Solar System somewhere, carrying enough power to wipe us off the face of the Earth if he wanted to."

"That's why I did it," protested Stutsman. "I knew Manning was around. I was afraid he'd start something, so I beat him to it. I thought it would throw a scare into the people, make them afraid to follow Manning when he acted."

"You have a low opinion of the human race, don't you?" Chambers said. "You think you can beat them into a mire of helplessness and fear."

Chambers rose from his chair, pounded his desk for emphasis.

"But you can't do it, Stutsman. Men have tried it before you, from the very dawn of history. You can destroy their homes and kill their children. You can burn them at the stake or in the electric chair, hang them or space-walk them or herd them into gas chambers. You can drive them like cattle into concentration camps, you can keep the torture racks bloody, but you can't break them.

"Because the people always survive. Their courage is greater than the courage of any one man or group of men. They always reach the man who has oppressed them, they always tear him down from the place he sits, and they do not deal gently with him when they do. In the end the people always win."

Chambers reached across the desk and caught Stutsman by the slack of the shirt. A twist of his hand tightened the fabric around Stutsman's neck. The financier thrust his face close to the wolfish scowl. "That is what is going to happen to you and me. We'll go down in history as just a couple of damn fools who tried to rule and couldn't make the grade. Thanks to you and your damned stupidity. You and your blood purges!"

Patches of anger burned on Stutsman's cheeks. His eyes glittered and his lips were white. But his whisper was bitter mockery. "Maybe we should have coddled and humored them. Made them just so awful happy that big bad old Interplanetary had them. So they could have set up little bronze images of you in their homes. So you could have been sort of a solar god!"

"I still think it would have been the better way." Chambers flung Stutsman from him with a straight-armed push. The man reeled and staggered across the carpeted floor. "Get out of my sight!"

Stutsman straightened his shirt, turned and left.

Chambers slumped into his chair, his hands grasping the arms on either side of his great body, his eyes staring out through the window from which flooded the last rays of the afternoon Sun.

Drums pounded in his brain ... the drums of rebellion out in space, of rebellion on those other worlds ... drums that were drowning out and shattering forever the dream that he had woven. He had wanted economic dictatorship ... not the cold, passionless, terrible dictatorship that Stutsman typified ... but one that would bring peace and prosperity and happiness to the Solar System.

He closed his eyes and thought. Snatches of ambition, snatches of hopes ... but it was useless to think, for the drums and the imagined shouting drowned out his thoughts.

Mankind didn't give a damn for good business administration, nor a hoot for prosperity or peace or happiness. Liberty and the right to rule, the right to go risk one's neck ... to climb a mountain or cross a desert or explore a swamp, the right to aim one's sights at distant stars, to fling a taunting challenge into the teeth of space, to probe with clumsy fingers and force nature to lay bare her secrets ... that was what mankind wanted. That was what those men out on Mars and Venus and in the Jovian worlds were fighting for. Not against Spencer Chambers or Ludwig Stutsman or Interplanetary Power, but for the thing that drove man on and made of him a flame that others might follow. Fighting for a heritage that was first expressed when the first man growled at the entrance to his cave and dared the world to take it from him.

Spencer Chambers closed his eyes and rocked back and forth in the tilting office chair.

It had been a good fight, a hard fight. He had had a lot of fun out of it. But he was licked, after all these years. He had held the biggest dream of any man who ever lived. Alexander and Napoleon, Hitler, Stalin and those other fellows had been pikers alongside of Spencer Chambers. They had only aimed at Earthly conquest while he had reached out to grab at all the worlds. But by heaven, he'd almost made it!

A door grated open.

"Chambers!" said a voice.

His feet hit the floor with a thud and he sat stiff and staring at the figure in the door.

It was Craven and the man was excited. His glasses were slid far down on his nose, his hair was standing on end, his tie was all awry.

"I have it!" Craven whooped. "I have it at last!"

Hope clutched at Chambers, but he was almost afraid to speak.

"Have what?" he whispered tensely.

"The collector field! It was under my nose all the time, but I didn't see it!"

Chambers was out of his chair and striding across the room. A tumult buzzed within his skull.

Licked? Hell, he hadn't even started! He'd win yet. He'd teach the people to revolt! He'd run Manning and Page out to the end of space and push them through!

CHAPTER XVII

It was a weird revolution. There were few battles, little blood shed. There seemed to be no secret plots. There were no skulking leaders, no passwords, nothing that in former years had marked rebellion against tyranny.

It was a revolution carried out with utter boldness. Secret police were helpless, for it was not a secret revolution. The regular police and the troopers were helpless because the men they wanted to arrest were shadows that flitter here and there … large and substantial shadows, but impossible to seize and imprison.

Every scheme that was hatched within the government circles was known almost at once to the ghostly leaders who stalked the land. Police detachments, armed with warrants for the arrests of men who had participated in some action which would stamp them as active rebels, found the suspects absent when they broke down the doors. Someone had warned them. Troops, hurried to points where riots had broken out, arrived to find peaceful scenes, but with evidence of recent battle. The rioters had been warned, had made their getaway.

When the rebels struck it was always at the most opportune time, when the government was off balance or off guard.

In the first day of the revolt, Ranthoor fell when the maddened populace, urged on by the words of a shadowy John Moore Mallory, charged the federation buildings. The government fled, leaving all records behind, to Satellite City on Ganymede.

In the first week three Martian cities fell, but Sandebar, the capital, still held out. On Venus, Radium City was taken by the rebels within twenty-four hours after the first call to revolt had rung across the worlds, but New Chicago, the seat of government, still was in the government's hands, facing a siege.

Government propagandists spread the word that the material energy engines were not safe. Reports were broadcast that on at least two occasions the engines had blown up, killing the men who operated them.

But this propaganda failed to gain credence, for in the cities that were in the rebel hands, technicians were at work manufacturing and setting up the material engines. Demonstrations were given. The people saw them, saw what enormous power they developed.

Russ Page stared incredulously at the television screen. It seemed to be shifting back and forth. One second it held the distorted view of Satellite City on Ganymede, and the next second the view of jumbled, icy desert somewhere outside the city.

"Look here, Greg," he said. "Something's wrong."

Greg Manning turned away from the calculator where he had been working and stared at the screen.

"How long has it been acting that way?" he asked.

"Just started," said Russ.

Greg straightened and glanced down the row of television machines. Some of them were dead, their switches closed, but on the screens of many of the others was the same effect as on this machine. Their operators were working frustratedly at the controls, trying to focus the image, bring it into sharp relief.

"Can't seem to get a thing, sir," said one of the men. "I was working on the fueling station out on Io, and the screen just went haywire."

"Mine seems to be all right," said another man. "I've had it on Sandebar for the last couple of hours and there's nothing wrong."

A swift check revealed one fact. The machines, when trained on the Jovian worlds, refused to function. Anywhere else in space, however, they worked perfectly.

Russ stoked and lit his pipe, snapped off his machine and swung around in the operator's chair.

"Somebody's playing hell with us out around Jupiter," he stated calmly.

"I've been expecting something like this," said Greg. "I have been afraid of this ever since Craven blanketed us out of the Interplanetary building."

"He really must have something this time," Russ agreed. "He's blanketing out the entire Jovian system. There's a space field of low intensity surrounding all of Jupiter, enclosing all the moons. He keeps shifting the intensity so that, even though we can force our way through his field, the irregular variations make it impossible to line up anything. It works, in principle, just as effectively as if we couldn't get through at all."

Greg whistled soundlessly through suddenly bared teeth.

"That takes power," he said, "and I'm afraid Craven has it. Power to burn."

"The collector field?" asked Russ.

Greg nodded. "A field that sucks in radiant energy. Free energy that he just reaches out and grabs. And it doesn't depend on the Sun alone. It probably makes use of every type of radiation in all of space."

Russ slumped in his chair, smoking, his forehead wrinkled in thought.

"If that's what he's got," he finally declared, "he's going to be hard to crack. He can suck in any radiant vibration form, any space vibration. He can shift them around, break them down and build them up. He can discharge them, direct them. He's got a vibration plant that's the handiest little war machine that ever existed."

Greg suddenly wheeled and walked to a wall cabinet. From it he took a box and, opening it, lifted out a tiny mechanism.

He chuckled deep in his throat. "The mechanical shadow. The little machine that always tells us where Craven is-as long as he's wearing his glasses."

"He always wears them," said Russ crisply. "He's blind as a bat without them."

Greg set the machine down on the table. "When we find Craven, we'll find the contraption that's blanketing Jupiter and its moons."

Dials spun and needles quivered. Rapidly Russ jotted down the readings on a sheet of paper. At the calculator, he tapped keys, depressed the activator. The machine hummed and snarled and chuckled.

Russ glanced at the result imprinted on the paper roll.

"Craven is out near Jupiter," he announced. "About 75,000 miles distant from its surface, in a plane normal to the Sun's rays."

"A spaceship," suggested Greg.

Russ nodded. "That's the only answer."

The two men looked at one another.

"That's something we can get hold of," said Greg.

He walked to the ship controls and lowered himself into the pilot's chair. A hand came out and hauled back a lever.

The *Invincible* moved.

From the engine rooms came the whine of the gigantic power plant as it built up and maintained the gravity concentration center suddenly created in front of the ship.

Russ, standing beside Greg at the control panel, looked out into space and marveled. They were flashing through space, their speed building up at a breath-taking rate, yet they had no real propulsion power. The discovery of the gravity concentrator had outdated such a method of driving a spaceship. Instead, they were falling, hurtling downward into the yawning maw of an artificial gravity field. And such a method made for speed, terrible speed.

Jupiter seemed to leap at them. It became a great crimson and yellow ball that filled almost half the vision plate.

The *Invincible's* speed was slacking off, slower and slower, until it barely crawled in comparison to its former speed.

Slowly they circled Jupiter's great girth, staring out of the vision port for a sight of Craven's ship. They were nearing the position the little mechanical shadow had indicated.

"There it is," said Russ suddenly, almost breathlessly.

Far out in space, tiny, almost like a dust mote against the great bulk of the monster planet, rode a tiny light. Slowly the *Invincible* crawled inward. The mote of light became a gleaming silver ship, a mighty ship-one that was fully as large as the *Invincible*!

"That's it all right," said Greg. "They're lying behind a log out here raising hell with our television apparatus. Maybe we better tickle them a little bit and see what they have."

Rising from the control board, he went to another control panel. Russ remained standing in front of the vision plate, staring down at the ship out in space.

Behind him came a shrill howl from the power plant. The *Invincible* staggered slightly. A beam of deep indigo lashed across space, a finger suddenly jabbing at the other ship.

Space was suddenly colored, for thousands of miles, as the beam struck Craven's ship and seemed to explode in a blast of dazzling indigo light. The ship reeled under the impact of the blow, reeled and weaved in space as the beam struck it and delivered to it the mighty power of the screaming engines back in the engine room.

"What happened?" Greg screamed above the roar.

Russ shrugged his shoulders. "You jarred him a little. Pushed him through space for several hundred miles. Made him know something had hit him, but it didn't seem to do any damage."

"That was pure cosmic I gave him! Five billion horsepower-and it just staggered him!"

"He's got a space lens that absorbs the energy," said Russ. "The lens concentrates it and pours it into a receiving chamber, probably a huge photo-cell. Nobody yet has burned out one of those things on a closed circuit."

Greg wrinkled his brow, perplexed. "What he must have is a special field of some sort that lowers the wave-length and the intensity. He's getting natural cosmics all the time and taking care of them."

"That wouldn't be much of a trick," Russ pointed out. "But when he takes care of cosmics backed by five billion horsepower ... that's something else!"

Greg grinned wickedly. "I'm going to hand him a long heat radiation. If his field shortens that any, he'll have radio beam and that will blow photo-cells all to hell."

He stabbed viciously at the keys on the board and once again the shrill howl of the engines came from the rear of the ship. A lance of red splashed out across space and touched the other ship. Again space was lit, this time with a crimson glow.

Russ shook his head. "Nothing doing."

Greg sat down and looked at Russ. "Funny thing about this. They just sat there and let us throw two charges at them, took everything we gave them and never tried to hand it back."

"Maybe they haven't anything to hand us," Russ suggested hopefully.

"They must have. Craven wouldn't take to space with just a purely defensive weapon. He knew we'd find him and he'd have a fight on his hands."

Russ found his pipe was dead. Snapping his lighter, he applied flame to the blackened tobacco. Walking slowly to the wall cabinet, he lifted two other boxes out, set them on the table and took from them two other mechanical shadows. He turned them on and leaned close, watching the spinning dials, the quivering needles.

"Greg," he whispered, "Chambers and Stutsman are there in that ship with Craven! Look, their shadows register identical with the one that spotted Craven."

"I suspected as much," Greg replied. "We got the whole pack cornered out here. If we can just get rid of them, the whole war would be won in one stroke."

Russ lifted a stricken face from the row of tiny mechanisms. "This is our big chance. We may never get it again. The next hour could decide who is going to win."

Greg rose from the chair and stood before the control board. Grimly he punched a series of keys. The engines howled again. Greg twisted a dial and the howl rose into a shrill scream.

From the *Invincible* another beam lashed out ... another and another. Space was speared with beam after beam hurtling from the great ship.

Swiftly the beams went through the range of radiation, through radio and short radio, infra-red, visible light, ultra-violet, X-ray, the gammas and the cosmics —a terrific flood of billions of horsepower.

Craven's ship buckled and careened under the lashing impacts of the bombardment, but it seemed unhurt!

Greg's face was bleaker than usual as he turned from the board to look at Russ.

"We've used everything we have," he said, "and he's stopped them all. We can't touch him."

Russ shivered. The control room suddenly seemed chilly with a frightening kind of cold.

"He's carrying photo-cells and several thousand tons of accumulator stacks. Not much power left in them. He could pour a billion horsepower into them for hours and still have room for more."

Greg nodded wearily. "All we've been doing is feeding him."

The engines were humming quietly now, singing the low song of power held in leash.

But then they screamed like a buzz saw biting into an iron-hard stick of white oak. Screamed in a single, frightful agony as they threw into the protecting wall that enclosed the *Invincible* all the power they could develop.

The air of the ship was instantaneously charged with a hazy, bluish glow, and the sharp, stinging odor of ozone filled the ship.

Outside, an enormous burst of blue-white flame splashed and spattered around the *Invincible*. Living lightning played in solid, snapping sheets around the vision port and ran in trickling blazing fire across the plates.

Russ cried out and backed away, holding his arm before his eyes. It was as if he had looked into a nova of energy exploding before his eyes.

In the instant the scream died and the splash of terrific fire had vanished. Only a rapidly dying glow remained.

"What was it?" asked Russ dazedly. "What happened? Ten engines every one of them capable of over five billion horsepower and every one of them screaming!"

"Craven," said Greg grimly. "He let us have everything he had. He simply drained his accumulator stacks and threw it all into our face. But he's done now. That was his only shot. He'll have to build up power now and that will take a while. But we couldn't have taken much more."

"Stalemate," said Russ. "We can't hurt him, he can't hurt us."

"Not by a damn sight," declared Greg. "I still have a trick or two in mind."

He tried them. From the *Invincible* a fifty-billion-horsepower bolt of living light and fire sprang out as all ten engines thundered with an insane voice that racked the ship.

Fireworks exploded in space when the bolt struck Craven's ship. Screen after screen exploded in glittering, flaming sparks, but the ship rode the lashing charge, finally halted the thrust of power. The beam glowed faintly, died out.

Perspiration streamed down Greg's face as he bent over a calculator and constructed the formula for a magnetic field. He sent out a field of such unimaginable intensity that it would have drawn any beryl-steel within a mile of it into a hard, compact mass. Even the *Invincible*, a hundred miles away, lurched under the strain. But Craven's ship, after the first wild jerk, did not move. A curious soft glow spread out from the ship, veered sharply and disappeared in the magnetic field.

Greg swore softly. "He's cutting it down as fast as I try to build it up," he explained, "and I can't move it any nearer."

From Craven's ship lashed out another thunderbolt and once again the engines screamed in terrible unison as they poured power into the ship's triple screen. The first screen stopped all material things. The second stopped radiations by refracting them into the fourth dimension. The third shield was akin to the anti-entropy field, which stopped all matter ...and yet the ten engines bellowed like things insane as Craven struck with flaming bolts, utilizing the power he had absorbed from the fifty billion horsepower Greg had thrown at him.

There was anger in Greg Manning's face ...a terrible anger. His fists knotted and he shook them at the gleaming ship that lay far down near Jupiter.

"I've got one trick left," he shouted, almost as if he expected Craven to hear. "Just one trick. Damn you, see if you can stop this one!"

He set up the pattern on the board and punched the activating lever. The ten engines thrummed with power. Then the howling died away.

Four times they screamed and four times they ebbed into a gentle hum.

"Get on the navigation controls!" yelled Greg. "Be ready to give the ship all you've got."

Greg leaped for the control chair, grasped the acceleration lever.

"Now," growled Greg, "look out, Craven, we're coming at you!"

Greg, teeth gritted, slammed the acceleration over.

Suddenly all space wrenched horribly with a nauseating, terrible thud that seemed to strain at the very anchors of the Universe.

CHAPTER XVIII

Jupiter and the Jovian worlds leaped suddenly backward, turned swiftly green, then blue, and faded in an instant into violet. The Sun spun crazily through space, retreating, dimming to a tiny ruby-tinted star.

The giant generators in the *Invincible* hummed louder now, continually louder, a steel-throated roar that trembled through every plate, through every girder, through every bit of metal in the ship.

The ship itself was plunging spaceward, streaking like a runaway star for the depths of space beyond the Solar System. And behind it, caught tight, gripped and held, Craven's ship trailed at the end of a tractor field that bound it to the space-rocketing *Invincible*.

The acceleration compensator, functioning perfectly, had taken up the slack as the ship had plunged from a standing start into a speed that neared the pace of light. But it had never been built to stand such sudden, intense acceleration, and for an instant Russ and Greg seemed to be crushed by a mighty weight that struck at them. The sensation swiftly lifted as the compensator took up the load.

Greg shook his head, flinging the trickling perspiration from his eyes.

"I hope their compensator worked as well as ours," he said.

"If it didn't," declared Russ, "we're towing a shipload of dead men."

Russ glanced at the speed dial. They were almost touching the speed of light. "He hasn't cut down our speed yet."

"We threw him off his balance. His drive depends largely on the mass of some planet as a body to take up the reaction of his ship. Jupiter is the ideal body for that ... but he's leaving Jupiter behind. He has to do something soon or it'll be too late."

"He's getting less energy, too," said Russ. "We're retreating from his main sources of energy, the Sun and Jupiter. Almost the speed of light and that would cut down his energy intake terrifically. He has to use what he's got in his accumulators, and after that last blast at us, they must be nearly drained."

As Russ watched, the speed needle fell off slightly. Russ held his breath. It edged back slowly, creeping. The speed was being cut down.

"Craven is using whatever power he has," he said. "They're alive back there, all right. He's trying to catch hold of Jupiter and make its gravity work for him."

The *Invincible* felt the strain of the other ship now. Felt it as Craven poured power into his drive, fighting to get free of the invisible hawser that had trapped him, fighting against being dragged into outer space at the tail-end of a mighty craft heading spaceward with frightening speed.

Girders groaned in the *Invincible*, the engines moaned and throbbed. The speed needle fell back, creeping down the dial, slowly, unwillingly, resisting any drop in speed. But Craven was cutting it down. And as he cut it, he was able to absorb more energy with his collector lens. But he was fighting two things ... momentum and the steadily decreasing gravitational pull of Jupiter and the Sun. The Sun's pull was dwindling slowly, Jupiter's rapidly.

The needle still crept downward.

"What's his point of equality to us?" demanded Greg. "Will we make it?"

Russ shook his head. "Won't know for hours. He'll be able to slow us up ... maybe he'll even stop us or be able to jerk free, although I doubt that. But every minute takes him farther away from his main source of power, the Solar System's radiation. He could collect power anywhere in space, you know, but the best place to collect it is near large radiant bodies."

Russ continued to crouch over the dial, begrudging every backward flicker of the needle.

This was the last play, the final hand. If they could drag Craven and his ship away from the Solar System, maroon him deep in space, far removed from any source of radiation, they would win, for they could go back and finish the work of smashing Interplanetary.

But if Craven won-if he could halt their mad dash for space, if he could shake free-they'd never have another chance. He would be studying that field they had wrapped around him, be ready for it next time, might even develop one like it and use it on the *Invincible*. If Craven could win his way back to the Sun, he would be stronger than they were, could top them in power, shatter all their plans, and once again the worlds would bow to Interplanetary and Spencer Chambers.

Russ watched the meter. The speed was little more than ten miles a second now and dropping rapidly. He sat motionless, hunched, sucking at his dead pipe, listening to the thrumming of the generators.

"If we only had a margin," he groaned. "If we just had a few more horsepower. Just a few. But we're wide open. Every engine is developing everything it can!"

Greg tapped him on the shoulder, gently. Russ turned his head and looked into the face of his friend, a face as bleak as ever, but with a hint of smile in the corners of the eyes.

"Why not let Jupiter help us?" he asked. "He could be a lot of help."

Russ stared for a moment, uncomprehending. Then with a sob of gladness he reached out a hand, shoved over a lever. Mirrors of anti-entropy shifted, assumed different angles, and the *Invincible* sheered off. They were no longer retreating directly from the Sun, but at an angle quartering off across the Solar System.

Greg grinned. "We're falling behind Jupiter now. Letting Jupiter run away from us as he circles his orbit, following the Sun. Adds miles per second to our velocity of retreat, even if it doesn't show on the dial."

The cosmic tug of war went on, grimly-two ships straining, fighting each other, one seeking to escape, the other straining to snake the second ship into the maw of open, hostile space.

The speed was down to five miles a second, then a fraction lower. The needle was flickering now, impossible to decide whether it was dropping or not. And in the engine rooms, ten great generators howled in their attempt to make that needle move up the dial again.

Russ lit his pipe, his eyes not leaving the dial. The needle was creeping lower again. Down to three miles a second now.

He puffed clouds of smoke and considered. Saturn fortunately was ninety degrees around in his orbit. On the present course, only Neptune remained between them and free space. Pluto was far away, but even if it had been, it really wouldn't count, for it was small and had little attraction.

In a short while Ganymede and Callisto would be moving around on the far side of Jupiter and that might help. Everything counted so much now.

The dial was down to two miles a second and there it hung. Hung and stayed. Russ watched it with narrowed eyes. By this time Craven certainly would have given up much hope of help from Jupiter. If the big planet couldn't have helped him before, it certainly couldn't now. In another hour or two Earth would transit the Sun and that would cut down the radiant energy to some degree. But in the meantime Craven was loading his photo-cells and accumulators, was laying up a power reserve. As a last desperate resort he would use that power, in a final attempt to break away from the *Invincible*.

Russ waited for that attempt. There was nothing that could be done about it. The engines were developing every watt of power that could be urged out of them. If Craven had the power to break away, he would break away ... that was all there would be to it.

An hour passed and the needle crept up a fraction of a point. Russ was still watching the dial, his mind foggy with concentration.

Suddenly the *Invincible* shuddered and seemed to totter in space, as if something, some mighty force, had struck the ship a terrific blow. The needle swung swiftly backward, reached one mile a second, dipped to half a mile.

Russ sat bolt upright, holding his breath, his teeth clenched with death grip upon the pipe-stem.

Craven had blasted with everything he had! He had used every last trickle of power in the accumulators ... all the power he had been storing up.

Russ leaped from the chair and raced to the periscopic mirror. Stooping, he stared into it. Far back in space, like a silver bauble, swung Craven's ship. It swung back and forth in space, like a mighty, cosmic pendulum. Breathlessly he watched. The ship was still in the grip of the space field!

"Greg," he shouted, "we've got him!"

He raced back to the control panel, snapped a glance at the speed dial. The needle was rising rapidly now, a full mile a second. Within another fifteen minutes, it had climbed to a mile and a half. The *Invincible* was starting to go places!

The engines still howled, straining, shrieking, roaring their defiance.

In an hour the needle indicated the speed of four miles a second. Two hours later it was ten and rising visibly as Jupiter fell far behind and the Sun became little more than a glowing cinder.

Russ swung the controls to provide side acceleration and the two ships swung far to the rear of Neptune. They would pass that massive planet at the safe distance of a full hundred million miles.

"He won't even make a pass at it," said Greg. "He knows he's licked."

"Probably trying to store some more power," suggested Russ.

"Sweet chance he has to do that," declared Greg. "Look at that needle walk, will you? We'll hit the speed of light in a few more hours and after that he may just as well shut off his lens. There just won't be any radiation for him to catch."

Craven didn't make a try at Neptune. The planet was far away when they intersected its orbit ... furthermore, a wall of darkness had closed in about the ships. They were going three times as fast as light and the speed was still accelerating!

Hour after hour, day after day, the *Invincible* and its trailing captive sped doggedly outward into space. Out into the absolute wastes of interstellar space, where the stars were flecks of light, like tiny eyes watching from very far away.

Russ lounged in the control chair and stared out the vision plate. There was nothing to see, nothing to do. There hadn't been anything to see or do for days. The controls were locked at maximum and the engines still hammered their roaring song of speed and power. Before them stretched an empty gulf that probably never before had been traversed by any intelligence, certainly not by man.

Out into the mystery of interstellar space. Only it didn't seem mysterious. It was very commonplace and ordinary, almost monotonous. Russ gripped his pipe and chuckled.

There had been a day when men had maintained one couldn't go faster than light. Also, men had claimed that it would be impossible to force nature to give up the secret of material energy. But here they were, speeding along faster than light, their engines roaring with the power of material energy.

They were plowing a new space road, staking out a new path across the deserts of space, pioneering far beyond the 'last frontier.'

Greg's steps sounded across the room. "We've gone a long way, Russ. Maybe we better begin to slow down a bit."

"Yes," agreed Russ. He leaned forward and grasped the controls. "We'll slow down now," he said.

Sudden silence smote the ship. Their ears, accustomed for days to the throaty roarings of the engines, rang with the torture of no sound.

Long minutes and then new sounds began to be heard ... the soft humming of the single engine that provided power for the interior apparatus and the maintenance of the outer screens.

"Soon as we slow down below the speed of light," said Greg, "we'll throw the televisor on Craven's ship and learn what we can about his apparatus. No use trying it now, for we couldn't use it, because we're in the same space condition it uses in normal operation."

"In fact," laughed Russ, "we can't do much of anything except move. Energies simply can't pass through this space we're in. We're marooned."

Greg sat down in a chair, gazed solemnly at Russ.

"Just what was our top speed?" he demanded.

Russ grinned. "Ten thousand times the speed of light," he said.

Greg whistled soundlessly. "A long way from home."

Far away, the stars were tiny pinpoints, like little crystals shining by the reflection of a light. Pinpoints of light and shimmering masses of lacy silver ... star dust that seemed ghostly and strange, but was in reality the massing of many million mighty stars. And great empty black spaces where there was not a single light, where the dark went on and on and did not stop.

Greg exhaled his breath softly. "Well, we're here."

"Wherever that might be," amended Russ.

There were no familiar constellations, not a single familiar star. Every sign post of the space they had known was wiped out.

"There really aren't any brilliant stars," said Russ. "None at all. We must be in a sort of hole in space, a place that's relatively empty of any stars."

Greg nodded soberly. "Good thing we have those mechanical shadows. Without them we'd never find our way back home. But we have several that will lead us back."

Outside the vision panel, they could see Craven's ship. Freed now of the space field, it was floating slowly, still under the grip of the momentum they had built up in their dash across space. It was so close that they could see the lettering across its bow.

"So they call it the *Interplanetarian*," said Russ.

Greg nodded. "Guess it's about time we talk to them. I'm afraid they're getting pretty nervous."

"Do you have any idea where we are?" demanded Ludwig Stutsman.

Craven shook his head. "No more idea than you have. Manning snaked us across billions of miles, clear out of the Solar System into interstellar space. Take a look at those stars and you get some idea."

Spencer Chambers stroked his gray mustache, asked calmly: "What do you figure our chances are of getting back?"

"That's something we'll know more about later," said Craven. "Doesn't look too bright right now. I'm not worrying about that. What I'm wondering about is what Manning and Page are going to do now that they have us out here."

"I thought you'd be," said a voice that came out of clear air.

They stared at the place from which the voice had seemed to come. There was a slight refraction in the air; then, swiftly, a man took shape. It was Manning. He stood before them, smiling.

"Hello, Manning," said Craven. "I figured you'd pay us a call when you got around to it."

"Look here," snarled Stutsman, but he stopped when Chambers' hand fell upon his shoulder, gripped it hard.

"Got plenty of air?" asked Greg.

"Air? Sure. Atmosphere machines working perfectly," Craven replied.

"Fine," said Greg. "How about food and water? Plenty of both?"

"Plenty," said Craven.

"Look here, Manning," broke in Chambers, "where's all this questioning leading? What have you got up your sleeve?"

"Just wanted to be sure," Greg told him. "Would hate to have you fellows starve on me, or go thirsty. Wouldn't want to come back and find you all dead."

"Come back?" asked Chambers wonderingly. "I'm afraid I don't understand. Is this a joke of some sort?"

"No joke," said Greg grimly. "I thought you might have guessed. I'm going to leave you here."

"Leave us here?" roared Stutsman.

"Keep your shirt on," snapped Greg. "Just for a while, until we can go back to the Solar System and finish a little job we're doing. Then we'll come back and get you."

Craven grimaced. "I thought it would be something like that." He squinted at Manning through the thick lenses. "You never miss a bet, do you?"

Greg laughed. "I try not to."

A little silence fell upon the three men and Manning's image.

Greg broke it. "How about your energy collector?" he asked Craven. "Will it maintain the ship out here? You get cosmic rays. Not too much else, I'm afraid."

Craven grinned wryly. "You're right, but we can get along. The accumulators are practically drained, though, and we won't be able to store anything. Would you mind shooting us over just a little power? Enough to charge the accumulators a little for emergency use."

He looked over his shoulder, almost apprehensively.

"There might be an emergency out here, you know. Nobody knows anything about this place."

"I'll give you a little power," Greg agreed.

"Thank you very much," said Craven, half in mockery. "No doubt you think yourself quite smart, Manning, getting us out here. You know you have us stranded, that we can't collect more than enough power to live on."

"That's why I did it," Greg said, and vanished.

CHAPTER XIX

Craven watched the *Invincible* gather speed and tear swiftly through the black, saw it grow tiny and then disappear entirely, either swallowed by the distance or snapping into the strange super-space that existed beyond the speed of light.

He turned from the window, chuckling.

Stutsman snarled at him: "What's so funny?"

The scientist glared at the wolfish face and without speaking, walked to the desk and sat down. He reached for pencil and paper.

Chambers walked over to watch him.

"You've found something, Doctor," he said quietly.

Craven laughed, throatily. "Yes, I have. I've found a lot. Manning thinks he can keep us out here, but he's wrong. We'll be in the Solar System less than a week after he gets there."

Chambers stifled a gasp, tried to speak calmly. "You mean this?"

"Of course I mean it. I don't waste my time with foolish jokes."

"You have the secret of material energy?"

"Not that," the scientist growled, "but I have something else as valuable. I have the secret of Manning's drive: I know what it is that enables him to exceed the speed of light ... to go ten thousand times as fast as light ... the Lord knows how much faster if he wanted to."

"No ordinary drive would do that," said Chambers. "It would take more than power to make a ship go that fast."

"You bet your life it would, and Manning is the boy who's got it. He uses a space field. I think I can duplicate it."

"And how long will it take you to do this work?"

"About a week," Craven told him. "Perhaps a little longer, perhaps a little less. But once we go, we'll go as fast as Manning does. We'll be short on power, but I think I can do something about that, too."

Chambers took a chair beside the desk. "But do we know the way home?"

"We can find it," said Craven.

"But there are no familiar constellations," objected Chambers. "He dragged us out so far that there isn't a single star that any one of us can identify."

"I said I'd find the Solar System," Craven declared impatiently, "and I will. Manning started out for it, didn't he? I saw the way he went. The Sun is a type G star and all I'll do is look for a type G star."

"But there may be more than one type G star," objected the financier.

"Probably are," Craven agreed, "but there are other ways of finding the Sun and identifying it."

He volunteered no further information, went back to work with the pad and pencil. Chambers rose wearily from his chair.

"Tell me when you know what we can do," he said.

"Sure," Craven grunted.

"That's the Sun," said Craven. "That faint star between those two brighter ones."

"Are you sure of it?" demanded Stutsman.

"Of course. I don't make blunders."

"It's the only type G star in that direction," suggested Chambers, helpfully.

"Not that, either," declared Craven. "In fact, there are several type G stars. I examined them all and I know I'm right."

"How do you know?" challenged Stutsman.

"Spectroscopic examination. That collector field of ours gathers energy just like a burning glass. You've seen a burning glass, haven't you?"

He stared at Stutsman, directing the question at him.

Stutsman shuffled awkwardly, unhappily.

"Well," Craven went on, "I used that for a telescope. Gathered the light from the suns and analyzed it. Of course it didn't act like a real telescope, produce an image or anything like that, but it was ideal for spectroscopic work."

They waited for him to explain. Finally, he continued:

"All of the stars I examined were just type G stars, nothing else, but there was a difference in one of them. First, the spectroscope showed lines of reflected light passing through oxygen and hydrogen, water vapor and carbon dioxide. Pure planetary phenomena, never found on a star itself. Also it showed that a certain per cent of the light was polarized. Now remember that I examined it for a long time and I found out something else from the length of observation which convinces me. The light varied with a periodic irregularity. The chronometers aren't working exactly right out here, so I can't give you any explanation in terms of hours. But I find a number of regularly recurring changes in light intensity and character ... and that proves the presence of a number of planetary bodies circling the star. That's the only way one could explain the fluctuations for the G-type star is a steady type. It doesn't vary greatly and has no light fluctuations to speak of. Not like the Cepheid and Mira types."

"And that proves it's our Sun?" asked Chambers.

Craven nodded. "Fairly definitely, I'd say."

"How far away is it?" Stutsman wanted to know.

Craven snorted. "You would ask something like that."

"But," declared Stutsman, "there are ways of measuring how far a star is away from any point, measuring both the distance and the size of the star."

"Okay," agreed Craven, "you find me something solid and within reach that's measurable. Something, preferably, about 200 million miles or so across. Then I'll tell you how far we are from the Sun. This ship is not in an orbit. It's not fixed in space. I have no accurate way of measuring distances and angles simultaneously and accurately. Especially angles as small as these would be."

Craven and Stutsman glared at one another.

"It's a long way however you look at it," the financier said. "If we're going to get there, we'll have to start as soon as possible. How soon can we start, Doctor?"

"Very soon. I have the gravity concentration field developed and Manning left me just enough power to get a good start." He chuckled, took off his glasses, wiped the lenses and put them back on again. "Imagine him giving me that power!"

"But after we use up that power, what are we going to do?" demanded Chambers. "This collector lens of yours won't furnish us enough to keep going."

"You're right," Craven conceded, "but we'll be able to get more. We'll build up what speed we can and then we'll shut off the drive and let momentum carry us along. In the meantime our collector will gather power for us. We're advancing toward the source of radiation now, instead of away from it. Out here, where there's little gravity stress, fewer conflicting lines of gravitation, we'll be able to spread out the field, widen it, make it thousands of miles across. And the new photo-cells will be a help as well."

"How are the photo-cells coming?" asked Chambers.

Craven grinned. "We'll have a bank of them in within a few hours, and replace the others as fast as we can. I have practically the whole crew at work on them. Manning doesn't know it, but he found the limit of those photo-cells when he was heaving energy at us back in the Solar System. He blistered them. I wouldn't have thought it possible, but it was. You have to hand it to Manning and Page. They are a couple of smart men."

To the eye there was only one slight difference between the old cells and the new ones. The new type cell, when on no load, appeared milky white, whereas the old cells on no load were silvery. The granular surface of the new units was responsible for the difference in appearance, for each minute section of the surface was covered with even more minute metallic hexagonal pyramids and prisms.

"Just a little matter of variation in the alloy," Craven explained. "Crystalization of the alloy, forming those little prisms and pyramids. As a result, you get a surface thousands of times greater than in the old type. Helps you absorb every bit of the energy."

The *Interplanetarian* arrowed swiftly starward, driving ahead with terrific momentum while the collector lens, sweeping up the oncoming radiations, charged the great banks of accumulators. The G-type star toward which they were heading was still pale, but the two brighter stars to either side blazed like fiery jewels against the black of space.

"You say we'll be only a week or so behind Manning?" asked Chambers.

Craven looked at the financier, his eyes narrowed behind the heavy lenses. He sucked in his loose lips and turned once again to the control board.

"Perhaps a little longer," he admitted finally. "We're losing time, having to go along on momentum in order to collect power. But the nearer we get to those stars, the more power we'll have and we'll be able to move faster."

Chambers drummed idly on the arm of his chair, thinking.

"Perhaps there's time yet," he said, half to himself. "With the power we'll have within the Solar System, we can stop Manning and the revolution. We can gain control again."

Craven was silent, watching the dials.

"Manning might even pass us on the way back to look for us," Chambers went on. "He thinks we're still out there. He wouldn't expect to find us where we are, light years from where we started."

Craven shot him a curious look. "I wouldn't be too sure of that. Manning has a string of some sort tied to us. He's got us tagged … good and proper. He's always been able to find us again, no matter where we were. I have a hunch he'll find us again, even way out here."

Chambers shrugged his shoulders. "It really doesn't matter. Just so we get close enough to the Sun so we can load those accumulators and jam the photo-cells full. With a load like that we can beat him hands down."

The financier fell into a silence. He stared out of the vision plate, watching the stars. Still far away, but so much nearer than they had been.

His brain hummed with dreams. Old dreams, revived again, old dreams of conquest and of empire, dreams of a power that held a solar system in its grip.

Craven broke his chain of thoughts. "Where's our friend Stutsman? I haven't seen him around lately."

Chambers chuckled good-naturedly. "He's sulking. He seems to have gotten the idea neither one of us likes him. He's been spending most of his time back in the engine room with the crew."

"Were you talking about me?" asked a silky voice.

They spun around to see Stutsman standing in the doorway of the control room. His face was twisted into a wolfish grin and in his right hand he held a heat gun.

Chambers' voice was sharp, like the note of a clanging bell. "What's this?"

Stutsman's face twisted into an even more exaggerated grin. "This," he said, "is mutiny. I'm taking over!" He laughed at them.

"No use calling the crew. They're with me."

"Damn you!" shouted Chambers, taking a step forward. He halted as Stutsman jerked the pistol up.

"Forget it, Chambers. You're just second man from now on. Maybe not even second man. You tried out this dictator business and you bungled it. You went soft. You're taking orders from me from now on. No questions, no back talk. You do as I say and maybe you won't get hurt."

"You're mad, Stutsman!" cried Chambers. "You can't get away with this."

Stutsman barked out a brittle laugh. "Who is going to stop me?"

"The people," Chambers shouted at him. "The people will. They won't allow this. When you get back to the Solar System…"

Stutsman growled, stepping toward Chambers, pistol leveled. "The people won't have anything to say about this. I'll rule the Solar System the way I want to. There won't be anyone else who'll have a thing to say about it. So you dreamed of empire, did you? You dreamed of a solar dictatorship. Well, watch me! I'll build a real empire. But I'll be the head of it ... not you."

Craven sat down in his chair, crossed his knees. "Just what do you plan to do, Dictator Stutsman?"

Stutsman fairly foamed at the mouth over the insolence of Craven's voice. "I'll smash Manning first. I'll wipe him out. This ship will do it. You said yourself it would. You have ten times the power he has. And then..."

Craven raised a hand and waved him into silence. "So you plan to reach the Solar System, do you? You plan to meet Manning, and destroy his ship. Nice plan."

"What's wrong with it?" challenged Stutsman.

"Nothing," said Craven calmly. "Absolutely nothing at all ... *except that we may never reach the Solar System!*"

Stutsman seemed to sag. The wolfish snarl on his lips drooped. His eyes stared. Then with an effort he braced himself.

"What do you mean? Why can't we?" He gestured toward the vision plate, toward the tiny yellow star between the two brighter stars.

"That," said Craven, "isn't our Sun. It has planets, but it isn't our Sun."

Chambers stepped quickly to Craven, reached out a hand and hoisted him from the chair, shook him.

"You must be joking! That has to be the Sun!"

Craven shrugged free of Chambers' clutch, spoke in an even voice. "I never joke. We made a mistake, that's all. I hadn't meant to tell you yet. I had intended to get in close to the star and take on a full load of power and then try to locate our Sun. But I'm afraid it's a hopeless task."

"A hopeless task?" shrieked Stutsman. "You are trying to trick me. This is put up between the two of you. That's the Sun over there. I know it is!"

"It isn't," said Craven. "Manning tricked us. He started off in the wrong direction. He made us think he was going straight back to the Solar System, but he didn't. He circled and went in some other direction."

The scientist eyed Stutsman calmly. Stutsman's knuckles were white with the grip he had upon the gun.

"We're lost," Craven told him, looking squarely at him. "We may never find the Solar System!"

CHAPTER XX

The revolution was over. Interplanetary officials and army heads had fled to the sanctuary of Earth. Interplanetary was ended ... ended forever, for on every world, including Earth, material energy engines were humming. The people had power to burn, to throw away, power so cheap that it was practically worthless as a commodity, but invaluable as a way to a new life, a greater life, a fuller life ... a broader destiny for the human race.

Interplanetary stocks were worthless. The mighty power plants on Venus and Mercury were idle. The only remaining tangible asset were the fleets of spaceships used less than a month before to ship the accumulators to the outer worlds, to bring them Sunward for recharging.

Patents protecting the rights to the material energy engines had been obtained from every government throughout the Solar System. New governments were being formed on the wreckage of the old. John Moore Mallory already had been inaugurated as president of the Jovian confederacy. The elections on Mars and Venus would be held within a week.

Mercury, its usefulness gone with the smashing of the accumulator trade, had been abandoned. No human foot now trod its surface. Its mighty domes were empty. It went its way, as it had gone for billions of years, a little burned out, worthless planet, ignored and shunned. For a brief moment it had known the conquering tread of mankind, had played its part in the commerce of the worlds, but now it had reverted to its former state ... a lonely wanderer of the regions near the Sun, a pariah among the other planets.

Russell Page looked across the desk at Gregory Manning. He heaved a sigh and dug the pipe out of his jacket pocket.

"It's finished, Greg," he said.

Greg nodded solemnly, watching Russ fill the bowl and apply the match.

Except for the small crew, they were alone in the *Invincible*. John Moore Mallory and the others were on their own worlds, forming their own governments, carrying out the dictates of the people, men who would go down in solar history.

The *Invincible* hung just off Callisto. Russ looked out at the mighty moon, saw the lonely stretches of its ice-bound surface, saw the silvery spot that was the dome of Ranthoor.

"All done," said Greg, "except for one thing."

"Go out and get Chambers and the others," said Russ, puffing at the pipe.

Greg nodded. "We may as well get started."

Russ rose slowly, went to the wall cabinet and lifted out a box, the mechanical shadow with its tiny space field surrounding the fleck of steel that would lead them to the *Interplanetarian*. Carefully he lifted the machine from its resting place and set it on the desk. Bending over it, he watched the dials.

Suddenly he whistled. "Greg, they've moved! They aren't where we left them!"

Greg sprang to his side and stared at the readings. "They're moving farther away from us ... out into space. Where can they be going?"

Russ straightened, scowling, pulling at the pipe. "They probably found another G-type star, and are heading for that. They must think it is old Sol."

"That sounds like it," said Greg. "We spun all over the map to throw Craven off and looped several times so he'd lose all sense of direction. Naturally he would be lost."

"But he's evidently got something," Russ pointed out. "We left him marooned ... dead center, out where he didn't have too much radiation and couldn't get leverage on any single body. Yet he's moving-and getting farther away all the time."

"He solved our gravitation concentration screen," said Greg. "He tricked us into giving him power to build it."

The two men looked at one another for a long minute.

"Well," said Russ, "that's that. Craven and Chambers and Stutsman. The three villains. All lost in space. Heading for the wrong star. Hopelessly lost. Maybe they'll never find their way back."

He stopped and relit his pipe. An aching silence fell in the room.

"Poetic justice," said Russ. "Hail and farewell."

Greg rubbed his fist indecisively along the desk. "I can't do it, Russ. We took them out there. We marooned them. We have to get them back or I couldn't sleep nights."

Russ laughed quietly, watching the bleak face that stared at him. "I knew that's what you'd say."

He knocked out the pipe, crushed a fleck of burning tobacco with his boot. Pocketing the pipe, he walked to the control panel, sat down and reached for the lever. The engines hummed louder and louder. The *Invincible* darted spaceward.

"It's too late now," said Chambers. "By the time we reach that planetary system and charge our accumulators, Manning and Page will have everything under control back in the Solar System. Even if we could locate the star that was our Sun, we wouldn't have a chance to get there in time."

"Too bad," Craven said, and wagged his head, looking like a solemn owl. "Too bad. Dictator Stutsman won't have a chance to strut his stuff."

Stutsman started to say something and thought better of it. He leaned back in his chair. From his belt hung a heat pistol.

Chambers eyed the pistol with ill-concealed disgust. "There's no point in playing soldier. We aren't going to try to upset your mutiny. So far your taking over the ship hasn't made any difference to us … so why should we fight you?"

"It isn't going to make any difference either," said Craven. "Because there are just two things that will happen to us. We're either lost forever, will never find our way back, will spend the rest of our days wandering from star to star, or Manning will come out and take us by the ear and lead us home again."

Chambers started, leaned forward and fastened his steely eyes on Craven. "Do you really think he could find us?"

"I have no doubt of it," Craven replied. "I don't know how he does it, but I'm convinced he can. Probably, however, he'll find that we are lost and get rid of us that way."

"No," said Chambers, "you're wrong there. Manning wouldn't do that. He'll come to get us."

"I don't know why he should," snapped Craven.

"Because he's that sort of man," declared Chambers.

"What you going to do when he does get out here?" demanded Stutsman. "Fall on his neck and kiss him?"

Chambers smiled, stroked his mustache. "Why, no," he said. "I imagine we'll fight. We'll give him everything we've got and he'll do the same. It wouldn't seem natural if we didn't."

"You're damned right we will," growled Stutsman. "Because I'm running this show. You seem to keep forgetting that. We have power enough, when we get those accumulators filled, to wipe him out. And that is exactly what I'm going to do."

"Fine," said Craven, mockingly, "just fine. There's just one thing you forget. Manning is the only man who can lead us back to the Solar System."

"Hell," stormed Stutsman, "that doesn't make any difference. I'll find my way back there some way."

"You're afraid of Manning," Chambers challenged.

Stutsman's hand went down to the heat pistol's grip. His eyes glazed and his face twisted itself into utter hatred. "I don't know why I keep on letting you live. Craven is valuable to me. I can't kill him. But you aren't. You aren't worth a damn to anyone."

Chambers matched his stare. Stutsman's hand dropped from the pistol and he slouched to his feet, walked from the room.

Afraid of Manning! He laughed, a hollow, gurgling laugh. Afraid of Manning!

But he was.

Within his brain hammered a single sentence. Words he had heard Manning speak as he watched over the television set at Manning's mocking invitation. Words that beat into his brain and seared his reason and made his soul shrivel and grow small.

Manning talking to Scorio. Talking to him matter-of-factly, but grimly: *"I promise you that we'll take care of Stutsman!"*

Manning had taken Scorio and his gangsters one by one and sent them to far corners of the Solar System. One out to the dreaded Vulcan Fleet, one to the Outpost, one to the Titan prison, and one to the hell-hole on Vesta, while Scorio had gone to a little mountain set in a Venus swamp. They hadn't a chance. They had been locked within a force shell and shunted through millions of miles of space. No trial, no hearing ... nothing. Just terrible, unrelenting judgment.

"I promise you that we'll take care of Stutsman!"

"Craven's only a few billion miles ahead now," said Gregory Manning. "With our margin of speed, we should overhaul him in a few more hours. He is still short on power, but he's remedying that rapidly. He's getting nearer to that sun every minute. Running in toward it as he is, he tends to sweep up outpouring radiations. That helps him collect a whole lot more than he would under ordinary circumstances."

Russ, sitting before the controls, pipe clenched in his teeth, watching the dials, nodded soberly.

"All I'm afraid of," he said, "is that he'll get too close to that sun before we catch up with him. If he gets close enough so he can fill those accumulators, he'll pack a bigger wallop than we do. It'll all be in one bolt, of course, for his power isn't continuous like ours. He has to collect it slowly. But when he's really loaded, he can give us aces and still win. I'd hate to take everything he could pack into those accumulators."

Greg shuddered. "So would I."

The *Invincible* was exceeding the speed of light, was enveloped in the mysterious darkness that characterized the speed. They could see nothing outside the ship, for there was nothing to see. But the tiny mechanical shadow, occupying a place of honor on the navigation board, kept them informed of the position and the distance of the *Interplanetarian*.

Greg lolled in his chair, watching Russ.

"I don't think we need to worry about him throwing the entire load of the accumulators at us," he said. "He wouldn't dare load those accumulators to peak capacity. He's got to leave enough carrying capacity in the cells to handle any jolts we send him and he knows we can send him plenty. He has to keep that handling margin at all times, over and above what he takes in for power, because his absorption screen is also a defensive screen. And he has to use some power to keep our television apparatus out."

Russ chuckled. "I suppose, at that, we have him plenty worried."

The thunder of the engines filled the control room. For days now that thunder had been in their ears. They had grown accustomed to it, now hardly noticed it. Ten mighty engines, driving the *Invincible* at a pace no other ship had ever obtained, except, possibly, the *Interplanetarian*, although lack of power should have held Craven's ship down to a lower speed. Craven wouldn't have dared to build up the acceleration they had now attained, for he would have drained his banks and been unable to charge them again.

"Maybe he won't fight," said Russ. "Maybe he's figured out by this time that he's heading for the wrong star. He may be glad to see us and follow us back to the Solar System."

"No chance of that. Craven and Chambers won't pass up a chance for a fight. They'll give us a few wallops if only for the appearance of things."

"We're crawling up all the time," said Russ. "If we can catch him within four or five billion miles of the star, he won't be too tough to handle. Be getting plenty of radiations even then, but not quite as much as he would like to have."

"He'll have to start decelerating pretty soon," Greg declared. "He can't run the chance of smashing into the planetary system at the speed he's going. He won't want to waste too much power using his field as a brake, because he must know by this time that we're after him and he'll want what power he has to throw at us."

Hours passed. The *Invincible* crept nearer and nearer, suddenly seemed to leap ahead as the *Interplanetarian* began deceleration.

"Keep giving her all you got," Greg urged Russ. "We've got plenty of power for braking. We can overhaul him and stop in a fraction of the time he does."

Russ nodded grimly. The distance indicator needle on the mechanical shadow slipped off rapidly. Greg, leaping from his chair, hung over it, breathlessly.

"I think," he said, "we better slow down now. If we don't, we'll be inside the planetary system."

"How far out is Craven?" asked Russ.

"Not far enough," Greg replied unhappily. "He can't be more than three billion miles from the star and that star's hot. A class G, all right, but a good deal younger than old Sol."

"We'll let them know we've arrived," grinned Greg. He sent a stabbing beam of half a billion horsepower slashing at the *Interplanetarian*.

The other ship staggered but steadied itself.

"They know," said Russ cryptically from his position in front of the vision plate. "We shook them up a bit."

They waited. Nothing happened.

Greg scratched his head. "Maybe you were right. Maybe they don't want to fight."

Together they watched the *Interplanetarian*. It was still moving in toward the distant sun, as if nothing had happened.

"We'll see," said Greg.

Back at the controls he threw out a gigantic tractor beam, catching the other ship in a net of forces that visibly cut its speed.

Space suddenly vomited lashing flame that slapped back and licked and crawled in living streamers over the surface of the *Invincible*. The engines moaned in their valiant battle to keep up the outer screen. The pungent odor of ozone filtered into the control room. The whole ship was bucking and vibrating, creaking, as if it were being pulled apart.

"So they don't want to fight, eh?" hooted Russ.

Greg gritted his teeth. "They snapped the tractor beam."

"They have power there," Russ declared.

"Too much," said Greg. "More power than they have any right to have."

His hand went out to the lever on the board and pulled it back. A beam smashed out, with the engines' screaming drive behind it, billions of horsepower driving with unleashed ferocity at the other ship.

Greg's hand spun a dial, while the generators roared thunderous defiance.

"I'm giving them the radiation scale," said Greg.

The *Interplanetarian* was staggering under the terrific bombardment, but its screen was handling every ounce of the power that Greg was pouring into it.

"Their photo-cells can't handle that," cried Russ. "No photo-cell would handle all that stuff you're shooting at them. Unless..."

"Unless what?"

"Unless Craven has improved on them."

"We'll have to find out. Get the televisor."

Russ leaped for the television machine.

A moment later he lifted a haggard face.

"I can't get through," he said. "Craven's got our beams stopped and now he has our television blocked out."

Greg nodded. "We might have expected that. When he could scramble our televisors back in the Jovian worlds, he certainly ought to be able to screen his ship against them."

He shoved the lever clear over, slamming the extreme limit of power into the beam. The engines screamed like demented things, howling and shrieking. Instantly a tremendous sheet of solid flame spun a fiery web around the *Interplanetarian*, turning it into a blazing inferno of lapping, leaping fire.

A dozen terrific beams, billions of horsepower in each, stabbed back at the *Invincible* as the *Interplanetarian* shunted the terrific energy influx from the overcharged accumulators to the various automatic energy discharges.

The *Invincible's* screen flared in defense and the ten great engines wailed in utter agony. More stabbing flame shot from the *Interplanetarian* in slow explosions.

The temperature in the *Invincible's* control room was rising. The ozone was sharp enough to make their eyes water and nostrils burn. The vision glass was blanked out by the lapping flames that crawled and writhed over the screen outside the glass.

Russ tore his collar open, wiped his face with his shirt sleeve. "Try a pure magnetic!"

Greg, his face set and bleak as a wall of stone, grunted agreement. His fingers danced over the control manual.

Suddenly the stars outside twisted and danced, like stars gone mad, as if they were dancing a riotous jig in space, some uproariously hopping up and down while others were applauding the show that was being provided for their unblinking eyes.

The magnetic field was tightening now, twisting the light from those distant stars and bending it straight again. The *Interplanetarian* reeled like a drunken thing and the great arcs of electric flame looped madly and plunged straight for the field's very heart.

The stars danced weirdly in far-off space again as the *Interplanetarian's* accumulators lashed out with tremendous force to oppose the energy of the field.

The field glowed softly and disappeared.

"They have us stopped at every turn," groaned Russ. "There must be some way, something we can do." He looked at Greg. Greg grinned without humor, wiping his face. "There is something we can do," said Russ grimly. "We should have thought of it long ago."

He strode to the desk, reached out one hand and drew a calculator near.

"You keep them busy," he snapped. "I'll have this thing figured out in just a while."

From the engine rooms came the roar and hum of the laboring units and the *Invincible* shuddered once again as Greg grimly hurled one beam after another, at the *Interplanetarian*.

The *Interplanetarian* struck back, using radio frequency that flamed fiercely against the *Invincible's* outer screen. Simultaneously the *Interplanetarian* leaped forward with a sudden surge of accumulated energy, driving at the star that lay not more than three billion miles away.

Greg worked desperately, cursing under his breath. He pulled down the outer screen that was fighting directly against the radio frequency, energy for energy, and allowed the beam to strike squarely on the second screen, the inversion field that shunted the major portion of the energy impacting against it through 90 degrees into another space.

The engines moaned softly and settled into a quieter rumble as the necessity of supplying the first screen was eliminated. But they screamed once again as Greg sent out a tractor beam that seized and held, dragged the *Interplanetarian* to a standstill. Craven's ship had gained millions of miles, though, and established a tremendous advantage by fighting nearer to its source of energy.

"Russ," gasped Greg, "if you don't get that scheme of yours figured out pretty soon, we're done for. They've stopped everything we've got. They're nearer the sun. We won't stand a chance if they make another break like that."

Russ glanced up to answer, but his mouth fell open in amazement and he did not speak. A streak of terrible light was striking at them from the *Interplanetarian*, blinding white light, and along that highway of light swarmed a horde of little green figures, like squirming green amebas. Swarming toward the *Invincible*, stretching out hungry, pale-green pseudopods toward the inversion barrier ... *and eating through it!*

Wherever they touched, holes appeared. They drifted through the inversion screen easily and began drilling into the inner screen of anti-entropy. Eating their way into the anti-entropy ... *into a state of matter which Russ and Greg had thought would resist all change!*

For seconds both men stood transfixed, unable to believe the evidence of their eyes. But the ameba things came on in ever-increasing throngs, creatures that gnawed and slobbered at the anti-entropy, eating into it, flaking it away, drilling their way through it.

When they pierced the anti-entropy, they would cut through the steel plates of the *Invincible* like so much paper!

And more were coming. More and more!

With a grunt of amazement, Greg slammed a beam straight into the heart of the amebas. They ate the beam and vanished as mistily as before, little glowing things that ate and died. But there were always more to take their place. They overwhelmed the beam and ate back along its length, attacked the screen again.

They ate through walls of force and walls of metal, and a rush of hissing air began to flame into ions in the terrific battle of energies outside the *Invincible*.

Russ was crouching over the manual of the televisor board. His breath moaned in his throat as his fingers flew.

"I have to have power, Greg," he said. "Lots of power."

"Take it." Greg replied. "I haven't been able to do anything with it. It isn't any use to me."

Russ's thumb reached out and tripped the activating lever. The giant engines shrieked and yowled.

Something was happening on the television screen ... something terrifying. Craven's ship seemed to retreat suddenly for millions of miles ... and as suddenly the *Invincible* appeared on the screen. For a single flashing instant, the view held; then it was gone in blank grayness. For seconds nothing happened on the screen, unnerving seconds while the two men held their breath.

The screen's grayness fled and they looked into the control room of the *Interplanetarian*. Craven was hunched in a chair, intent upon a series of controls. Behind him and to one side stood Stutsman, a heat pistol dangled from his hand, his face twisted into a sneer of triumph. There was no sign of Chambers.

"You damn fool," Craven was snapping at Stutsman. "You're cheating us out of the only chance we ever had of getting home."

"Shut up," snarled Stutsman, the pistol jerking in his hand. "Have you got that apparatus on full power?"

"It's been on full power for minutes now," said Craven. "It must be eating holes straight through Manning's ship."

"See you keep it that way. I really don't need you any more, anyhow. I've watched and I know all the tricks. I could carry on this battle single-handed."

Craven did not reply, merely hunched closer over the controls, eyes watching flickering dials.

Greg jogged Russ's elbow. "That must be the apparatus over there, in the corner of the room. That triangular affair. A condenser of some sort. That stuff they're throwing at us must be super-saturated force fields and they'd need a space-field condenser for that."

Russ nodded. "We'll take care of that."

His fingers moved swiftly and a transport beam whipped out, riding the television beam. Bands of force wrapped around the triangular machine and wrenched viciously. In the screen the apparatus disappeared ... simply was gone. It now lay within the *Invincible's* control room, jerked there by the tele-transport.

The flood of dazzling light reaching out from the *Interplanetarian* snapped off and the little green ameba things were gone. The shrill whistle of escaping air stopped as the eaten screens clamped down again, sealing in the atmosphere despite the holes bored through the metal plates.

In the television screen, Craven leaped from his chair, was staring with Stutsman at the place where the concentrator had stood. The machine had been ripped from a welded base and jagged, bright, torn metal gleamed in the control room lights. Snapped cables and broken busbars lay piled about the room.

"What happened?" Stutsman was screaming. They heard Craven laugh at the terror in the other's voice. "Manning just walked in and grabbed it away from us."

"But he couldn't! We had the screen up! He couldn't get through!"

Craven shrugged his shoulders. "I don't know how he did it, but he did. Probably he could clean out the whole place if he wanted to."

"That's a good idea," said Russ, judiciously.

He stripped bank after bank of the other ship's photo-cells from their moorings, wrecked the force field controls, ripped cables from the engines and left the ship without means of collecting power, without means of using power, without means of movement, of offense or defense.

He leaned back in his chair and regarded the screen with deep satisfaction.

"That," he decided, "should hold them for a while."

He hauled the pipe out of his pocket and filled it from the battered leather pouch.

Greg regarded him with a quizzical stare. "You sent the televisor back in time. You got it inside the *Interplanetarian* before Craven had run up his screen and then you brought it forward."

"You guessed it," said Russ, tamping the tobacco into the bowl. "We should have thought of that long ago. We have a time factor there. In fact, the whole thing revolves around time. We move the televisor, we use the tele-transport, by giving the objects we wish to move an acceleration in time."

Greg wrinkled his brow. "Maybe that means we can really investigate the past, or even the future. Can sit here before our screen and see everything that has happened, everything that is going to happen."

Russ shook his head. "I don't know, Greg. Notice, though, that we got no screen response until the televisor came up out of the past and actually reached the point which coincided with the present. That is, the screen and the televisor itself have to be on the same time level for them to operate. We might modify the screen, even modify the televisor so that we could travel in time, but it will take a lot of research, a lot of work. And especially it will take a whale of a lot of power."

"We have the power," said Greg.

Russ moved the lighter back and forth over the tobacco, igniting it carefully. Clouds of blue smoke swirled around his head. He spoke out of the smoke.

"Right now," he said, "we better see how Craven and our other friends are getting along. I didn't like the way Stutsman was talking or the way he was swinging that gun around. And Chambers wasn't anywhere in sight. There's something screwy about the entire thing."

"What are we going to do now?" demanded Stutsman.

Craven grinned at him. "That's up to you. Remember, you're the master mind around here. You took over and said you were going to run things." He waved a casual hand at the shattered machines, the ripped-out apparatus. "Well, there you are. Go ahead and run the joint."

"But you will have to help," pleaded Stutsman, his face twisted until it seemed that he was suffering intense physical agony. "You know what to do. I don't."

Craven shook his head. "There isn't any use starting. Manning will be along almost anytime now. We'll wait and see what he has in mind."

"Manning!" shrieked Stutsman, waving the pistol wildly. "Always Manning. One would think you were working for Manning."

"He's the big shot out in this little corner of space right now," Craven pointed out. "There isn't any way you can get around that."

Stutsman backed carefully away. His gun came up and he looked at Craven appraisingly, as if selecting his targets.

"Put down that gun," said a voice.

Gregory Manning stood between Stutsman and Craven. There had been no foggy forerunner of his appearance. He had just snapped out of empty air.

Stutsman stared at him, his eyes widening, but the gun remained steady in his hand.

"Look out, Craven," warned Greg. "He's going to fire and it will go right through me and hit you."

There was the thump of a falling body as Craven hurled himself out of his chair, hit the floor and rolled. Stutsman's gun vomited flame. The spouting flame passed through Greg's image, blasted against the chair in which Craven had sat, fused it until it fell in on itself.

"Russ," said Greg quietly, "disarm this fellow before he hurts somebody."

An unseen force reached out and twisted the gun from Stutsman's hand, flung it to one side. Swiftly Stutsman's hands were forced behind his back and held there by invisible bonds.

Stutsman cried out, tried to struggle, but he was unable to move. It was as if giant hands had gripped him, were holding him in a viselike clutch.

"Thanks, Manning," said Craven, getting up off the floor. "The fool would have shot this time. He's threatened it for days. He has been developing a homicidal mania."

"We don't need to worry about him now," declared Greg. He turned around to face Craven. "Where's Chambers?"

"Stutsman locked him up," said Craven. "I imagine he has the key in his pocket. Locked him up in the stateroom. Chambers jumped him and tried to take the gun away from him and Stutsman laid him out, hit him over the head. He kept Chambers locked up after that. Hasn't allowed anyone to go near the room. Hasn't even given him food and water. That was three days ago."

"Get the key out of his pocket," directed Greg. "Go and see how Chambers is."

Alone in the control room with Stutsman, Greg looked at him.

"I have a score to settle with you, Stutsman," he said. "I had intended to let it ride, but not now."

"You can't touch me," blustered Stutsman. "You wouldn't dare."

"What makes you think I wouldn't?"

"You're bluffing. You've got a lot of tricks, but you can't do the things you would like me to think you can. You've got Chambers and Craven fooled, but not me."

"It may be that I can offer you definite proof."

Chambers staggered over the threshold. His clothing was rumpled. A rude bandage was wound around his head. His face was haggard and his eyes red.

"Hello, Manning," he said. "I suppose you've won. The Solar System must be in your control by now."

He lifted his hand to his mustache, brushed it, a feeble attempt at playing the old role he'd acted so long.

"We've won," said Greg quietly, "but you're wrong about our being in control. The governments are in the hands of the people, where they should be."

Chambers nodded. "I see," he mumbled. "Different people, different ideas." His eyes rested on Stutsman and Greg saw sudden rage sweep across the gray, haggard face. "So you've got him, have you? What are you going to do with him? What are you going to do with all of us?"

"I haven't had time to think about it," said Greg. "I've principally been thinking about Stutsman here."

"He mutinied," rasped Chambers. "He seized the ship, turned the crew against me."

"And the penalty for that," said Greg, quietly, "is death. Death by walking in space."

Stutsman writhed within the bands of force that held him tight. His face contorted. "No, damn you! You can't do that! Not to me, you can't!"

"Shut up," roared Chambers and Stutsman quieted.

"I was thinking, too," said Greg, "that at his order thousands of people were mercilessly shot down back in the Solar System. Stood against a wall and mowed down. Others were killed like wild animals in the street. Thousands of them."

He moved slowly toward Stutsman and the man cringed.

"Stutsman," he said, "you're a butcher. You're a stench in the nostrils of humanity. You aren't fit to live."

"Those," said Craven, "are my sentiments exactly."

"You hate me," screamed Stutsman. "All of you hate me. You are doing this because you hate me."

"Everyone hates you, Stutsman," said Greg. "Every living person hates you. You have a cloud of hate hanging over you as black and wide as space."

The man closed his eyes, trying to break free of the bonds.

"Bring me a spacesuit," snapped Greg, watching Stutsman's face.

Craven brought it and dropped it at Stutsman's feet.

"All right, Russ," said Greg. "Turn him loose."

Stutsman swayed and almost fell as the bands of force released him.

"Get into that suit," ordered Greg.

Stutsman hesitated, but something he saw in Greg's face made him lift the suit, step into it, fasten it about his body.

"What are you going to do with me?" he whimpered. "You aren't going to take me back to Earth again, are you? You aren't going to make me stand trial?"

"No," said Greg, gravely, "we aren't taking you back to Earth. And you're standing trial right now."

Stutsman read his fate in the cold eyes that stared into his. Chattering frightenedly, he rushed at Greg, plunged through him, collided with the wall of the ship and toppled over, feebly attempting to rise.

Invisible hands hoisted him to his feet, gripped him, held him upright. Greg walked toward him, stood facing him.

"Stutsman," he said, "you have four hours of air. That will give you four hours to think, to make your peace with death." He turned toward the other two. Chambers nodded grimly. Craven said nothing.

"And now," said Greg to Craven, "if you will fasten down his helmet."

The helmet clanged shut, shutting out the pleas and threats that came from Stutsman's throat.

Stutsman saw distant stars, cruel, gleaming eyes that glared at him. Empty space fell away on all sides.

Numbed by fear, he realized where he was. Manning had picked him up and thrown him far into space ... out into that waste where for hundreds of light years there was only the awful nothingness of space.

He was less than a speck of dust, in this great immensity of emptiness. There was no up or down, no means of orientation.

Loneliness and terror closed in on him, a terrible agony of fear. In four hours his air would be gone and then he would die! His body would swirl and eddy through this great cosmic ocean. It would never be found. It would remain here, embalmed by the cold of space, until the last clap of eternity.

There was one way, the easy way. His hand reached up and grasped the connection between his helmet and the air tank. One wrench and he would die swiftly, quickly ... instead of letting death stalk him through the darkness for the next four hours.

He shivered and his hand loosened its hold, dropped away. He was afraid to hasten death. He wanted to put it off. He was afraid of death ... horribly afraid.

The stars mocked him and he seemed to hear hooting laughter from somewhere far away. Curiously, it sounded like his own laughter....

"I'll make it easy for you, Manning," Chambers said. "I know that all of us are guilty. Guilty in the eyes of the people and the law. Guilty in your eyes. If we had won, there would have been no penalty. There's never a penalty for the one who wins."

"Penalty," said Greg, his eyes half smiling. "Why, yes, I think there is. I'm going to order you aboard the *Invincible* for something to eat and to get some rest."

"You mean to say that we aren't prisoners?"

Greg shook his head. "Not prisoners," he said. "Why, I came out here to guide you back to Earth. I hauled you out here and got you into this jam. It was up to me to get you out of it. I would have done the same for Stutsman, too, but..."

He hesitated and looked at Chambers.

Chambers stared back and slowly nodded.

"Yes, Manning," he said. "I think I understand."

CHAPTER XXI

Chambers lit his cigar and leaned back in his chair.

"I wish you could see it my way, Manning," he said. "There's no place for me on Earth, no place for me in the Solar System. You see, I tried and failed. I'm just a has-been back there."

He laughed quietly. "Somehow, I can't imagine myself coming back in the role of the defeated tribal leader, chained to your chariot, so to speak."

"But it wouldn't be that way," protested Greg. "Your company is gone, true, and your stocks are worthless, but you haven't lost everything. You still have a fleet of ships. With our new power, the Solar System will especially need ships. Lots of ships. For the spacelanes will be filled with commerce. You'd be coming back to a new deal, a new Solar System, a place that has been transformed almost overnight by power that's practically free."

"Yes, yes, I know all that," said Chambers. "But I climbed too high. I got too big. I can't come back now as something small, a failure."

"You have things we need," said Greg. "The screen that blankets out our television and tele-transport, for example. We need your screen as a safeguard against the very thing we have created. Think of what criminal uses could be made of the tele-transport. No vault, no net of charged wires, nothing, could stop a thief from taking anything he wanted. Prisons would cease to be prisons. Criminals could reach in and pick up their friends, no matter how many guards there were. Prisons and bank vaults and national treasuries could be cleaned out in a single day."

"Then there's the super-saturated space fields," added Russ, ruefully. "Those almost got us. If I hadn't thought of moving the televisor through time, we would have had to pull stakes and run for it."

"No, you wouldn't," pointed out Craven. "You could have wiped us out in a moment. You can disintegrate matter. Send it up in a puff of smoke ... rip every electron apart and send it hurtling away."

"Of course we could have, Craven," said Greg, "but we wouldn't."

Chambers laughed softly. "Not quite mad enough at us to do that, eh?"

Greg looked at him. "I guess that must have been it."

"But I'm curious about the green space fields," persisted Russ.

"Simple," said Craven. "They were just fields that had more energy packed into a certain portion of space than space could take. Space fields that had far more than their share of energy, more than they could hold. A super-saturated solution will crystalize almost immediately onto the tiniest crystal put into it. Those fields acted the same way. They crystalized instantly into hyper-space the moment they came into contact with other energy, whether as photons of radiation, matter or other space fields. Your anti-entropy didn't stand a chance under those conditions. When they crystalized, they took a chunk of the field along with them, a small chunk, but one after another they ate a hole right through your screen."

"Something like that would have a commercial value," said Greg. "Useful in war, too, and now that mankind has taken to space, now that we're spreading out, we must think of possible attack. There must be life on other planets throughout the Galaxy. Someday they'll come. If they don't, someday we'll go to them. And we may need every type of armament we can get our hands on."

Chambers knocked the ash off his cigar and was staring out the vision port. The ship had swung so that through the port could be seen the distant star toward which the *Interplanetarian* had been driving.

"For my part," said Chambers, slowly, measuring each word, "you can have those findings of ours. We'll give them to you, knowing you will use them as they should be used. Craven can tell you how they work. That is, if Craven wants to. He is the man who developed them."

"Certainly," said Craven. "They'll be something to remember us by."

"But you are coming back with us, aren't you?" asked Greg.

Craven shook his head. "No, I'm going with Chambers. I don't know what he's thinking of, but whatever it is, it's all right with me. We've been together too long. I'd miss someone to fight with."

Chambers was still staring out the vision port. He was talking, but he did not seem to be talking to them.

"I had a dream, you see. I saw the people struggling against the inefficiency and stupidity of popular government. I saw the periodic rise of bad leaders. I saw them lead the people into blunders. I read history and I saw that since the time man had risen from the ape, this had been going on. So I proposed to give the people scientific government … a business administration. An administration that would have run the government exactly as a successful businessman runs his business. The people would have resented it if I had told them they didn't know how to run their affairs. There was only one way to do it … gain control and force it down their throats."

Chambers was no longer a beaten man, no longer a man with a white bandage around his head and his power stripped from him. Once again he was the fighting financier who had sat back at the desk in the Interplanetary building on Earth and issued orders … orders that sped across millions of miles of space.

He shrugged his shoulders. "They didn't want it. Man doesn't want to live under scientific government. He doesn't want to be protected against blunders. He wants what he calls freedom. The right to do the things he wants to do, even if it means making a damn fool of himself. The right to rise to great heights and tumble to equally low depths. That's human nature and I ruled it out. But you can't rule out human nature."

They sat in silence, no one speaking. Russ cupped his pipe bowl in his hand and watched Chambers. Chambers leaned back and slowly puffed at the cigar. Greg just sat, his face unchanging.

Craven finally broke the silence. "Just what are you planning to do?"

Chambers flicked his hand toward the distant sun that gleamed through the vision port.

"There's a new solar system out there," he said. "New worlds, a new sun. A place to start over again. You and I discovered it. It's ours by right of discovery. We'll go there and stake out our claim."

"But there may be nothing there," protested Greg. "That sun is younger than our Sun. The planets may not have cooled as yet. Life may not have developed."

"In such a case," said Chambers, "we shall find another planetary system around another sun. A system that has cooled, where there is life."

Russ gasped. Here was something important, something that should set a precedent. The first men to roam from star to star seeking new worlds. The first men to turn their backs on the old solar system and strike out in search of new worlds swinging in their paths around distant suns.

Greg was saying, "All right, if that's the way you want it. I was hoping you'd come back with us. But we'll help you repair your ship. We'll give you all the supplies we can spare."

Russ rose to his feet. "That," he said, "calls for a little drink."

He opened a cabinet and took out bottles and glasses.

"Only three," said Chambers. "Craven doesn't drink."

Craven interrupted. "Pour one for me, too, Page."

Chambers looked at the scientist, astounded. "I never knew you to take a drink in your life."

Craven twisted his face into a grin. "This is a special occasion."

The *Invincible* was nearing Mars, heading for Earth, which was still a greenish sphere far to one side of the flaming Sun.

Russ watched the little green globe, thinking.

Earth was home. To him it always would be home. But that would be changed soon. Just a few more generations, and, to millions upon millions of human beings, Earth no longer would be home.

With the new material energy engines, life on every planet would be possible now, even easy. The cost of manufacture, mining, shipping across the vast distances between the planets would be only a fraction of what it had been when man had been forced to rely upon the unwieldy, expensive accumulator system of supplying life-giving power.

Now Mars would have power of her own. Even Pluto could generate her own. And power was ... well, it was power. The power to live, the power to work, to establish and maintain commerce, to adjust gravity to Earth standard or to any standard. The power to remake and reshape and rebuild planetary conditions to suit man exactly.

Earthmen and Earthwomen would be moving out en masse now to the new and virgin fields of endeavor-to the farms of Venus, to the manufacturing centers that were springing up on Mars, to the mines of the Jovian worlds, to the great laboratory plants that would spring up on Titan and on Pluto and on the other colder worlds.

The migration of races had started long ago. In the Old Stone Age, the Cro-Magnon had swept out of nowhere to oust the Neanderthal. Centuries later the barbarians of the north, in another of those restless migrations, had overwhelmed and swept away the Roman Empire. And many centuries later, migration had turned from Europe to a new world across the sea, and fighting Americans had battled their way from east to west, conquering a continent.

And now another great migration was on-man was leaving the Earth, moving into space. He was leaving behind him the world that had reared and fostered him. He was striking out and out. First the planets would be overrun, and then man would leap from the planets to the stars!

For years after America had become a country, had built a tradition of her own, Europe was regarded by millions as the homeland. But as the years swept by, this had ceased to be and the Americas were a world unto themselves, owing nothing to Europe.

And that was the way it would be with Earth. For centuries, for thousands of years, Earth would be the Mother Planet, the homeland for all the millions of roaming men and women who dared the gulfs of space and the strangeness of new worlds. There would be trips back to the Earth for sentimental reasons ... to see the place where one's ancestors were born and had lived, to goggle at the monument which marked the point from which the first spaceship had taken off for the Moon, to visit old museums and see old cities and breathe the air that men and women had breathed for thousands of years before they found the power to take them anywhere.

In the end, Earth would be just a worn-out planet. Even now her minerals were rapidly being exhausted; her oil wells were dry and all her coal was mined; her industry stabilized and filled; her businesses interlocking and highly competitive. A world that was too full, that had too many things, too many activities, too many people. A world that didn't need men and women. A world where even genius was kept from rising to the top.

And this was what was driving mankind away from the Earth. The competition, the crowded conditions, in business and industrial fields, the lack of opportunity for new development, the everlasting struggle to get ahead, fighting for a place to live when millions of others were fighting for the same thing. But not entirely that, not that alone. There was something else-that old adventuresome spirit, the driving urge to face new dangers, to step over old frontiers, to do and dare, to make a damn fool of one's self, or to surpass the greatest accomplishments of history.

But Earth would never die, for there was a part of Earth in every man and woman who would go forth into space, part of Earth's courage, part of Earth's ideals, part of Earth's dreams. The habits and the virtues and the faults that Earth had spawned and fostered ... these were things that would never die. Old Earth would live forever. Even when she was drifting dust and the Sun was a dead, cold star, Earth would live on in the courage and the dreams that by that time would be spreading to the far corners of the Galaxy.

Russ dug the pipe out of his pocket, searched for the pouch, found it on the desk behind him. It was empty.

"Hell," he said, "my tobacco's all gone."

Greg grinned. "You won't have to wait long. We'll be back on Earth in a few more hours."

Russ put the stem between his teeth, bit down on it savagely. "I guess that's right. I can dry smoke her until we get there."

Earth was larger now. Mars had swung astern.

Suddenly a winking light stabbed out into space from the night side of Earth. Signaling ... signaling ... clearing the spacelanes for a greater future than any human prophet had ever predicted.

The World That Couldn't Be

Like every farmer on every planet, Duncan had to hunt down anything that damaged his crops-even though he was aware this was —

CHAPTER I

The tracks went up one row and down another, and in those rows the *vua* plants had been sheared off an inch or two above the ground. The raider had been methodical; it had not wandered about haphazardly, but had done an efficient job of harvesting the first ten rows on the west side of the field. Then, having eaten its fill, it had angled off into the bush-and that had not been long ago, for the soil still trickled down into the great pug marks, sunk deep into the finely cultivated loam.

Somewhere a sawmill bird was whirring through a log, and down in one of the thorn-choked ravines, a choir of chatterers was clicking through a ghastly morning song. It was going to be a scorcher of a day. Already the smell of desiccated dust was rising from the ground and the glare of the newly risen sun was dancing off the bright leaves of the hula-trees, making it appear as if the bush were filled with a million flashing mirrors.

Gavin Duncan hauled a red bandanna from his pocket and mopped his face.

"No, mister," pleaded Zikkara, the native foreman of the farm. "You cannot do it, mister. You do not hunt a Cytha."

"The hell I don't," said Duncan, but he spoke in English and not the native tongue.

He stared out across the bush, a flat expanse of sun-cured grass interspersed with thickets of hula-scrub and thorn and occasional groves of trees, criss-crossed by treacherous ravines and spotted with infrequent waterholes.

It would be murderous out there, he told himself, but it shouldn't take too long. The beast probably would lay up shortly after its pre-dawn feeding and he'd overhaul it in an hour or two. But if he failed to overhaul it, then he must keep on.

"Dangerous," Zikkara pointed out. "No one hunts the Cytha."

"I do," Duncan said, speaking now in the native language. "I hunt anything that damages my crop. A few nights more of this and there would be nothing left."

* * * * *

Jamming the bandanna back into his pocket, he tilted his hat lower across his eyes against the sun.

"It might be a long chase, mister. It is the *skun* season now. If you were caught out there...."

"Now listen," Duncan told it sharply. "Before I came, you'd feast one day, then starve for days on end; but now you eat each day. And you like the doctoring. Before, when you got sick, you died. Now you get sick, I doctor you, and you live. You like staying in one place, instead of wandering all around."

"Mister, we like all this," said Zikkara, "but we do not hunt the Cytha."

"If we do not hunt the Cytha, we lose all this," Duncan pointed out. "If I don't make a crop, I'm licked. I'll have to go away. Then what happens to you?"

"We will grow the corn ourselves."

"That's a laugh," said Duncan, "and you know it is. If I didn't kick your backsides all day long, you wouldn't do a lick of work. If I leave, you go back to the bush. Now let's go and get that Cytha."

"But it is such a little one, mister! It is such a young one! It is scarcely worth the trouble. It would be a shame to kill it."

Probably just slightly smaller than a horse, thought Duncan, watching the native closely.

It's scared, he told himself. It's scared dry and spitless.

"Besides, it must have been most hungry. Surely, mister, even a Cytha has the right to eat."

"Not from my crop," said Duncan savagely. "You know why we grow the *vua*, don't you? You know it is great medicine. The berries that it grows cures those who are sick inside their heads. My people need that medicine-need it very badly. And what is more, out there —" he swept his arm toward the sky —"out there they pay very much for it."

"But, mister...."

"I tell you this," said Duncan gently, "you either dig me up a bush-runner to do the tracking for me or you can all get out, the kit and caboodle of you. I can get other tribes to work the farm."

"No, mister!" Zikkara screamed in desperation.

"You have your choice," Duncan told it coldly.

* * * * *

He plodded back across the field toward the house. Not much of a house as yet. Not a great deal better than a native shack. But someday it would be, he told himself. Let him sell a crop or two and he'd build a house that would really be a house. It would have a bar and swimming pool and a garden filled with flowers, and at last, after years of wandering, he'd have a home and broad acres and everyone, not just one lousy tribe, would call him mister.

Gavin Duncan, planter, he said to himself, and liked the sound of it. Planter on the planet Layard. But not if the Cytha came back night after night and ate the *vua* plants.

He glanced over his shoulder and saw that Zikkara was racing for the native village.

Called their bluff, Duncan informed himself with satisfaction.

He came out of the field and walked across the yard, heading for the house. One of Shotwell's shirts was hanging on the clothes-line, limp in the breathless morning.

Damn the man, thought Duncan. Out here mucking around with those stupid natives, always asking questions, always under foot. Although, to be fair about it, that was Shotwell's job. That was what the Sociology people had sent him out to do.

Duncan came up to the shack, pushed the door open and entered. Shotwell, stripped to the waist, was at the wash bench.

Breakfast was cooking on the stove, with an elderly native acting as cook.

Duncan strode across the room and took down the heavy rifle from its peg. He slapped the action open, slapped it shut again.

Shotwell reached for a towel.

"What's going on?" he asked.

102

"Cytha got into the field."

"Cytha?"

"A kind of animal," said Duncan. "It ate ten rows of *vua*."

"Big? Little? What are its characteristics?"

The native began putting breakfast on the table. Duncan walked to the table, laid the rifle across one corner of it and sat down. He poured a brackish liquid out of a big stew pan into their cups.

God, he thought, what I would give for a cup of coffee.

* * * * *

Shotwell pulled up his chair. "You didn't answer me. What is a Cytha like?"

"I wouldn't know," said Duncan.

"Don't know? But you're going after it, looks like, and how can you hunt it if you don't know —"

"Track it. The thing tied to the other end of the trail is sure to be the Cytha. Well find out what it's like once we catch up to it."

"We?"

"The natives will send up someone to do the tracking for me. Some of them are better than a dog."

"Look, Gavin. I've put you to a lot of trouble and you've been decent with me. If I can be any help, I would like to go."

"Two make better time than three. And we have to catch this Cytha fast or it might settle down to an endurance contest."

"All right, then. Tell me about the Cytha."

Duncan poured porridge gruel into his bowl, handed the pan to Shotwell. "It's a sort of special thing. The natives are scared to death of it. You hear a lot of stories about it. Said to be unkillable. It's always capitalized, always a proper noun. It has been reported at different times from widely scattered places."

"No one's ever bagged one?"

"Not that I ever heard of." Duncan patted the rifle. "Let me get a bead on it."

He started eating, spooning the porridge into his mouth, munching on the stale corn bread left from the night before. He drank some of the brackish beverage and shuddered.

"Some day," he said, "I'm going to scrape together enough money to buy a pound of coffee. You'd think —"

"It's the freight rates," Shotwell said. "I'll send you a pound when I go back."

"Not at the price they'd charge to ship it out," said Duncan. "I wouldn't hear of it."

They ate in silence for a time. Finally Shotwell said: "I'm getting nowhere, Gavin. The natives are willing to talk, but it all adds up to nothing."

"I tried to tell you that. You could have saved your time."

Shotwell shook his head stubbornly. "There's an answer, a logical explanation. It's easy enough to say you cannot rule out the sexual factor, but that's exactly what has happened here on Layard. It's easy to exclaim that a sexless animal, a sexless race, a sexless planet is impossible, but that is what we have. Somewhere there is an answer and I have to find it."

* * * * *

"Now hold up a minute," Duncan protested. "There's no use blowing a gasket. I haven't got the time this morning to listen to your lecture."

"But it's not the lack of sex that worries me entirely," Shotwell said, "although it's the central factor. There are subsidiary situations deriving from that central fact which are most intriguing."

"I have no doubt of it," said Duncan, "but if you please —"

"Without sex, there is no basis for the family, and without the family there is no basis for a tribe, and yet the natives have an elaborate tribal setup, with taboos by way of regulation. Somewhere there must exist some underlying, basic unifying factor, some common loyalty, some strange relationship which spells out to brotherhood."

"Not brotherhood," said Duncan, chuckling. "Not even sisterhood. You must watch your terminology. The word you want is ithood."

The door pushed open and a native walked in timidly.

"Zikkara said that mister want me," the native told them. "I am Sipar. I can track anything but screamers, stilt-birds, longhorns and donovans. Those are my taboos."

"I am glad to hear that," Duncan replied. "You have no Cytha taboo, then."

"Cytha!" yipped the native. "Zikkara did not tell me Cytha!"

Duncan paid no attention. He got up from the table and went to the heavy chest that stood against one wall. He rummaged in it and came out with a pair of binoculars, a hunting knife and an extra drum of ammunition. At the kitchen cupboard, he rummaged once again, filling a small leather sack with a gritty powder from a can he found.

"Rockahominy," he explained to Shotwell. "Emergency rations thought up by the primitive North American Indians. Parched corn, ground fine. It's no feast exactly, but it keeps a man going."

"You figure you'll be gone that long?"

"Maybe overnight. I don't know. Won't stop until I get it. Can't afford to. It could wipe me out in a few days."

"Good hunting," Shotwell said. "I'll hold the fort."

Duncan said to Sipar: "Quit sniveling and come on."

He picked up the rifle, settled it in the crook of his arm. He kicked open the door and strode out.

Sipar followed meekly.

CHAPTER II

Duncan got his first shot late in the afternoon of that first day.

In the middle of the morning, two hours after they had left the farm, they had flushed the Cytha out of its bed in a thick ravine. But there had been no chance for a shot. Duncan saw no more than a huge black blur fade into the bush.

Through the bake-oven afternoon, they had followed its trail, Sipar tracking and Duncan bringing up the rear, scanning every piece of cover, with the sun-hot rifle always held at ready.

Once they had been held up for fifteen minutes while a massive donovan tramped back and forth, screaming, trying to work up its courage for attack. But after a quarter hour of showing off, it decided to behave itself and went off at a shuffling gallop.

Duncan watched it go with a lot of thankfulness. It could soak up a lot of lead, and for all its awkwardness, it was handy with its feet once it set itself in motion. Donovans had killed a lot of men in the twenty years since Earthmen had come to Layard.

With the beast gone, Duncan looked around for Sipar. He found it fast asleep beneath a hula-shrub. He kicked the native awake with something less than gentleness and they went on again.

The bush swarmed with other animals, but they had no trouble with them.

Sipar, despite its initial reluctance, had worked well at the trailing. A misplaced bunch of grass, a twig bent to one side, a displaced stone, the faintest pug mark were Sipar's stock in trade. It worked like a lithe, well-trained hound. This bush country was its special province; here it was at home.

With the sun dropping toward the west, they had climbed a long, steep hill and as they neared the top of it, Duncan hissed at Sipar. The native looked back over its shoulder in surprise. Duncan made motions for it to stop tracking.

The native crouched and as Duncan went past it, he saw that a look of agony was twisting its face. And in the look of agony he thought he saw as well a touch of pleading and a trace of hatred. It's scared, just like the rest of them, Duncan told himself. But what the native thought or felt had no significance; what counted was the beast ahead.

Duncan went the last few yards on his belly, pushing the gun ahead of him, the binoculars bumping on his back. Swift, vicious insects ran out of the grass and swarmed across his hands and arms and one got on his face and bit him.

* * * * *

He made it to the hilltop and lay there, looking at the sweep of land beyond. It was more of the same, more of the blistering, dusty slogging, more of thorn and tangled ravine and awful emptiness.

He lay motionless, watching for a hint of motion, for the fitful shadow, for any wrongness in the terrain that might be the Cytha.

But there was nothing. The land lay quiet under the declining sun. Far on the horizon, a herd of some sort of animals was grazing, but there was nothing else.

Then he saw the motion, just a flicker, on the knoll ahead-about halfway up.

He laid the rifle carefully on the ground and hitched the binoculars around. He raised them to his eyes and moved them slowly back and forth. The animal was there where he had seen the motion.

It was resting, looking back along the way that it had come, watching for the first sign of its trailers. Duncan tried to make out the size and shape, but it blended with the grass and the dun soil and he could not be sure exactly what it looked like.

He let the glasses down and now that he had located it, he could distinguish its outline with the naked eye.

His hand reached out and slid the rifle to him. He fitted it to his shoulder and wriggled his body for closer contact with the ground. The cross-hairs centered on the faint outline on the knoll and then the beast stood up.

It was not as large as he had thought it might be-perhaps a little larger than Earth lion-size, but it certainly was no lion. It was a square-set thing and black and inclined to lumpiness and it had an awkward look about it, but there were strength and ferociousness as well.

Duncan tilted the muzzle of the rifle so that the cross-hairs centered on the massive neck. He drew in a breath and held it and began the trigger squeeze.

The rifle bucked hard against his shoulder and the report hammered in his head and the beast went down. It did not lurch or fall; it simply melted down and disappeared, hidden in the grass.

"Dead center," Duncan assured himself.

He worked the mechanism and the spent cartridge case flew out. The feeding mechanism snicked and the fresh shell clicked as it slid into the breech.

He lay for a moment, watching. And on the knoll where the thing had fallen, the grass was twitching as if the wind were blowing, only there was no wind. But despite the twitching of the grass, there was no sign of the Cytha. It did not struggle up again. It stayed where it had fallen.

Duncan got to his feet, dug out the bandanna and mopped at his face. He heard the soft thud of the step behind him and turned his head. It was the tracker.

"It's all right, Sipar," he said. "You can quit worrying. I got it. We can go home now."

* * * * *

It had been a long, hard chase, longer than he had thought it might be. But it had been successful and that was the thing that counted. For the moment, the *vua* crop was safe.

He tucked the bandanna back into his pocket, went down the slope and started up the knoll. He reached the place where the Cytha had fallen. There were three small gouts of torn, mangled fur and flesh lying on the ground and there was nothing else.

He spun around and jerked his rifle up. Every nerve was screamingly alert. He swung his head, searching for the slightest movement, for some shape or color that was not the shape or color of the bush or grass or ground. But there was nothing. The heat droned in the hush of afternoon. There was not a breath of moving air. But there was danger —a saw-toothed sense of danger close behind his neck.

"Sipar!" he called in a tense whisper, "Watch out!"

The native stood motionless, unheeding, its eyeballs rolling up until there was only white, while the muscles stood out along its throat like straining ropes of steel.

Duncan slowly swiveled, rifle held almost at arm's length, elbows crooked a little, ready to bring the weapon into play in a fraction of a second.

Nothing stirred. There was no more than emptiness-the emptiness of sun and molten sky, of grass and scraggy bush, of a brown-and-yellow land stretching into foreverness.

Step by step, Duncan covered the hillside and finally came back to the place where the native squatted on its heels and moaned, rocking back and forth, arms locked tightly across its chest, as if it tried to cradle itself in a sort of illusory comfort.

The Earthman walked to the place where the Cytha had fallen and picked up, one by one, the bits of bleeding flesh. They had been mangled by his bullet. They were limp and had no shape. And it was queer, he thought. In all his years of hunting, over many planets, he had never known a bullet to rip out hunks of flesh.

He dropped the bloody pieces back into the grass and wiped his hand upon his thighs. He got up a little stiffly.

He'd found no trail of blood leading through the grass, and surely an animal with a hole of that size would leave a trail.

And as he stood there upon the hillside, with the bloody fingerprints still wet and glistening upon the fabric of his trousers, he felt the first cold touch of fear, as if the fingertips of fear might momentarily, almost casually, have trailed across his heart.

He turned around and walked back to the native, reached down and shook it.

"Snap out of it," he ordered.

He expected pleading, cowering, terror, but there was none.

Sipar got swiftly to its feet and stood looking at him and there was, he thought, an odd glitter in its eyes.

"Get going," Duncan said. "We still have a little time. Start circling and pick up the trail. I will cover you."

He glanced at the sun. An hour and a half still left-maybe as much as two. There might still be time to get this buttoned up before the fall of night.

A half mile beyond the knoll, Sipar picked up the trail again and they went ahead, but now they traveled more cautiously, for any bush, any rock, any clump of grass might conceal the wounded beast.

Duncan found himself on edge and cursed himself savagely for it. He'd been in tight spots before. This was nothing new to him. There was no reason to get himself tensed up. It was a deadly business, sure, but he had faced others calmly and walked away from them. It was those frontier tales he'd heard about the Cytha-the kind of superstitious chatter that one always heard on the edge of unknown land.

He gripped the rifle tighter and went on.

No animal, he told himself, was unkillable.

Half an hour before sunset, he called a halt when they reached a brackish waterhole. The light soon would be getting bad for shooting. In the morning, they'd take up the trail again, and by that time the Cytha would be at an even greater disadvantage. It would be stiff and slow and weak. It might be even dead.

Duncan gathered wood and built a fire in the lee of a thorn-bush thicket. Sipar waded out with the canteens and thrust them at arm's length beneath the surface to fill them. The water still was warm and evil-tasting, but it was fairly free of scum and a thirsty man could drink it.

The sun went down and darkness fell quickly. They dragged more wood out of the thicket and piled it carefully close at hand.

Duncan reached into his pocket and brought out the little bag of rockahominy.

"Here," he said to Sipar. "Supper."

The native held one hand cupped and Duncan poured a little mound into its palm.

"Thank you, mister," Sipar said. "Food-giver."

"Huh?" asked Duncan, then caught what the native meant. "Dive into it," he said, almost kindly. "It isn't much, but it gives you strength. We'll need strength tomorrow."

Food-giver, eh? Trying to butter him up, perhaps. In a little while, Sipar would start whining for him to knock off the hunt and head back for the farm.

Although, come to think of it, he really was the food-giver to this bunch of sexless wonders. Corn, thank God, grew well on the red and stubborn soil of Layard-good old corn from North America. Fed to hogs, made into corn-pone for breakfast back on Earth, and here, on Layard, the staple food crop for a gang of shiftless varmints who still regarded, with some good solid skepticism and round-eyed wonder, this unorthodox idea that one should take the trouble to grow plants to eat rather than go out and scrounge for them.

Corn from North America, he thought, growing side by side with the *vua* of Layard. And that was the way it went. Something from one planet and something from another and still something further from a third and so was built up through the wide social confederacy of space a truly cosmic culture which in the end, in another ten thousand years or so, might spell out some way of life with more sanity and understanding than was evident today.

He poured a mound of rockahominy into his own hand and put the bag back into his pocket.

"Sipar."

"Yes, mister?"

"You were not scared today when the donovan threatened to attack us."

"No, mister. The donovan would not hurt me."

"I see. You said the donovan was taboo to you. Could it be that you, likewise, are taboo to the donovan?"

"Yes, mister. The donovan and I grew up together."

"Oh, so that's it," said Duncan.

He put a pinch of the parched and powdered corn into his mouth and took a sip of brackish water. He chewed reflectively on the resultant mash.

He might go ahead, he knew, and ask why and how and where Sipar and the donovan had grown up together, but there was no point to it. This was exactly the kind of tangle that Shotwell was forever getting into.

Half the time, he told himself, I'm convinced the little stinkers are doing no more than pulling our legs.

What a fantastic bunch of jerks! Not men, not women, just things. And while there were never babies, there were children, although never less than eight or nine years old. And if there were no babies, where did the eight-and nine-year-olds come from?

* * * * *

"I suppose," he said, "that these other things that are your taboos, the stilt-birds and the screamers and the like, also grew up with you."

"That is right, mister."

"Some playground that must have been," said Duncan.

He went on chewing, staring out into the darkness beyond the ring of firelight.

"There's something in the thorn bush, mister."

"I didn't hear a thing."

"Little pattering. Something is running there."

Duncan listened closely. What Sipar said was true. A lot of little things were running in the thicket.

"More than likely mice," he said.

He finished his rockahominy and took an extra swig of water, gagging on it slightly.

"Get your rest," he told Sipar. "I'll wake you later so I can catch a wink or two."

"Mister," Sipar said, "I will stay with you to the end."

"Well," said Duncan, somewhat startled, "that is decent of you."

"I will stay to the death," Sipar promised earnestly.

"Don't strain yourself," said Duncan.

He picked up the rifle and walked down to the waterhole.

The night was quiet and the land continued to have that empty feeling. Empty except for the fire and the waterhole and the little micelike animals running in the thicket.

And Sipar-Sipar lying by the fire, curled up and sound asleep already. Naked, with not a weapon to its hand-just the naked animal, the basic humanoid, and yet with underlying purpose that at times was baffling. Scared and shivering this morning at mere mention of the Cytha, yet never faltering on the trail; in pure funk back there on the knoll where they had lost the Cytha, but now ready to go on to the death.

Duncan went back to the fire and prodded Sipar with his toe. The native came straight up out of sleep.

"Whose death?" asked Duncan. "Whose death were you talking of?"

"Why, ours, of course," said Sipar, and went back to sleep.

Duncan did not see the arrow coming. He heard the swishing whistle and felt the wind of it on the right side of his throat and then it thunked into a tree behind him.

He leaped aside and dived for the cover of a tumbled mound of boulders and almost instinctively his thumb pushed the fire control of the rifle up to automatic.

He crouched behind the jumbled rocks and peered ahead. There was not a thing to see. The hula-trees shimmered in the blaze of sun and the thorn-bush was gray and lifeless and the only things astir were three stilt-birds walking gravely a quarter of a mile away.

"Sipar!" he whispered.

"Here, mister."

"Keep low. It's still out there."

Whatever it might be. Still out there and waiting for another shot. Duncan shivered, remembering the feel of the arrow flying past his throat. A hell of a way for a man to die-out at the tail-end of nowhere with an arrow in his throat and a scared-stiff native heading back for home as fast as it could go.

He flicked the control on the rifle back to single fire, crawled around the rock pile and sprinted for a grove of trees that stood on higher ground. He reached them and there he flanked the spot from which the arrow must have come.

He unlimbered the binoculars and glassed the area. He still saw no sign. Whatever had taken the pot shot at them had made its getaway.

He walked back to the tree where the arrow still stood out, its point driven deep into the bark. He grasped the shaft and wrenched the arrow free.

"You can come out now," he called to Sipar. "There's no one around."

The arrow was unbelievably crude. The unfeathered shaft looked as if it had been battered off to the proper length with a jagged stone. The arrowhead was unflaked flint picked up from some outcropping or dry creek bed, and it was awkwardly bound to the shaft with the tough but pliant inner bark of the hula-tree.

"You recognize this?" he asked Sipar.

The native took the arrow and examined it. "Not my tribe."

"Of course not your tribe. Yours wouldn't take a shot at us. Some other tribe, perhaps?"

"Very poor arrow."

"I know that. But it could kill you just as dead as if it were a good one. Do you recognize it?"

"No tribe made this arrow," Sipar declared.

"Child, maybe?"

"What would child do way out here?"

"That's what I thought, too," said Duncan.

* * * * *

He took the arrow back, held it between his thumbs and forefingers and twirled it slowly, with a terrifying thought nibbling at his brain. It couldn't be. It was too fantastic. He wondered if the sun was finally getting him that he had thought of it at all.

He squatted down and dug at the ground with the makeshift arrow point. "Sipar, what do you actually know about the Cytha?"

"Nothing, mister. Scared of it is all."

"We aren't turning back. If there's something that you know-something that would help us...."

It was as close as he could come to begging aid. It was further than he had meant to go. He should not have asked at all, he thought angrily.

"I do not know," the native said.

Duncan cast the arrow to one side and rose to his feet. He cradled the rifle in his arm. "Let's go."

He watched Sipar trot ahead. Crafty little stinker, he told himself. It knows more than it's telling.

They toiled into the afternoon. It was, if possible, hotter and drier than the day before. There was a sense of tension in the air-no, that was rot. And even if there were, a man must act as if it were not there. If he let himself fall prey to every mood out in this empty land, he only had himself to blame for whatever happened to him.

The tracking was harder now. The day before, the Cytha had only run away, straight-line fleeing to keep ahead of them, to stay out of their reach. Now it was becoming tricky. It backtracked often in an attempt to throw them off. Twice in the afternoon, the trail blanked out entirely and it was only after long searching that Sipar picked it up again-in one instance, a mile away from where it had vanished in thin air.

That vanishing bothered Duncan more than he would admit. Trails do not disappear entirely, not when the terrain remains the same, not when the weather is unchanged. Something was going on, something, perhaps, that Sipar knew far more about than it was willing to divulge.

He watched the native closely and there seemed nothing suspicious. It continued at its work. It was, for all to see, the good and faithful hound.

* * * * *

Late in the afternoon, the plain on which they had been traveling suddenly dropped away. They stood poised on the brink of a great escarpment and looked far out to great tangled forests and a flowing river.

It was like suddenly coming into another and beautiful room that one had not expected.

This was new land, never seen before by any Earthman. For no one had ever mentioned that somewhere to the west a forest lay beyond the bush. Men coming in from space had seen it, probably, but only as a different color-marking on the planet. To them, it made no difference.

But to the men who lived on Layard, to the planter and the trader, the prospector and the hunter, it was important. And I, thought Duncan with a sense of triumph, am the man who found it.

"Mister!"

"Now what?"

"Out there. *Skun!*"

"I don't —"

"Out there, mister. Across the river."

Duncan saw it then —a haze in the blueness of the rift —a puff of copper moving very fast, and as he watched, he heard the far-off keening of the storm, a shiver in the air rather than a sound.

He watched in fascination as it moved along the river and saw the boiling fury it made out of the forest. It struck and crossed the river, and the river for a moment seemed to stand on end, with a sheet of silvery water splashed toward the sky.

Then it was gone as quickly as it had happened, but there was a tumbled slash across the forest where the churning winds had traveled.

Back at the farm, Zikkara had warned him of the *skun*. This was the season for them, it had said, and a man caught in one wouldn't have a chance.

Duncan let his breath out slowly.

"Bad," said Sipar.

"Yes, very bad."

"Hit fast. No warning."

"What about the trail?" asked Duncan. "Did the Cytha —"

Sipar nodded downward.

"Can we make it before nightfall?"

"I think so," Sipar answered.

It was rougher than they had thought. Twice they went down blind trails that pinched off, with sheer rock faces opening out into drops of hundreds of feet, and were forced to climb again and find another way.

They reached the bottom of the escarpment as the brief twilight closed in and they hurried to gather firewood. There was no water, but a little was still left in their canteens and they made do with that.

* * * * *

After their scant meal of rockahominy, Sipar rolled himself into a ball and went to sleep immediately.

Duncan sat with his back against a boulder which one day, long ago, had fallen from the slope above them, but was now half buried in the soil that through the ages had kept sifting down.

Two days gone, he told himself.

Was there, after all, some truth in the whispered tales that made the rounds back at the settlements-that no one should waste his time in tracking down a Cytha, since a Cytha was unkillable?

Nonsense, he told himself. And yet the hunt had toughened, the trail become more difficult, the Cytha a much more cunning and elusive quarry. Where it had run from them the day before, now it fought to shake them off. And if it did that the second day, why had it not tried to throw them off the first? And what about the third day-tomorrow?

He shook his head. It seemed incredible that an animal would become more formidable as the hunt progressed. But that seemed to be exactly what had happened. More spooked, perhaps, more frightened-only the Cytha did not act like a frightened beast. It was acting like an animal that was gaining savvy and determination, and that was somehow frightening.

From far off to the west, toward the forest and the river, came the laughter and the howling of a pack of screamers. Duncan leaned his rifle against the boulder and got up to pile more wood on the fire. He stared out into the western darkness, listening to the racket. He made a wry face and pushed a hand absent-mindedly through his hair. He put out a silent hope that the screamers would decide to keep their distance. They were something a man could do without.

Behind him, a pebble came bumping down the slope. It thudded to a rest just short of the fire.

Duncan spun around. Foolish thing to do, he thought, to camp so near the slope. If something big should start to move, they'd be out of luck.

He stood and listened. The night was quiet. Even the screamers had shut up for the moment. Just one rolling rock and he had his hackles up. He'd have to get himself in hand.

He went back to the boulder, and as he stooped to pick up the rifle, he heard the faint beginning of a rumble. He straightened swiftly to face the scarp that blotted out the star-strewn sky-and the rumble grew!

* * * * *

In one leap, he was at Sipar's side. He reached down and grasped the native by an arm, jerked it erect, held it on its feet. Sipar's eyes snapped open, blinking in the firelight.

The rumble had grown to a roar and there were thumping noises, as of heavy boulders bouncing, and beneath the roar the silky, ominous rustle of sliding soil and rock.

Sipar jerked its arm free of Duncan's grip and plunged into the darkness. Duncan whirled and followed.

They ran, stumbling in the dark, and behind them the roar of the sliding, bouncing rock became a throaty roll of thunder that filled the night from brim to brim. As he ran, Duncan could feel, in dread anticipation, the gusty breath of hurtling debris blowing on his neck, the crushing impact of a boulder smashing into him, the engulfing flood of tumbling talus snatching at his legs.

A puff of billowing dust came out and caught them and they ran choking as well as stumbling. Off to the left of them, a mighty chunk of rock chugged along the ground in jerky, almost reluctant fashion.

Then the thunder stopped and all one could hear was the small slitherings of the lesser debris as it trickled down the slope.

Duncan stopped running and slowly turned around. The campfire was gone, buried, no doubt, beneath tons of overlay, and the stars had paled because of the great cloud of dust which still billowed up into the sky.

He heard Sipar moving near him and reached out a hand, searching for the tracker, not knowing exactly where it was. He found the native, grasped it by the shoulder and pulled it up beside him.

Sipar was shivering.

"It's all right," said Duncan.

And it *was* all right, he reassured himself. He still had the rifle. The extra drum of ammunition and the knife were on his belt, the bag of rockahominy in his pocket. The canteens were all they had lost-the canteens and the fire.

"We'll have to hole up somewhere for the night," Duncan said. "There are screamers on the loose."

* * * * *

He didn't like what he was thinking, nor the sharp edge of fear that was beginning to crowd in upon him. He tried to shrug it off, but it still stayed with him, just out of reach.

Sipar plucked at his elbow.

"Thorn thicket, mister. Over there. We could crawl inside. We would be safe from screamers."

It was torture, but they made it.

"Screamers and you are taboo," said Duncan, suddenly remembering. "How come you are afraid of them?"

"Afraid for you, mister, mostly. Afraid for myself just a little. Screamers could forget. They might not recognize me until too late. Safer here."

"I agree with you," said Duncan.

The screamers came and padded all about the thicket. The beasts sniffed and clawed at the thorns to reach them, but finally went away.

When morning came, Duncan and Sipar climbed the scarp, clambering over the boulders and the tons of soil and rock that covered their camping place. Following the gash cut by the slide, they clambered up the slope and finally reached the point of the slide's beginning.

There they found the depression in which the poised slab of rock had rested and where the supporting soil had been dug away so that it could be started, with a push, down the slope above the campfire.

And all about were the deeply sunken pug marks of the Cytha!

CHAPTER IV

Now it was more than just a hunt. It was knife against the throat, kill or be killed. Now there was no stopping, when before there might have been. It was no longer sport and there was no mercy.

"And that's the way I like it," Duncan told himself.

He rubbed his hand along the rifle barrel and saw the metallic glints shine in the noonday sun. One more shot, he prayed. Just give me one more shot at it. This time there will be no slip-up. This time there will be more than three sodden hunks of flesh and fur lying in the grass to mock me.

He squinted his eyes against the heat shimmer rising from the river, watching Sipar hunkered beside the water's edge.

The native rose to its feet and trotted back to him.

"It crossed," said Sipar. "It walked out as far as it could go and it must have swum."

"Are you sure? It might have waded out to make us think it crossed, then doubled back again."

He stared at the purple-green of the trees across the river. Inside that forest, it would be hellish going.

"We can look," said Sipar.

"Good. You go downstream. I'll go up."

An hour later, they were back. They had found no tracks. There seemed little doubt the Cytha had really crossed the river.

They stood side by side, looking at the forest.

"Mister, we have come far. You are brave to hunt the Cytha. You have no fear of death."

"The fear of death," Duncan said, "is entirely infantile. And it's beside the point as well. I do not intend to die."

They waded out into the stream. The bottom shelved gradually and they had to swim no more than a hundred yards or so.

They reached the forest bank and threw themselves flat to rest.

Duncan looked back the way that they had come. To the east, the escarpment was a dark-blue smudge against the pale-blue burnished sky. And two days back of that lay the farm and the *vua* field, but they seemed much farther off than that. They were lost in time and distance; they belonged to another existence and another world.

All his life, it seemed to him, had faded and become inconsequential and forgotten, as if this moment in his life were the only one that counted; as if all the minutes and the hours, all the breaths and heartbeats, wake and sleep, had pointed toward this certain hour upon this certain stream, with the rifle molded to his hand and the cool, calculated bloodlust of a killer riding in his brain.

* * * * *

Sipar finally got up and began to range along the stream. Duncan sat up and watched.

Scared to death, he thought, and yet it stayed with me. At the campfire that first night, it had said it would stick to the death and apparently it had meant exactly what it said. It's hard, he thought, to figure out these jokers, hard to know what kind of mental operation, what seethings of emotion, what brand of ethics and what variety of belief and faith go to make them and their way of life.

It would have been so easy for Sipar to have missed the trail and swear it could not find it. Even from the start, it could have refused to go. Yet, fearing, it had gone. Reluctant, it had trailed. Without any need for faithfulness and loyalty, it had been loyal and faithful. But loyal to what, Duncan wondered, to him, the outlander and intruder? Loyal to itself? Or perhaps, although that seemed impossible, faithful to the Cytha?

What does Sipar think of me, he asked himself, and maybe more to the point, what do I think of Sipar? Is there a common meeting ground? Or are we, despite our humanoid forms, condemned forever to be alien and apart?

He held the rifle across his knees and stroked it, polishing it, petting it, making it even more closely a part of him, an instrument of his deadliness, an expression of his determination to track and kill the Cytha.

Just another chance, he begged. Just one second, or even less, to draw a steady bead. That is all I want, all I need, all I'll ask.

Then he could go back across the days that he had left behind him, back to the farm and field, back into that misty other life from which he had been so mysteriously divorced, but which in time undoubtedly would become real and meaningful again.

Sipar came back. "I found the trail."

Duncan heaved himself to his feet. "Good."

They left the river and plunged into the forest and there the heat closed in more mercilessly than ever-humid, stifling heat that felt like a soggy blanket wrapped tightly round the body.

The trail lay plain and clear. The Cytha now, it seemed, was intent upon piling up a lead without recourse to evasive tactics. Perhaps it had reasoned that its pursuers would lose some time at the river and it may have been trying to stretch out that margin even further. Perhaps it needed that extra time, he speculated, to set up the necessary machinery for another dirty trick.

Sipar stopped and waited for Duncan to catch up. "Your knife, mister?"

Duncan hesitated. "What for?"

"I have a thorn in my foot," the native said. "I have to get it out."

Duncan pulled the knife from his belt and tossed it. Sipar caught it deftly.

Looking straight at Duncan, with the flicker of a smile upon its lips, the native cut its throat.

CHAPTER V

He should go back, he knew. Without the tracker, he didn't have a chance. The odds were now with the Cytha-if, indeed, they had not been with it from the very start.

Unkillable? Unkillable because it grew in intelligence to meet emergencies? Unkillable because, pressed, it could fashion a bow and arrow, however crude? Unkillable because it had a sense of tactics, like rolling rocks at night upon its enemy? Unkillable because a native tracker would cheerfully kill itself to protect the Cytha?

A sort of crisis-beast, perhaps? One able to develop intelligence and abilities to meet each new situation and then lapsing back to the level of non-intelligent contentment? That, thought Duncan, would be a sensible way for anything to live. It would do away with the inconvenience and the irritability and the discontentment of intelligence when intelligence was unneeded. But the intelligence, and the abilities which went with it, would be there, safely tucked away where one could reach in and get them, like a necklace or a gun-something to be used or to be put away as the case might be.

Duncan hunched forward and with a stick of wood pushed the fire together. The flames blazed up anew and sent sparks flying up into the whispering darkness of the trees. The night had cooled off a little, but the humidity still hung on and a man felt uncomfortable —a little frightened, too.

Duncan lifted his head and stared up into the fire-flecked darkness. There were no stars because the heavy foliage shut them out. He missed the stars. He'd feel better if he could look up and see them.

When morning came, he should go back. He should quit this hunt which now had become impossible and even slightly foolish.

But he knew he wouldn't. Somewhere along the three-day trail, he had become committed to a purpose and a challenge, and he knew that when morning came, he would go on again. It was not hatred that drove him, nor vengeance, nor even the trophy-urge —the hunter-lust that prodded men to kill something strange or harder to kill or bigger than any man had ever killed before. It was something more than that, some weird entangling of the Cytha's meaning with his own.

He reached out and picked up the rifle and laid it in his lap. Its barrel gleamed dully in the flickering campfire light and he rubbed his hand along the stock as another man might stroke a woman's throat.

"Mister," said a voice.

* * * * *

It did not startle him, for the word was softly spoken and for a moment he had forgotten that Sipar was dead-dead with a half-smile fixed upon its face and with its throat laid wide open.

"Mister?"

Duncan stiffened.

Sipar was dead and there was no one else-and yet someone had spoken to him, and there could be only one thing in all this wilderness that might speak to him.

"Yes," he said.

He did not move. He simply sat there, with the rifle in his lap.

"You know who I am?"

"I suppose you are the Cytha."

"You have done well," the Cytha said. "You've made a splendid hunt. There is no dishonor if you should decide to quit. Why don't you go back? I promise you no harm."

It was over there, somewhere in front of him, somewhere in the brush beyond the fire, almost straight across the fire from him, Duncan told himself. If he could keep it talking, perhaps even lure it out —

"Why should I?" he asked. "The hunt is never done until one gets the thing one is after."

"I can kill you," the Cytha told him. "But I do not want to kill. It hurts to kill."

"That's right," said Duncan. "You are most perceptive."

For he had it pegged now. He knew exactly where it was. He could afford a little mockery.

His thumb slid up the metal and nudged the fire control to automatic and he flexed his legs beneath him so that he could rise and fire in one single motion.

"Why did you hunt me?" the Cytha asked. "You are a stranger on my world and you had no right to hunt me. Not that I mind, of course. In fact, I found it stimulating. We must do it again. When I am ready to be hunted, I shall come and tell you and we can spend a day or two at it."

"Sure we can," said Duncan, rising. And as he rose into his crouch, he held the trigger down and the gun danced in insane fury, the muzzle flare a flicking tongue of hatred and the hail of death hissing spitefully in the underbrush.

"Anytime you want to," yelled Duncan gleefully, "I'll come and hunt you! You just say the word and I'll be on your tail. I might even kill you. How do you like it, chump!"

And he held the trigger tight and kept his crouch so the slugs would not fly high, but would cut their swath just above the ground, and he moved the muzzle back and forth a lot so that he covered extra ground to compensate for any miscalculations he might have made.

* * * * *

The magazine ran out and the gun clicked empty and the vicious chatter stopped. Powder smoke drifted softly in the campfire light and the smell of it was perfume in the nostrils and in the underbrush many little feet were running, as if a thousand frightened mice were scurrying from catastrophe.

Duncan unhooked the extra magazine from where it hung upon his belt and replaced the empty one. Then he snatched a burning length of wood from the fire and waved it frantically until it burst into a blaze and became a torch. Rifle grasped in one hand and the torch in the other, he plunged into the underbrush. Little chittering things fled to escape him.

He did not find the Cytha. He found chewed-up bushes and soil churned by flying metal, and he found five lumps of flesh and fur, and these he brought back to the fire.

Now the fear that had been stalking him, keeping just beyond his reach, walked out from the shadows and hunkered by the campfire with him.

He placed the rifle within easy reach and arranged the five bloody chunks on the ground close to the fire and he tried with trembling fingers to restore them to the shape they'd been before the bullets struck them. And that was a good one, he thought with grim irony, because they had no shape. They had been part of the Cytha and you killed a Cytha inch by inch, not with a single shot. You knocked a pound of meat off it the first time, and the next time you shot off another pound or two, and if you got enough shots at it, you finally carved it down to size and maybe you could kill it then, although he wasn't sure.

He was afraid. He admitted that he was and he squatted there and watched his fingers shake and he kept his jaws clamped tight to stop the chatter of his teeth.

The fear had been getting closer all the time; he knew it had moved in by a step or two when Sipar cut its throat, and why in the name of God had the damn fool done it? It made no sense at all. He had wondered about Sipar's loyalties, and the very loyalties that he had dismissed as a sheer impossibility had been the answer, after all. In the end, for some obscure reason-obscure to humans, that is-Sipar's loyalty had been to the Cytha.

But then what was the use of searching for any reason in it? Nothing that had happened made any sense. It made no sense that a beast one was pursuing should up and talk to one-although it did fit in with the theory of the crisis-beast he had fashioned in his mind.

* * * * *

Progressive adaptation, he told himself. Carry adaptation far enough and you'd reach communication. But might not the Cytha's power of adaptation be running down? Had the Cytha gone about as far as it could force itself to go? Maybe so, he thought. It might be worth a gamble. Sipar's suicide, for all its casualness, bore the overtones of last-notch desperation. And the Cytha's speaking to Duncan, its attempt to parley with him, contained a note of weakness.

The arrow had failed and the rockslide had failed and so had Sipar's death. What next would the Cytha try? Had it anything to try?

Tomorrow he'd find out. Tomorrow he'd go on. He couldn't turn back now.

He was too deeply involved. He'd always wonder, if he turned back now, whether another hour or two might not have seen the end of it. There were too many questions, too much mystery-there was now far more at stake than ten rows of *vua*.

Another day might make some sense of it, might banish the dread walker that trod upon his heels, might bring some peace of mind.

As it stood right at the moment, none of it made sense.

But even as he thought it, suddenly one of the bits of bloody flesh and mangled fur made sense.

Beneath the punching and prodding of his fingers, it had assumed a shape.

Breathlessly, Duncan bent above it, not believing, not even wanting to believe, hoping frantically that it should prove completely wrong.

But there was nothing wrong with it. The shape was there and could not be denied. It had somehow fitted back into its natural shape and it was a baby screamer-well, maybe not a baby, but at least a tiny screamer.

Duncan sat back on his heels and sweated. He wiped his bloody hands upon the ground. He wondered what other shapes he'd find if he put back into proper place the other hunks of limpness that lay beside the fire.

He tried and failed. They were too smashed and torn.

He picked them up and tossed them in the fire. He took up his rifle and walked around the fire, sat down with his back against a tree, cradling the gun across his knees.

* * * * *

Those little scurrying feet, he wondered-like the scampering of a thousand busy mice. He had heard them twice, that first night in the thicket by the waterhole and again tonight.

And what could the Cytha be? Certainly not the simple, uncomplicated, marauding animal he had thought to start with.

A hive-beast? A host animal? A thing masquerading in many different forms?

Shotwell, trained in such deductions, might make a fairly accurate guess, but Shotwell was not here. He was at the farm, fretting, more than likely, over Duncan's failure to return.

Finally the first light of morning began to filter through the forest and it was not the glaring, clean white light of the open plain and bush, but a softened, diluted, fuzzy green light to match the smothering vegetation.

The night noises died away and the noises of the day took up-the sawings of unseen insects, the screechings of hidden birds and something far away began to make a noise that sounded like an empty barrel falling slowly down a stairway.

What little coolness the night had brought dissipated swiftly and the heat clamped down, a breathless, relentless heat that quivered in the air.

Circling, Duncan picked up the Cytha trail not more than a hundred yards from camp.

The beast had been traveling fast. The pug marks were deeply sunk and widely spaced. Duncan followed as rapidly as he dared. It was a temptation to follow at a run, to match the Cytha's speed, for the trail was plain and fresh and it fairly beckoned.

And that was wrong, Duncan told himself. It was too fresh, too plain-almost as if the animal had gone to endless trouble so that the human could not miss the trail.

He stopped his trailing and crouched beside a tree and studied the tracks ahead. His hands were too tense upon the gun, his body keyed too high and fine. He forced himself to take slow, deep breaths. He had to calm himself. He had to loosen up.

He studied the tracks ahead-four bunched pug marks, then a long leap interval, then four more bunched tracks, and between the sets of marks the forest floor was innocent and smooth.

Too smooth, perhaps. Especially the third one from him. Too smooth and somehow artificial, as if someone had patted it with gentle hands to make it unsuspicious.

Duncan sucked his breath in slowly.

Trap?

Or was his imagination playing tricks on him?

And if it were a trap, he would have fallen into it if he had kept on following as he had started out.

Now there was something else, a strange uneasiness, and he stirred uncomfortably, casting frantically for some clue to what it was.

* * * * *

He rose and stepped out from the tree, with the gun at ready. What a perfect place to set a trap, he thought. One would be looking at the pug marks, never at the space between them, for the space between would be neutral ground, safe to stride out upon.

Oh, clever Cytha, he said to himself. Oh, clever, clever Cytha!

And now he knew what the other trouble was-the great uneasiness. It was the sense of being watched.

Somewhere up ahead, the Cytha was crouched, watching and waiting-anxious or exultant, maybe even with laughter rumbling in its throat.

He walked slowly forward until he reached the third set of tracks and he saw that he had been right. The little area ahead was smoother than it should be.

"Cytha!" he called.

His voice was far louder than he had meant it to be and he stood astonished and a bit abashed.

Then he realized why it was so loud.

It was the only sound there was!

The forest suddenly had fallen silent. The insects and birds were quiet and the thing in the distance had quit falling down the stairs. Even the leaves were silent. There was no rustle in them and they hung limp upon their stems.

There was a feeling of doom and the green light had changed to a copper light and everything was still.

And the light was *copper*!

Duncan spun around in panic. There was no place for him to hide.

Before he could take another step, the *skun* came and the winds rushed out of nowhere. The air was clogged with flying leaves and debris. Trees snapped and popped and tumbled in the air.

The wind hurled Duncan to his knees, and as he fought to regain his feet, he remembered, in a blinding flash of total recall, how it had looked from atop the escarpment-the boiling fury of the winds and the mad swirling of the coppery mist and how the trees had whipped in whirlpool fashion.

He came half erect and stumbled, clawing at the ground in an attempt to get up again, while inside his brain an insistent, clicking voice cried out for him to run, and somewhere another voice said to lie flat upon the ground, to dig in as best he could.

Something struck him from behind and he went down, pinned flat, with his rifle wedged beneath him. He cracked his head upon the ground and the world whirled sickeningly and plastered his face with a handful of mud and tattered leaves.

He tried to crawl and couldn't, for something had grabbed him by the ankle and was hanging on.

* * * * *

With a frantic hand, he clawed the mess out of his eyes, spat it from his mouth.

Across the spinning ground, something black and angular tumbled rapidly. It was coming straight toward him and he saw it was the Cytha and that in another second it would be on top of him.

He threw up an arm across his face, with the elbow crooked, to take the impact of the wind-blown Cytha and to ward it off.

But it never reached him. Less than a yard away, the ground opened up to take the Cytha and it was no longer there.

Suddenly the wind cut off and the leaves once more hung motionless and the heat clamped down again and that was the end of it. The *skun* had come and struck and gone.

Minutes, Duncan wondered, or perhaps no more than seconds. But in those seconds, the forest had been flattened and the trees lay in shattered heaps.

He raised himself on an elbow and looked to see what was the matter with his foot and he saw that a fallen tree had trapped his foot beneath it.

He tugged a few times experimentally. It was no use. Two close-set limbs, branching almost at right angles from the hole, had been driven deep into the ground and his foot, he saw, had been caught at the ankle in the fork of the buried branches.

The foot didn't hurt-not yet. It didn't seem to be there at all. He tried wiggling his toes and felt none.

He wiped the sweat off his face with a shirt sleeve and fought to force down the panic that was rising in him. Getting panicky was the worst thing a man could do in a spot like this. The thing to do was to take stock of the situation, figure out the best approach, then go ahead and try it.

The tree looked heavy, but perhaps he could handle it if he had to, although there was the danger that if he shifted it, the bole might settle more solidly and crush his foot beneath it. At the moment, the two heavy branches, thrust into the ground on either side of his ankle, were holding most of the tree's weight off his foot.

The best thing to do, he decided, was to dig the ground away beneath his foot until he could pull it out.

He twisted around and started digging with the fingers of one hand. Beneath the thin covering of humus, he struck a solid surface and his fingers slid along it.

With mounting alarm, he explored the ground, scratching at the humus. There was nothing but rock-some long-buried boulder, the top of which lay just beneath the ground.

His foot was trapped beneath a heavy tree and a massive boulder, held securely in place by forked branches that had forced their splintering way down along the boulder's sides.

* * * * *

He lay back, propped on an elbow. It was evident that he could do nothing about the buried boulder. If he was going to do anything, his problem was the tree.

To move the tree, he would need a lever and he had a good, stout lever in his rifle. It would be a shame, he thought a little wryly, to use a gun for such a purpose, but he had no choice.

He worked for an hour and it was no good. Even with the rifle as a pry, he could not budge the tree.

He lay back, defeated, breathing hard, wringing wet with perspiration.

He grimaced at the sky.

All right, Cytha, he thought, you won out in the end. But it took a *skun* to do it. With all your tricks, you couldn't do the job until....

Then he remembered.

He sat up hurriedly.

"Cytha!" he called.

The Cytha had fallen into a hole that had opened in the ground. The hole was less than an arm's length away from him, with a little debris around its edges still trickling into it.

Duncan stretched out his body, lying flat upon the ground, and looked into the hole. There, at the bottom of it, was the Cytha.

It was the first time he'd gotten a good look at the Cytha and it was a crazily put-together thing. It seemed to have nothing functional about it and it looked more like a heap of something, just thrown on the ground, than it did an animal.

The hole, he saw, was more than an ordinary hole. It was a pit and very cleverly constructed. The mouth was about four feet in diameter and it widened to roughly twice that at the bottom. It was, in general, bottle-shaped, with an incurving shoulder at the top so that anything that fell in could not climb out. Anything falling into that pit was in to stay.

This, Duncan knew, was what had lain beneath that too-smooth interval between the two sets of Cytha tracks. The Cytha had worked all night to dig it, then had carried away the dirt dug out of the pit and had built a flimsy camouflage cover over it. Then it had gone back and made the trail that was so loud and clear, so easy to make out and follow. And having done all that, having labored hard and stealthily, the Cytha had settled down to watch, to make sure the following human had fallen in the pit.

* * * * *

"Hi, pal," said Duncan. "How are you making out?"

The Cytha did not answer.

"Classy pit," said Duncan. "Do you always den up in luxury like this?"

But the Cytha didn't answer.

Something queer was happening to the Cytha. It was coming all apart.

Duncan watched with fascinated horror as the Cytha broke down into a thousand lumps of motion that scurried in the pit and tried to scramble up its sides, only to fall back in tiny showers of sand.

Amid the scurrying lumps, one thing remained intact, a fragile object that resembled nothing quite so much as the stripped skeleton of a Thanksgiving turkey. But it was a most extraordinary Thanksgiving skeleton, for it throbbed with pulsing life and glowed with a steady violet light.

Chitterings and squeakings came out of the pit and the soft patter of tiny running feet, and as Duncan's eyes became accustomed to the darkness of the pit, he began to make out the forms of some of the scurrying shapes. There were tiny screamers and some donovans and sawmill birds and a bevy of kill-devils and something else as well.

Duncan raised a hand and pressed it against his eyes, then took it quickly away. The little faces still were there, looking up as if beseeching him, with the white shine of their teeth and the white rolling of their eyes.

He felt horror wrenching at his stomach and the sour, bitter taste of revulsion welled into his throat, but he fought it down, harking back to that day at the farm before they had started on the hunt.

"I can track down anything but screamers, stilt-birds, longhorns and donovans," Sipar had told him solemnly. "These are my taboos."

And Sipar was also their taboo, for he had not feared the donovan. Sipar had been, however, somewhat fearful of the screamers in the dead of night because, the native had told him reasonably, screamers were forgetful.

Forgetful of what!

Forgetful of the Cytha-mother? Forgetful of the motley brood in which they had spent their childhood?

For that was the only answer to what was running in the pit and the whole, unsuspected answer to the enigma against which men like Shotwell had frustratedly banged their heads for years.

* * * * *

Strange, he told himself. All right, it might be strange, but if it worked, what difference did it make? So the planet's denizens were sexless because there was no need of sex-what was wrong with that? It might, in fact, Duncan admitted to himself, head off a lot of trouble. No family spats, no triangle trouble, no fighting over mates. While it might be unexciting, it did seem downright peaceful.

And since there was no sex, the Cytha species was the planetary mother-but more than just a mother. The Cytha, more than likely, was mother-father, incubator, nursery, teacher and perhaps many other things besides, all rolled into one.

In many ways, he thought, it might make a lot of sense. Here natural selection would be ruled out and ecology could be controlled in considerable degree and mutation might even be a matter of deliberate choice rather than random happenstance.

And it would make for a potential planetary unity such as no other world had ever known. Everything here was kin to everything else. Here was a planet where Man, or any other alien, must learn to tread most softly. For it was not inconceivable that, in a crisis or a clash of interests, one might find himself faced suddenly with a unified and cooperating planet, with every form of life making common cause against the interloper.

The little scurrying things had given up; they'd gone back to their places, clustered around the pulsing violet of the Thanksgiving skeleton, each one fitting into place until the Cytha had taken shape again. As if, Duncan told himself, blood and nerve and muscle had come back from a brief vacation to form the beast anew.

"Mister," asked the Cytha, "what do we do now?"

"You should know," Duncan told it. "You were the one who dug the pit."

"I split myself," the Cytha said. "A part of me dug the pit and the other part that stayed on the surface got me out when the job was done."

"Convenient," grunted Duncan.

And it *was* convenient. That was what had happened to the Cytha when he had shot at it-it had split into all its component parts and had got away. And that night beside the waterhole, it had spied on him, again in the form of all its separate parts, from the safety of the thicket.

"You are caught and so am I," the Cytha said. "Both of us will die here. It seems a fitting end to our association. Do you not agree with me?"

"I'll get you out," said Duncan wearily. "I have no quarrel with children."

* * * * *

He dragged the rifle toward him and unhooked the sling from the stock. Carefully he lowered the gun by the sling, still attached to the barrel, down into the pit.

The Cytha reared up and grasped it with its forepaws.

"Easy now," Duncan cautioned. "You're heavy. I don't know if I can hold you."

But he needn't have worried. The little ones were detaching themselves and scrambling up the rifle and the sling. They reached his extended arms and ran up them with scrabbling claws. Little sneering screamers and the comic stilt-birds and the mouse-size kill-devils that snarled at him as they climbed. And the little grinning natives-not babies, scarcely children, but small editions of full-grown humanoids. And the weird donovans scampering happily.

They came climbing up his arms and across his shoulders and milled about on the ground beside him, waiting for the others.

And finally the Cytha, not skinned down to the bare bones of its Thanksgiving-turkey-size, but far smaller than it had been, climbed awkwardly up the rifle and the sling to safety.

Duncan hauled the rifle up and twisted himself into a sitting position.

The Cytha, he saw, was reassembling.

He watched in fascination as the restless miniatures of the planet's life swarmed and seethed like a hive of bees, each one clicking into place to form the entire beast.

And now the Cytha was complete. Yet small-still small-no more than lion-size.

"But it is such a little one," Zikkara had argued with him that morning at the farm. "It is such a young one."

Just a young brood, no more than suckling infants-if suckling was the word, or even some kind of wild approximation. And through the months and years, the Cytha would grow, with the growing of its diverse children, until it became a monstrous thing.

It stood there looking at Duncan and the tree.

"Now," said Duncan, "if you'll push on the tree, I think that between the two of us —"

"It is too bad," the Cytha said, and wheeled itself about.

He watched it go loping off.

"Hey!" he yelled.

But it didn't stop.

He grabbed up the rifle and had it halfway to his shoulder before he remembered how absolutely futile it was to shoot at the Cytha.

He let the rifle down.

"The dirty, ungrateful, double-crossing —"

He stopped himself. There was no profit in rage. When you were in a jam, you did the best you could. You figured out the problem and you picked the course that seemed best and you didn't panic at the odds.

He laid the rifle in his lap and started to hook up the sling and it was not till then that he saw the barrel was packed with sand and dirt.

He sat numbly for a moment, thinking back to how close he had been to firing at the Cytha, and if that barrel was packed hard enough or deep enough, he might have had an exploding weapon in his hands.

He had used the rifle as a crowbar, which was no way to use a gun. That was one way, he told himself, that was guaranteed to ruin it.

* * * * *

Duncan hunted around and found a twig and dug at the clogged muzzle, but the dirt was jammed too firmly in it and he made little progress.

He dropped the twig and was hunting for another stronger one when he caught the motion in a nearby clump of brush.

He watched closely for a moment and there was nothing, so he resumed the hunt for a stronger twig. He found one and started poking at the muzzle and there was another flash of motion.

He twisted around. Not more than twenty feet away, a screamer sat easily on its haunches. Its tongue was lolling out and it had what looked like a grin upon its face.

And there was another, just at the edge of the clump of brush where he had caught the motion first.

There were others as well, he knew. He could hear them sliding through the tangle of fallen trees, could sense the soft padding of their feet.

The executioners, he thought.

The Cytha certainly had not wasted any time.

He raised the rifle and rapped the barrel smartly on the fallen tree, trying to dislodge the obstruction in the bore. But it didn't budge; the barrel still was packed with sand.

But no matter-he'd have to fire anyhow and take whatever chance there was.

He shoved the control to automatic, and tilted up the muzzle.

There were six of them now, sitting in a ragged row, grinning at him, not in any hurry. They were sure of him and there was no hurry. He'd still be there when they decided to move in.

And there were others-on all sides of him.

Once it started, he wouldn't have a chance.

"It'll be expensive, gents," he told them.

And he was astonished at how calm, how coldly objective he could be, now that the chips were down. But that was the way it was, he realized.

He'd thought, a while ago, how a man might suddenly find himself face to face with an aroused and cooperating planet. Maybe this was it in miniature.

The Cytha had obviously passed the word along: *Man back there needs killing. Go and get him.*

Just like that, for a Cytha would be the power here. A life force, the giver of life, the decider of life, the repository of all animal life on the entire planet.

There was more than one of them, of course. Probably they had home districts, spheres of influence and responsibility mapped out. And each one would be a power supreme in its own district.

Momism, he thought with a sour grin. Momism at its absolute peak.

Nevertheless, he told himself, it wasn't too bad a system if you wanted to consider it objectively.

But he was in a poor position to be objective about that or anything else.

* * * * *

The screamers were inching closer, hitching themselves forward slowly on their bottoms.

"I'm going to set up a deadline for you critters," Duncan called out. "Just two feet farther, up to that rock, and I let you have it."

He'd get all six of them, of course, but the shots would be the signal for the general rush by all those other animals slinking in the brush.

If he were free, if he were on his feet, possibly he could beat them off. But pinned as he was, he didn't have a chance. It would be all over less than a minute after he opened fire. He might, he figured, last as long as that.

The six inched closer and he raised the rifle.

But they stopped and moved no farther. Their ears lifted just a little, as if they might be listening, and the grins dropped from their faces. They squirmed uneasily and assumed a look of guilt and, like shadows, they were gone, melting away so swiftly that he scarcely saw them go.

Duncan sat quietly, listening, but he could hear no sound.

Reprieve, he thought. But for how long? Something had scared them off, but in a while they might be back. He had to get out of here and he had to make it fast.

If he could find a longer lever, he could move the tree. There was a branch slanting up from the topside of the fallen tree. It was almost four inches at the butt and it carried its diameter well.

He slid the knife from his belt and looked at it. Too small, too thin, he thought, to chisel through a four-inch branch, but it was all he had. When a man was desperate enough, though, when his very life depended on it, he would do anything.

He hitched himself along, sliding toward the point where the branch protruded from the tree. His pinned leg protested with stabs of pain as his body wrenched it around. He gritted his teeth and pushed himself closer. Pain slashed through his leg again and he was still long inches from the branch.

He tried once more, then gave up. He lay panting on the ground.

There was just one thing left.

He'd have to try to hack out a notch in the trunk just above his leg. No, that would be next to impossible, for he'd be cutting into the whorled and twisted grain at the base of the supporting fork.

Either that or cut off his foot, and that was even more impossible. A man would faint before he got the job done.

It was useless, he knew. He could do neither one. There was nothing he could do.

* * * * *

For the first time, he admitted to himself: He would stay here and die. Shotwell, back at the farm, in a day or two might set out hunting for him. But Shotwell would never find him. And anyhow, by nightfall, if not sooner, the screamers would be back.

He laughed gruffly in his throat-laughing at himself.

The Cytha had won the hunt hands down. It had used a human weakness to win and then had used that same human weakness to achieve a viciously poetic vengeance.

After all, what could one expect? One could not equate human ethics with the ethics of the Cytha. Might not human ethics, in certain cases, seem as weird and illogical, as infamous and ungrateful, to an alien?

He hunted for a twig and began working again to clean the rifle bore.

A crashing behind him twisted him around and he saw the Cytha. Behind the Cytha stalked a donovan.

He tossed away the twig and raised the gun.

"No," said the Cytha sharply.

The donovan tramped purposefully forward and Duncan felt the prickling of the skin along his back. It was a frightful thing. Nothing could stand before a donovan. The screamers had turned tail and run when they had heard it a couple of miles or more away.

The donovan was named for the first known human to be killed by one. That first was only one of many. The roll of donovan-victims ran long, and no wonder, Duncan thought. It was the closest he had ever been to one of the beasts and he felt a coldness creeping over him. It was like an elephant and a tiger and a grizzly bear wrapped in the selfsame hide. It was the most vicious fighting machine that ever had been spawned.

He lowered the rifle. There would be no point in shooting. In two quick strides, the beast could be upon him.

The donovan almost stepped on him and he flinched away. Then the great head lowered and gave the fallen tree a butt and the tree bounced for a yard or two. The donovan kept on walking. Its powerfully muscled stern moved into the brush and out of sight.

"Now we are even," said the Cytha. "I had to get some help."

Duncan grunted. He flexed the leg that had been trapped and he could not feel the foot. Using his rifle as a cane, he pulled himself erect. He tried putting weight on the injured foot and it screamed with pain.

He braced himself with the rifle and rotated so that he faced the Cytha.

"Thanks, pal," he said. "I didn't think you'd do it."

"You will not hunt me now?"

Duncan shook his head. "I'm in no shape for hunting. I am heading home."

"It was the *vua*, wasn't it? That was why you hunted me?"

"The *vua* is my livelihood," said Duncan. "I cannot let you eat it."

The Cytha stood silently and Duncan watched it for a moment. Then he wheeled. Using the rifle for a crutch, he started hobbling away.

The Cytha hurried to catch up with him.

"Let us make a bargain, mister. I will not eat the *vua* and you will not hunt me. Is that fair enough?"

"That is fine with me," said Duncan. "Let us shake on it."

He put down a hand and the Cytha lifted up a paw. They shook, somewhat awkwardly, but very solemnly.

"Now," the Cytha said, "I will see you home. The screamers would have you before you got out of the woods."

CHAPTER VI

They halted on a knoll. Below them lay the farm, with the *vua* rows straight and green in the red soil of the fields.

"You can make it from here," the Cytha said. "I am wearing thin. It is an awful effort to keep on being smart. I want to go back to ignorance and comfort."

"It was nice knowing you," Duncan told it politely. "And thanks for sticking with me."

He started down the hill, leaning heavily on the rifle-crutch. Then he frowned troubledly and turned back.

"Look," he said, "you'll go back to animal again. Then you will forget. One of these days, you'll see all that nice, tender *vua* and —"

"Very simple," said the Cytha. "If you find me in the *vua*, just begin hunting me. With you after me, I will quickly get smart and remember once again and it will be all right."

"Sure," agreed Duncan. "I guess that will work."

The Cytha watched him go stumping down the hill.

Admirable, it thought. Next time I have a brood, I think I'll raise a dozen like him.

It turned around and headed for the deeper brush.

It felt intelligence slipping from it, felt the old, uncaring comfort coming back again. But it glowed with anticipation, seethed with happiness at the big surprise it had in store for its new-found friend.

Won't he be happy and surprised when I drop them at his door, it thought.

Will he be ever pleased!

—Clifford D. Simak

Hellhounds of the Cosmos

He glimmered momentarily, then vanished.

Weird are the conditions of the interdimensional struggle faced by Dr.
White's ninety-nine men.

The paper had gone to press, graphically describing the latest of the many horrible events which had been enacted upon the Earth in the last six months. The headlines screamed that Six Corners, a little hamlet in Pennsylvania, had been wiped out by the Horror. Another front-page story told of a Terror in the Amazon Valley which had sent the natives down the river in babbling fear. Other stories told of deaths here and there, all attributable to the "Black Horror," as it was called.

The telephone rang.

"Hello," said the editor.

"London calling," came the voice of the operator.

"All right," replied the editor.

He recognized the voice of Terry Masters, special correspondent. His voice came clearly over the transatlantic telephone.

"The Horror is attacking London in force," he said. "There are thousands of them and they have completely surrounded the city. All roads are blocked. The government declared the city under martial rule a quarter of an hour ago and efforts are being made to prepare for resistance against the enemy."

"Just a second," the editor shouted into the transmitter.

He touched a button on his desk and in a moment an answering buzz told him he was in communication with the press-room.

"Stop the presses!" he yelled into the speaking tube. "Get ready for a new front make-up!"

"O.K.," came faintly through the tube, and the editor turned back to the phone.

"Now let's have it," he said, and the voice at the London end of the wire droned on, telling the story that in another half hour was read by a world which shuddered in cold fear even as it scanned the glaring headlines.

"Woods," said the editor of the *Press* to a reporter, "run over and talk to Dr. Silas White. He phoned me to send someone. Something about this Horror business."

Henry Woods rose from his chair without a word and walked from the office. As he passed the wire machine it was tapping out, with a maddeningly methodical slowness, the story of the fall of London. Only half an hour before it had rapped forth the flashes concerning the attack on Paris and Berlin.

He passed out of the building into a street that was swarming with terrified humanity. Six months of terror, of numerous mysterious deaths, of villages blotted out, had set the world on edge. Now with London in possession of the Horror and Paris and Berlin fighting hopelessly for their lives, the entire population of the world was half insane with fright.

Exhorters on street corners enlarged upon the end of the world, asking that the people prepare for eternity, attributing the Horror to the act of a Supreme Being enraged with the wickedness of the Earth.

Expecting every moment an attack by the Horror, people left their work and gathered in the streets. Traffic, in places, had been blocked for hours and law and order were practically paralyzed. Commerce and transportation were disrupted as fright-ridden people fled from the larger cities, seeking doubtful hiding places in rural districts from the death that stalked the land.

A loudspeaker in front of a music store blared forth the latest news flashes.

"It has been learned," came the measured tones of the announcer, "that all communication with Berlin ceased about ten minutes ago. At Paris all efforts to hold the Horror at bay have been futile. Explosives blow it apart, but have the same effect upon it as explosion has on gas. It flies apart and then reforms again, not always in the same shape as it was before. A new gas, one of the most deadly ever conceived by man, has failed to have any effect on the things. Electric guns and heat guns have absolutely no effect upon them.

"A news flash which has just come in from Rome says that a large number of the Horrors has been sighted north of that city by airmen. It seems they are attacking the capitals of the world first. Word comes from Washington that every known form of defense is being amassed at that city. New York is also preparing...."

Henry Woods fought his way through the crowd which milled in front of the loudspeaker. The hum of excitement was giving away to a silence, the silence of a stunned people, the fearful silence of a populace facing a presence it is unable to understand, an embattled world standing with useless weapons before an incomprehensible enemy.

In despair the reporter looked about for a taxi, but realized, with a groan of resignation, that no taxi could possibly operate in that crowded street. A street car, blocked by the stream of humanity which jostled and elbowed about it, stood still, a defeated thing.

Seemingly the only man with a definite purpose in that whirlpool of terror-stricken men and women, the newspaperman settled down to the serious business of battling his way through the swarming street.

"Before I go to the crux of the matter," said Dr. Silas White, about half an hour later, "let us first review what we know of this so-called Horror. Suppose you tell me exactly what you know of it."

Henry Woods shifted uneasily in his chair. Why didn't the old fool get down to business? The chief would raise hell if this story didn't make the regular edition. He stole a glance at his wrist-watch. There was still almost an hour left. Maybe he could manage it. If the old chap would only snap into it!

"I know no more," he said, "than is common knowledge."

The gimlet eyes of the old white-haired scientist regarded the newspaperman sharply.

"And that is?" he questioned.

There was no way out of it, thought Henry. He'd have to humor the old fellow.

"The Horror," he replied, "appeared on Earth, so far as the knowledge of man is concerned, about six months ago."

Dr. White nodded approvingly.

"You state the facts very aptly," he said.

"How so?"

"When you say 'so far as the knowledge of man is concerned.'"

"Why is that?"

"You will understand in due time. Please proceed."

Vaguely the newspaperman wondered whether he was interviewing the scientist or the scientist interviewing him.

"They were first reported," Woods said, "early this spring. At that time they wiped out a small village in the province of Quebec. All the inhabitants, except a few fugitives, were found dead, killed mysteriously and half eaten, as if by wild beasts. The fugitives were demented, babbling of black shapes that swept down out of the dark forest upon the little town in the small hours of the morning.

"The next that was heard of them was about a week later, when they struck in an isolated rural district in Poland, killing and feeding on the population of several farms. In the next week more villages were wiped out, in practically every country on the face of the Earth. From the hinterlands came tales of murder done at midnight, of men and women horribly mangled, of livestock slaughtered, of buildings crushed as if by some titanic force.

"At first they worked only at night and then, seeming to become bolder and more numerous, attacked in broad daylight."

The newspaperman paused.

"Is that what you want?" he asked.

"That's part of it," replied Dr. White, "but that's not all. What do these Horrors look like?"

"That's more difficult," said Henry. "They have been reported as every conceivable sort of monstrosity. Some are large and others are small. Some take the form of animals, others of birds and reptiles, and some are cast in appalling shapes such as might be snatched out of the horrid imagery of a thing which resided in a world entirely alien to our own."

Dr. White rose from his chair and strode across the room to confront the other.

"Young man," he asked, "do you think it possible the Horror might have come out of a world entirely alien to our own?"

"I don't know," replied Henry. "I know that some of the scientists believe they came from some other planet, perhaps even from some other solar system. I know they are like nothing ever known before on Earth. They are always inky black, something like black tar, you know, sort of sticky-looking, a disgusting sight. The weapons of mankind can't affect them. Explosives are useless and so are projectiles. They wade through poison gas and fiery chemicals and seem to enjoy them. Elaborate electrical barriers have failed. Heat doesn't make them turn a hair."

"And you think they came from some other planet, perhaps some other solar system?"

"I don't know what to think," said Henry. "If they came out of space they must have come in some conveyance, and that would certainly have been sighted, picked up long before it arrived, by our astronomers. If they came in small conveyances, there must have been many of them. If they came in a single conveyance, it would be too large to escape detection. That is, unless —"

"Unless what?" snapped the scientist.

"Unless it traveled at the speed of light. Then it would have been invisible."

"Not only invisible," snorted the old man, "but non-existent."

A question was on the tip of the newspaperman's tongue, but before it could be asked the old man was speaking again, asking a question:

"Can you imagine a fourth dimension?"

"No, I can't," said Henry.

"Can you imagine a thing of only two dimensions?"

"Vaguely, yes."

The scientist smote his palms together.

"Now we're coming to it!" he exclaimed.

Henry Woods regarded the other narrowly. The old man must be turned. What did fourth and second dimensions have to do with the Horror?

"Do you know anything about evolution?" questioned the old man.

"I have a slight understanding of it. It is the process of upward growth, the stairs by which simple organisms climb to become more complex organisms."

Dr. White grunted and asked still another question:

"Do you know anything about the theory of the exploding universe? Have you ever noted the tendency of the perfectly balanced to run amuck?"

The reporter rose slowly to his feet.

"Dr. White," he said, "you phoned my paper you had a story for us. I came here to get it, but all you have done is ask me questions. If you can't tell me what you want us to publish, I will say good-day."

The doctor put forth a hand that shook slightly.

"Sit down, young man," he said. "I don't blame you for being impatient, but I will now come to my point."

The newspaperman sat down again.

"I have developed a hypothesis," said Dr. White, "and have conducted several experiments which seem to bear it out. I am staking my reputation upon the supposition that it is correct. Not only that, but I am also staking the lives of several brave men who believe implicitly in me and my theory. After all, I suppose it makes little difference, for if I fail the world is doomed, if I succeed it is saved from complete destruction.

"Have you ever thought that our evolutionists might be wrong, that evolution might be downward instead of upward? The theory of the exploding universe, the belief that all of creation is running down, being thrown off balance by the loss of energy, spurred onward by cosmic accidents which tend to disturb its equilibrium, to a time when it will run wild and space will be filled with swirling dust of disintegrated worlds, would bear out this contention.

"This does not apply to the human race. There is no question that our evolution is upward, that we have arisen from one-celled creatures wallowing in the slime of primal seas. Our case is probably paralleled by thousands of other intelligences on far-flung planets and island universes. These instances, however, running at cross purposes to the general evolutional trend of the entire cosmos, are mere flashes in the eventual course of cosmic evolution, comparing no more to eternity than a split second does to a million years.

"Taking these instances, then, as inconsequential, let us say that the trend of cosmic evolution is downward rather than upward, from complex units to simpler units rather than from simple units to more complex ones.

"Let us say that life and intelligence have degenerated. How would you say such a degeneration would take place? In just what way would it be manifested? What sort of transition would life pass through in passing from one stage to a lower one? Just what would be the nature of these stages?"

The scientist's eyes glowed brightly as he bent forward in his chair. The newspaperman said simply: "I have no idea."

"Man," cried the old man, "can't you see that it would be a matter of dimensions? From the fourth dimension to the third, from the third to the second, from the second to the first, from the first to a questionable existence or plane which is beyond our understanding or perhaps to oblivion and the end of life. Might not the fourth have evolved from a fifth, the fifth from a sixth, the sixth from a seventh, and so on to no one knows what multidimension?"

Dr. White paused to allow the other man to grasp the importance of his statements. Woods failed lamentably to do so.

"But what has this to do with the Horror?" he asked.

"Have you absolutely no imagination?" shouted the old man.

"Why, I suppose I have, but I seem to fail to understand."

"We are facing an invasion of fourth-dimensional creatures," the old man whispered, almost as if fearful to speak the words aloud. "We are being attacked by life which is one dimension above us in evolution. We are fighting, I tell you, a tribe of hellhounds out of the cosmos. They are unthinkably above us in the matter of intelligence. There is a chasm of knowledge between us so wide and so deep that it staggers the imagination. They regard us as mere animals, perhaps not even that. So far as they are concerned we are just fodder, something to be eaten as we eat vegetables and cereals or the flesh of domesticated animals. Perhaps they have watched us for years, watching life on the world increase, lapping their monstrous jowls over the fattening of the Earth. They have awaited the proper setting of the banquet table and now they are dining.

"Their thoughts are not our thoughts, their ideals not our ideals. Perhaps they have nothing in common with us except the primal basis of all life, self-preservation, the necessity of feeding.

"Maybe they have come of their own will. I prefer to believe that they have. Perhaps they are merely following the natural course of events, obeying some immutable law legislated by some higher being who watches over the cosmos and dictates what shall be and what shall not be. If this is true it means that there has been a flaw in my reasoning, for I believed that the life of each plane degenerated in company with the degeneration of its plane of existence, which would obey the same evolutional laws which govern the life upon it. I am quite satisfied that this invasion is a well-planned campaign, that some fourth-dimensional race has found a means of breaking through the veil of force which separates its plane from ours."

"But," pointed out Henry Woods, "you say they are fourth-dimensional things. I can't see anything about them to suggest an additional dimension. They are plainly three-dimensional."

"Of course they are three-dimensional. They would have to be to live in this world of three dimensions. The only two-dimensional objects which we know of in this world are merely illusions, projections of the third dimension, like a shadow. It is impossible for more than one dimension to live on any single plane.

"To attack us they would have to lose one dimension. This they have evidently done. You can see how utterly ridiculous it would be for you to try to attack a two-dimensional thing. So far as you were concerned it would have no mass. The same is true of the other dimensions. Similarly a being of a lesser plane could not harm an inhabitant of a higher plane. It is apparent that while the Horror has lost one material dimension, it has retained certain fourth-dimensional properties which make it invulnerable to the forces at the command of our plane."

The newspaperman was now sitting on the edge of his chair.

"But," he asked breathlessly, "it all sounds so hopeless. What can be done about it?"

Dr. White hitched his chair closer and his fingers closed with a fierce grasp upon the other's knee. A militant boom came into his voice.

"My boy," he said, "we are to strike back. We are going to invade the fourth-dimensional plane of these hellhounds. We are going to make them feel our strength. We are going to strike back."

Henry Woods sprang to his feet.

"How?" he shouted. "Have you...?"

Dr. White nodded.

"I have found a way to send the third-dimensional into the fourth. Come and I will show you."

The machine was huge, but it had an appearance of simple construction. A large rectangular block of what appeared to be a strange black metal was set on end and flanked on each side by two smaller ones. On the top of the large block was set a half-globe of a strange substance, somewhat, Henry thought, like frosted glass. On one side of the large cube was set a lever, a long glass panel, two vertical tubes and three clock-face indicators. The control board, it appeared, was relatively simple.

Beside the mass of the five rectangles, on the floor, was a large plate of transparent substance, ground to a concave surface, through which one could see an intricate tangle of wire mesh.

Hanging from the ceiling, directly above the one on the floor, was another concave disk, but this one had a far more pronounced curvature.

Wires connected the two disks and each in turn was connected to the rectangular machine.

"It is a matter of the proper utilization of two forces, electrical and gravitational," proudly explained Dr. White. "Those two forces, properly used, warp the third-dimensional into the fourth. A reverse process is used to return the object to the third. The principle of the machine is —"

The old man was about to launch into a lengthy discussion, but Henry interrupted him. A glance at his watch had shown him press time was drawing perilously close.

"Just a second," he said. "You propose to warp a third-dimensional being into a fourth dimension. How can a third-dimensional thing exist there? You said a short time ago that only a specified dimension could exist on one single plane."

"You have missed my point," snapped Dr. White. "I am not sending a third-dimensional thing to a fourth dimension. I am changing the third-dimensional being into a fourth-dimensional being. I add a dimension, and automatically the being exists on a different plane. I am reversing evolution. This third dimension we now exist on evolved, millions of eons ago, from a fourth dimension. I am sending a lesser entity back over those millions of eons to a plane similar to one upon which his ancestors lived inconceivably long ago."

"But, man, how do you know you can do it?"

The doctor's eyes gleamed and his fingers reached out to press a bell.

A servant appeared almost at once.

"Bring me a dog," snapped the old man. The servant disappeared.

"Young man," said Dr. White, "I am going to show you how I know I can do it. I have done it before, now I am going to do it for you. I have sent dogs and cats back to the fourth dimension and returned them safely to this room. I can do the same with men."

The servant reappeared, carrying in his arms a small dog. The doctor stepped to the control board of his strange machine.

"All right, George," he said.

The servant had evidently worked with the old man enough to know what was expected of him. He stepped close to the floor disk and waited. The dog whined softly, sensing that all was not exactly right.

The old scientist slowly shoved the lever toward the right, and as he did so a faint hum filled the room, rising to a stupendous roar as he advanced the lever. From both floor disk and upper disk leaped strange cones of blue light, which met midway to form an hour-glass shape of brilliance.

The light did not waver or sparkle. It did not glow. It seemed hard and brittle, like straight bars of force. The newspaperman, gazing with awe upon it, felt that terrific force was there. What had the old man said? Warp a third-dimensional being into another dimension! That would take force!

As he watched, petrified by the spectacle, the servant stepped forward and, with a flip, tossed the little dog into the blue light. The animal could be discerned for a moment through the light and then it disappeared.

"Look in the globe!" shouted the old man; and Henry jerked his eyes from the column of light to the half-globe atop the machine.

He gasped. In the globe, deep within its milky center, glowed a picture that made his brain reel as he looked upon it. It was a scene such as no man could have imagined unaided. It was a horribly distorted projection of an eccentric landscape, a landscape hardly analogous to anything on Earth.

"That's the fourth dimension, sir," said the servant.

"That's not the fourth dimension," the old man corrected him. "That's a third-dimensional impression of the fourth dimension. It is no more the fourth dimension than a shadow is three-dimensional. It, like a shadow, is merely a projection. It gives us a glimpse of what the fourth plane is like. It is a shadow of that plane."

Slowly a dark blotch began to grow in the landscape. Slowly it assumed definite form. It puzzled the reporter. It looked familiar. He could have sworn he had seen it somewhere before. It was alive, for it had moved.

"That, sir, is the dog," George volunteered.

"That was the dog," Dr. White again corrected him. "God knows what it is now."

He turned to the newspaperman.

"Have you seen enough?" he demanded.

Henry nodded.

The other slowly began to return the lever to its original position. The roaring subsided, the light faded, the projection in the half-globe grew fainter.

"How are you going to use it?" asked the newspaperman.

"I have ninety-eight men who have agreed to be projected into the fourth dimension to seek out the entities that are attacking us and attack them in turn. I shall send them out in an hour."

"Where is there a phone?" asked the newspaperman.

"In the next room," replied Dr. White.

As the reporter dashed out of the door, the light faded entirely from between the two disks and on the lower one a little dog crouched, quivering, softly whimpering.

The old man stepped from the controls and approached the disk. He scooped the little animal from where it lay into his arms and patted the silky head.

"Good dog," he murmured; and the creature snuggled close to him, comforted, already forgetting that horrible place from which it had just returned.

"Is everything ready, George?" asked the old man.

"Yes, sir," replied the servant. "The men are all ready, even anxious to go. If you ask me, sir, they are a tough lot."

"They are as brave a group of men as ever graced the Earth," replied the scientist gently. "They are adventurers, every one of whom has faced danger and will not shrink from it. They are born fighters. My one regret is that I have not been able to secure more like them. A thousand men such as they should be able to conquer any opponent. It was impossible. The others were poor soft fools. They laughed in my face. They thought I was an old fool —I, the man who alone stands between them and utter destruction."

His voice had risen to almost a scream, but it again sank to a normal tone.

"I may be sending ninety-eight brave men to instant death. I hope not."

"You can always jerk them back, sir," suggested George.

"Maybe I can, maybe not," murmured the old man.

Henry Woods appeared in the doorway.

"When do we start?" he asked.

"We?" exclaimed the scientist.

"Certainly, you don't believe you're going to leave me out of this. Why, man, it's the greatest story of all time. I'm going as special war correspondent."

"They believed it? They are going to publish it?" cried the old man, clutching at the newspaperman's sleeve.

"Well, the editor was skeptical at first, but after I swore on all sorts of oaths it was true, he ate it up. Maybe you think that story didn't stop the presses!"

"I didn't expect them to. I just took a chance. I thought they, too, would laugh at me."

"But when do we start?" persisted Henry.

"You are really in earnest? You really want to go?" asked the old man, unbelievingly.

"I am going. Try to stop me."

Dr. White glanced at his watch.

"We will start in exactly thirty-four minutes," he said.

"Ten seconds to go." George, standing with watch in hand, spoke in a precise manner, the very crispness of his words betraying the excitement under which he labored.

The blue light, hissing, drove from disk to disk; the room thundered with the roar of the machine, before which stood Dr. White, his hand on the lever, his eyes glued on the instruments before him.

In a line stood the men who were to fling themselves into the light to be warped into another dimension, there to seek out and fight an unknown enemy. The line was headed by a tall man with hands like hams, with a weather-beaten face and a wild mop of hair. Behind him stood a belligerent little cockney. Henry Woods stood fifth in line. They were a motley lot, adventurers every one of them, and some were obviously afraid as they stood before that column of light, with only a few seconds of the third dimension left to them. They had answered a weird advertisement, and had but a limited idea of what they were about to do. Grimly, though, they accepted it as a job, a bizarre job, but a job. They faced it as they had faced other equally dangerous, but less unusual, jobs.

"Five seconds," snapped George.

The lever was all the way over now. The half-globe showed, within its milky interior, a hideously distorted landscape. The light had taken on a hard, brittle appearance and its hiss had risen to a scream. The machine thundered steadily with a suggestion of horrible power.

"Time up!"

The tall man stepped forward. His foot reached the disk; another step and he was bathed in the light, a third and he glimmered momentarily, then vanished. Close on his heels followed the little cockney.

With his nerves at almost a snapping point, Henry moved on behind the fourth man. He was horribly afraid, he wanted to break from the line and run, it didn't matter where, any place to get away from that steady, steely light in front of him. He had seen three men step into it, glow for a second, and then disappear. A fourth man had placed his foot on the disk.

Cold sweat stood out on his brow. Like an automaton he placed one foot on the disk. The fourth man had already disappeared.

"Snap into it, pal," growled the man behind.

Henry lifted the other foot, caught his toe on the edge of the disk and stumbled headlong into the column of light.

He was conscious of intense heat which was instantly followed by equally intense cold. For a moment his body seemed to be under enormous pressure, then it seemed to be expanding, flying apart, bursting, exploding....

* * * * *

He felt solid ground under his feet, and his eyes, snapping open, saw an alien land. It was a land of somber color, with great gray moors, and beetling black cliffs. There was something queer about it, an intangible quality that baffled him.

He looked about him, expecting to see his companions. He saw no one. He was absolutely alone in that desolate brooding land. Something dreadful had happened! Was he the only one to be safely transported from the third dimension? Had some horrible accident occurred? Was he alone?

Sudden panic seized him. If something had happened, if the others were not here, might it not be possible that the machine would not be able to bring him back to his own dimension? Was he doomed to remain marooned forever in this terrible plane?

He looked down at his body and gasped in dismay. It was not his body!

It was a grotesque caricature of a body, a horrible profane mass of flesh, like a phantasmagoric beast snatched from the dreams of a lunatic.

It was real, however. He felt it with his hands, but they were not hands. They were something like hands; they served the same purpose that hands served in the third dimension. He was, he realized, a being of the fourth dimension, but in his fourth-dimensional brain still clung hard-fighting remnants of that faithful old third-dimensional brain. He could not, as yet, see with fourth-dimensional eyes, think purely fourth-dimensional thoughts. He had not oriented himself as yet to this new plane of existence. He was seeing the fourth dimension through the blurred lenses of millions of eons of third-dimensional existence. He was seeing it much more clearly than he had seen it in the half-globe atop the machine in Dr. White's laboratory, but he would not see it clearly until every vestige of the third dimension was wiped from him. That, he knew, would come in time.

He felt his weird body with those things that served as hands, and he found, beneath his groping, unearthly fingers, great rolling muscles, powerful tendons, and hard, well-conditioned flesh. A sense of well-being surged through him and he growled like an animal, like an animal of that horrible fourth plane.

But the terrible sounds that came from between his slobbering lips were not those of his own voice, they were the voices of many men.

Then he knew. He was not alone. Here, in this one body were the bodies, the brains, the power, the spirit, of those other ninety-eight men. In the fourth dimension, all the millions of third-dimensional things were one. Perhaps that particular portion of the third dimension called the Earth had sprung from, or degenerated from, one single unit of a dissolving, worn-out fourth dimension. The third dimension, warped back to a higher plane, was automatically obeying the mystic laws of evolution by reforming in the shape of that old ancestor, unimaginably removed in time from the race he had begot. He was no longer Henry Woods, newspaperman; he was an entity that had given birth, in the dim ages when the Earth was born, to a third dimension. Nor was he alone. This body of his was composed of other sons of that ancient entity.

He felt himself grow, felt his body grow vaster, assume greater proportions, felt new vitality flow through him. It was the other men, the men who were flinging themselves into the column of light in the laboratory to be warped back to this plane, to be incorporated in his body.

It was not his body, however. His brain was not his alone. The pronoun, he realized, represented the sum total of those other men, his fellow adventurers.

Suddenly a new feeling came, a feeling of completeness, a feeling of supreme fitness. He knew that the last of the ninety-eight men had stepped across the disk, that all were here in this giant body.

Now he could see more clearly. Things in the landscape, which had escaped him before, became recognizable. Awful thoughts ran through his brain, heavy, ponderous, black thoughts. He began to recognize the landscape as something familiar, something he had seen before, a thing with which he was intimate. Phenomena, which his third-dimensional intelligence would have gasped at, became commonplace. He was finally seeing through fourth-dimensional eyes, thinking fourth-dimensional thoughts.

Memory seeped into his brain and he had fleeting visions, visions of dark caverns lit by hellish flames, of huge seas that battered remorselessly with mile-high waves against towering headlands that reared titanic toward a glowering sky. He remembered a red desert scattered with scarlet boulders, he remembered silver cliffs of gleaming metallic stone. Through all his thoughts ran something else, a scarlet thread of hate, an all-consuming passion, a fierce lust after the life of some other entity.

He was no longer a composite thing built of third-dimensional beings. He was a creature of another plane, a creature with a consuming hate, and suddenly he knew against whom this hate was directed and why. He knew also that this creature was near and his great fists closed and then spread wide as he knew it. How did he know it? Perhaps through some sense which he, as a being of another plane, held, but which was alien to the Earth. Later, he asked himself this question. At the time, however, there was no questioning on his part. He only knew that somewhere near was a hated enemy and he did not question the source of his knowledge....

Mumbling in an idiom incomprehensible to a third-dimensional being, filled with rage that wove redly through his brain, he lumbered down the hill onto the moor, his great strides eating up the distance, his footsteps shaking the ground.

At the foot of the hill he halted and from his throat issued a challenging roar that made the very crags surrounding the moor tremble. The rocks flung back the roar as if in mockery.

Again he shouted and in the shout he framed a lurid insult to the enemy that lurked there in the cliffs.

Again the crags flung back the insult, but this time the echoes, booming over the moor, were drowned by another voice, the voice of the enemy.

At the far end of the moor appeared a gigantic form, a form that shambled on grotesque, misshapen feet, growling angrily as he came.

He came rapidly despite his clumsy gait, and as he came he mouthed terrific threats.

Close to the other he halted and only then did recognition dawn in his eyes.

"You, Mal Shaff?" he growled in his guttural tongue, and surprise and consternation were written large upon his ugly face.

"Yes, it is I, Mal Shaff," boomed the other. "Remember, Ouglat, the day you destroyed me and my plane. I have returned to wreak my vengeance. I have solved a mystery you have never guessed and I have come back. You did not imagine you were attacking me again when you sent your minions to that other plane to feed upon the beings there. It was I you were attacking, fool, and I am here to kill you."

Ouglat leaped and the thing that had been Henry Woods, newspaperman, and ninety-eight other men, but was now Mal Shaff of the fourth dimension, leaped to meet him.

Mal Shaff felt the force of Ouglat, felt the sharp pain of a hammering fist, and lashed out with those horrible arms of his to smash at the leering face of his antagonist. He felt his fists strike solid flesh, felt the bones creak and tremble beneath his blow.

His nostrils were filled with the terrible stench of the other's foul breath and his filthy body. He teetered on his gnarled legs and side-stepped a vicious kick and then stepped in to gouge with straightened thumb at the other's eye. The thumb went true and Ouglat howled in pain.

Mal Shaff leaped back as his opponent charged head down, and his knotted fist beat a thunderous tattoo as the misshapen beast closed in. He felt clawing fingers seeking his throat, felt ghastly nails ripping at his shoulders. In desperation he struck blindly, and Ouglat reeled away. With a quick stride he shortened the distance between them and struck Ouglat a hard blow squarely on his slavering mouth. Pressing hard upon the reeling figure, he swung his fists like sledge-hammers, and Ouglat stumbled, falling in a heap on the sand.

Mal Shaff leaped upon the fallen foe and kicked him with his taloned feet, ripping him wickedly. There was no thought of fair play, no faintest glimmer of mercy. This was a battle to the death: there could be no quarter.

The fallen monster howled, but his voice cut short as his foul mouth, with its razor-edged fangs, closed on the other's body. His talons, seeking a hold, clawed deep.

Mal Shaff, his brain a screaming maelstrom of weird emotions, aimed pile-driver blows at the enemy, clawed and ripped. Together the two rolled, locked tight in titanic battle, on the sandy plain and a great cloud of heavy dust marked where they struggled.

In desperation Ouglat put every ounce of his strength into a heave that broke the other's grip and flung him away.

The two monstrosities surged to their feet, their eyes red with hate, glaring through the dust cloud at one another.

Slowly Ouglat's hand stole to a black, wicked cylinder that hung on a belt at his waist. His fingers closed upon it and he drew the weapon. As he leveled it at Mal Shaff, his lips curled back and his features distorted into something that was not pleasant to see.

Mal Shaff, with doubled fists, saw the great thumb of his enemy slowly depressing a button on the cylinder, and a great fear held him rooted in his tracks. In the back of his brain something was vainly trying to explain to him the horror of this thing which the other held.

Then a multicolored spiral, like a corkscrew column of vapor, sprang from the cylinder and flashed toward him. It struck him full on the chest and even as it did so he caught the ugly fire of triumph in the red eyes of his enemy.

He felt a stinging sensation where the spiral struck, but that was all. He was astounded. He had feared this weapon, had been sure it portended some form of horrible death. But all it did was to produce a slight sting.

For a split second he stood stock-still, then he surged forward and advanced upon Ouglat, his hands outspread like claws. From his throat came those horrible sounds, the speech of the fourth dimension.

"Did I not tell you, foul son of Sargouthe, that I had solved a mystery you have never guessed at? Although you destroyed me long ago, I have returned. Throw away your puny weapon. I am of the lower dimension and am invulnerable to your engines of destruction. You bloated...." His words trailed off into a stream of vileness that could never have occurred to a third-dimensional mind.

Ouglat, with every line of his face distorted with fear, flung the weapon from him, and turning, fled clumsily down the moor, with Mal Shaff at his heels.

Steadily Mal Shaff gained and with only a few feet separating him from Ouglat, he dived with outspread arms at the other's legs.

The two came down together, but Mal Shaff's grip was broken by the fall and the two regained their feet at almost the same instant.

The wild moor resounded to their throaty roaring and the high cliffs flung back the echoes of the bellowing of the two gladiators below. It was sheer strength now and flesh and bone were bruised and broken under the life-shaking blows that they dealt. Great furrows were plowed in the sand by the sliding of heavy feet as the two fighters shifted to or away from attack. Blood, blood of fourth-dimensional creatures, covered the bodies of the two and stained the sand with its horrible hue. Perspiration streamed from them and their breath came in gulping gasps.

The lurid sun slid across the purple sky and still the two fought on. Ouglat, one of the ancients, and Mal Shaff, reincarnated. It was a battle of giants, a battle that must have beggared even the titanic tilting of forgotten gods and entities in the ages when the third-dimensional Earth was young.

Mal Shaff had no conception of time. He may have fought seconds or hours. It seemed an eternity. He had attempted to fight scientifically, but had failed to do so. While one part of him had cried out to elude his opponent, to wait for openings, to conserve his strength, another part had shouted at him to step in and smash, smash, smash at the hated monstrosity pitted against him.

It seemed Ouglat was growing in size, had become more agile, that his strength was greater. His punches hurt more; it was harder to hit him.

Still Mal Shaff drilled in determinedly, head down, fists working like pistons. As the other seemed to grow stronger and larger, he seemed to become smaller and weaker.

It was queer. Ouglat should be tired, too. His punches should be weaker. He should move more slowly, be heavier on his feet.

There was no doubt of it. Ouglat was growing larger, was drawing on some mysterious reserve of strength. From somewhere new force and life were flowing into his body. But from where was this strength coming?

A huge fist smashed against Mal Shaff's jaw. He felt himself lifted, and the next moment he skidded across the sand.

Lying there, gasping for breath, almost too fagged to rise, with the black bulk of the enemy looming through the dust cloud before him, he suddenly realized the source of the other's renewed strength.

Ouglat was recalling his minions from the third dimension! They were incorporating in his body, returning to their parent body!

They were coming back from the third dimension to the fourth dimension to fight a third-dimensional thing reincarnated in the fourth-dimensional form it had lost millions of eons ago!

This was the end, thought Mal Shaff. But he staggered to his feet to meet the charge of the ancient enemy and a grim song, a death chant immeasurably old, suddenly and dimly remembered from out of the mists of countless millenniums, was on his lips as he swung a pile-driver blow into the suddenly astonished face of the rushing Ouglat....

* * * * *

The milky globe atop the machine in Dr. White's laboratory glowed softly, and within that glow two figures seemed to struggle.

Before the machine, his hands still on the controls, stood Dr. Silas White. Behind him the room was crowded with newspapermen and photographers.

Hours had passed since the ninety-eight men-ninety-nine, counting Henry Woods-had stepped into the brittle column of light to be shunted back through unguessed time to a different plane of existence. The old scientist, during all those hours, had stood like a graven image before his machine, eyes staring fixedly at the globe.

Through the open windows he had heard the cry of the newsboy as the *Press* put the greatest scoop of all time on the street. The phone had rung like mad and George answered it. The doorbell buzzed repeatedly and George ushered in newspapermen who had asked innumerable questions, to which he had replied briefly, almost mechanically. The reporters had fought for the use of the one phone in the house and had finally drawn lots for it. A few had raced out to use other phones.

Photographers came and flashes popped and cameras clicked. The room was in an uproar. On the rare occasions when the reporters were not using the phone the instrument buzzed shrilly. Authoritative voices demanded Dr. Silas White. George, his eyes on the old man, stated that Dr. Silas White could not be disturbed, that he was busy.

From the street below came the heavy-throated hum of thousands of voices. The street was packed with a jostling crowd of awed humanity, every eye fastened on the house of Dr. Silas White. Lines of police held them back.

"What makes them move so slowly?" asked a reporter, staring at the globe. "They hardly seem to be moving. It looks like a slow motion picture."

"They are not moving slowly," replied Dr. White. "There must be a difference in time in the fourth dimension. Maybe what is hours to us is only seconds to them. Time must flow more slowly there. Perhaps it is a bigger place than this third plane. That may account for it. They aren't moving slowly, they are fighting savagely. It's a fight to the death! Watch!"

The grotesque arm of one of the figures in the milky globe was moving out slowly, loafing along, aimed at the head of the other. Slowly the other twisted his body aside, but too slowly. The fist finally touched the head, still moving slowly forward, the body following as slowly. The head of the creature twisted, bent backward, and the body toppled back in a leisurely manner.

"What does White say?...Can't you get a statement of some sort from him? Won't he talk at all? A hell of a fine reporter you are-can't even get a man to open his mouth. Ask him about Henry Woods. Get a human-interest slant on Woods walking into the light. Ask him how long this is going to last. Damn it all, man, do something, and don't bother me again until you have a real story-yes, I said a real story-are you hard of hearing? For God's sake, do something!"

The editor slammed the receiver on the hook.

"Brooks," he snapped, "get the War Department at Washington. Ask them if they're going to back up White. Go on, go on. Get busy.... How will you get them? I don't know. Just get them, that's all. Get them!"

Typewriters gibbered like chuckling morons through the roaring tumult of the editorial rooms. Copy boys rushed about, white sheets clutched in their grimy hands. Telephones jangled and strident voices blared through the haze that arose from the pipes and cigarettes of perspiring writers who feverishly transferred to paper the startling events that were rocking the world.

The editor, his necktie off, his shirt open, his sleeves rolled to the elbow, drummed his fingers on the desk. It had been a hectic twenty-four hours and he had stayed at the desk every minute of the time. He was dead tired. When the moment of relaxation came, when the tension snapped, he knew he would fall into an exhausted stupor of sleep, but the excitement was keeping him on his feet. There was work to do. There was news such as the world had never known before. Each new story meant a new front make-up, another extra. Even now the presses were thundering, even now papers with the ink hardly dry upon them were being snatched by the avid public from the hands of screaming newsboys.

A man raced toward the city desk, waving a sheet of paper in his hand. Sensing something unusual the others in the room crowded about as he laid the sheet before the editor.

"Just came in," the man gasped.

The paper was a wire dispatch. It read:

> "Rome-The Black Horror is in full retreat. Although still apparently immune to the weapons being used against it, it is lifting the siege of this city. The cause is unknown."

The editor ran his eye down the sheet. There was another dateline:

> "Madrid-The Black Horror, which has enclosed this city in a ring of dark terror for the last two days, is fleeing, rapidly disappearing...."

The editor pressed a button. There was an answering buzz.

"Composing room," he shouted, "get ready for a new front! Yes, another extra. This will knock their eyes out!"

A telephone jangled furiously. The editor seized it.

"Yes. What was that?... White says he must have help. I see. Woods and the others are weakening. Being badly beaten, eh?... More men needed to go out to the other plane. Wants reinforcements. Yes. I see. Well, tell him that he'll have them. If he can wait half an hour we'll have them walking by thousands into that light. I'll be damned if we won't! Just tell White to hang on! We'll have the whole nation coming to the rescue!"

He jabbed up the receiver.

"Richards," he said, "write a streamer, 'Help Needed,' 'Reinforcements Called' —something of that sort, you know. Make it scream. Tell the foreman to dig out the biggest type he has. A foot high. If we ever needed big type, we need it now!"

He turned to the telephone.

"Operator," he said, "get me the Secretary of War at Washington. The secretary in person, you understand. No one else will do."

He turned again to the reporters who stood about the desk.

"In two hours," he explained, banging the desk top for emphasis, "we'll have the United States Army marching into that light Woods walked into!"

* * * * *

The bloody sun was touching the edge of the weird world, seeming to hesitate before taking the final plunge behind the towering black crags that hung above the ink-pot shadows at their base. The purple sky had darkened until it was almost the color of soft, black velvet. Great stars were blazing out.

Ouglat loomed large in the gathering twilight, a horrible misshapen ogre of an outer world. He had grown taller, broader, greater. Mal Shaff's head now was on a level with the other's chest; his huge arms seemed toylike in comparison with those of Ouglat, his legs mere pipestems.

Time and time again he had barely escaped as the clutching hands of Ouglat reached out to grasp him. Once within those hands he would be torn apart.

The battle had become a game of hide and seek, a game of cat and mouse, with Mal Shaff the mouse.

Slowly the sun sank and the world became darker. His brain working feverishly, Mal Shaff waited for the darkness. Adroitly he worked the battle nearer and nearer to the Stygian darkness that lay at the foot of the mighty crags. In the darkness he might escape. He could no longer continue this unequal fight. Only escape was left.

The sun was gone now. Blackness was dropping swiftly over the land, like a great blanket, creating the illusion of the glowering sky descending to the ground. Only a few feet away lay the total blackness under the cliffs.

Like a flash Mal Shaff darted into the blackness, was completely swallowed in it. Roaring, Ouglat followed.

His shoulders almost touching the great rock wall that shot straight up hundreds of feet above him, Mal Shaff ran swiftly, fear lending speed to his shivering legs. Behind him he heard the bellowing of his enemy. Ouglat was searching for him, a hopeless search in that total darkness. He would never find him. Mal Shaff felt sure.

Fagged and out of breath, he dropped panting at the foot of the wall. Blood pounded through his head and his strength seemed to be gone. He lay still and stared out into the less dark moor that stretched before him.

For some time he lay there, resting. Aimlessly he looked out over the moor, and then he suddenly noted, some distance to his right, a hill rising from the moor. The hill was vaguely familiar. He remembered it dimly as being of great importance.

A sudden inexplicable restlessness filled him. Far behind him he heard the enraged bellowing of Ouglat, but that he scarcely noticed. So long as darkness lay upon the land he knew he was safe from his enemy.

The hill had made him restless. He must reach the top. He could think of no logical reason for doing so. Obviously he was safer here at the base of the cliff, but a voice seemed to be calling, a friendly voice from the hilltop.

He rose on aching legs and forged ahead. Every fiber of his being cried out in protest, but resolutely he placed one foot ahead of the other, walking mechanically.

Opposite the hill he disregarded the strange call that pulsed down upon him, long enough to rest his tortured body. He must build up his strength for the climb.

He realized that danger lay ahead. Once he quitted the blackness of the cliff's base, Ouglat, even in the darkness that lay over the land, might see him. That would be disastrous. Once over the top of the hill he would be safe.

Suddenly the landscape was bathed in light, a soft green radiance. One moment it had been pitch dark, the next it was light, as if a giant search-light had been snapped on.

In terror, Mal Shaff looked for the source of the light. Just above the horizon hung a great green orb, which moved up the ladder of the sky even as he watched.

A moon! A huge green satellite hurtling swiftly around this cursed world!

A great, overwhelming fear sat upon Mal Shaff and with a high, shrill scream of anger he raced forward, forgetful of aching body and outraged lungs.

His scream was answered from far off, and out of the shadows of the cliffs toward the far end of the moor a black figure hurled itself. Ouglat was on the trail!

Mal Shaff tore madly up the slope, topped the crest, and threw himself flat on the ground, almost exhausted.

A queer feeling stole over him, a queer feeling of well-being. New strength was flowing into him, the old thrill of battle was pounding through his blood once more.

Not only were queer things happening to his body, but also to his brain. The world about him looked queer, held a sort of an intangible mystery he could not understand. A half question formed in the back of his brain. Who and what was he? Queer thoughts to be thinking! He was Mal Shaff, but had he always been Mal Shaff?

He remembered a brittle column of light, creatures with bodies unlike his body, walking into it. He had been one of those creatures. There was something about dimensions, about different planes, a plan for one plane to attack another!

He scrambled to his bowed legs and beat his great chest with mighty, long-nailed hands. He flung back his head and from his throat broke a sound to curdle the blood of even the bravest.

On the moor below Ouglat heard the cry and answered it with one equally ferocious.

Mal Shaff took a step forward, then stopped stock-still. Through his brain went a sharp command to return to the spot where he had stood, to wait there until attacked. He stepped back, shifting his feet impatiently.

He was growing larger; every second fresh vitality was pouring into him. Before his eyes danced a red curtain of hate and his tongue roared forth a series of insulting challenges to the figure that was even now approaching the foot of the hill.

As Ouglat climbed the hill, the night became an insane bedlam. The challenging roars beat like surf against the black cliffs.

Ouglat's lips were flecked with foam, his red eyes were mere slits, his mouth worked convulsively.

They were only a few feet apart when Ouglat charged.

Mal Shaff was ready for him. There was no longer any difference in their size and they met like the two forward walls of contending football teams.

Mal Shaff felt the soft throat of the other under his fingers and his grip tightened. Maddened, Ouglat shot terrific blow after terrific blow into Mal Shaff's body.

Try as he might, however, he could not shake the other's grip.

It was silent now. The night seemed brooding, watching the struggle on the hilltop.

Larger and larger grew Mal Shaff, until he overtopped Ouglat like a giant.

Then he loosened his grip and, as Ouglat tried to scuttle away, reached down to grasp him by the nape of his neck.

High above his head he lifted his enemy and dashed him to the ground. With a leap he was on the prostrate figure, trampling it apart, smashing it into the ground. With wild cries he stamped the earth, treading out the last of Ouglat, the Black Horror.

When no trace of the thing that had been Ouglat remained, he moved away and viewed the trampled ground.

Then, for the first time he noticed that the crest of the hill was crowded with other monstrous figures. He glared at them, half in surprise, half in anger. He had not noticed their silent approach.

"It is Mal Shaff!" cried one.

"Yes, I am Mal Shaff. What do you want?"

"But, Mal Shaff, Ouglat destroyed you once long ago!"

"And I, just now," replied Mal Shaff, "have destroyed Ouglat."

The figures were silent, shifting uneasily. Then one stepped forward.

"Mal Shaff," it said, "we thought you were dead. Apparently it was not so. We welcome you to our land again. Ouglat, who once tried to kill you and apparently failed, you have killed, which is right and proper. Come and live with us again in peace. We welcome you."

Mal Shaff bowed.

Gone was all thought of the third dimension. Through Mal Shaff's mind raced strange, haunting memories of a red desert scattered with scarlet boulders, of silver cliffs of gleaming metallic stone, of huge seas battering against towering headlands. There were other things, too. Great palaces of shining jewels, and weird nights of inhuman joy where hellish flames lit deep, black caverns.

He bowed again.

"I thank you, Bathazar," he said.

Without a backward look he shambled down the hill with the others.

* * * * *

"Yes?" said the editor. "What's that you say? Doctor White is dead! A suicide! Yeah, I understand. Worry, hey! Here, Roberts, take this story."

He handed over the phone.

"When you write it," he said, "play up the fact he was worried about not being able to bring the men back to the third dimension. Give him plenty of praise for ending the Black Horror. It's a big story."

"Sure," said Roberts, then spoke into the phone: "All right, Bill, shoot the works."

www.ingramcontent.com/pod-product-compliance
Lightning Source LLC
Chambersburg PA
CBHW050530160726
48003CB00002B/538